WINTER SOLSTICE

WINTER SOLSTICE

A NOVEL

Elin Hilderbrand

Little, Brown and Company

New York   Boston   London

Copyright © 2017 by Elin Hilderbrand
Excerpt from *Winter in Paradise* copyright © 2018 by Elin Hilderbrand

Little, Brown and Company
Hachette Book Group
1290 Avenue of the Americas, New York, NY 10104
littlebrown.com

Originally published in hardcover by Little, Brown and Company, October 2017

The publisher is not responsible for websites (or their content) that are not owned by the publisher.

First Little, Brown mass market edition, September 2019

10 9 8 7 6 5 4 3 2 1

OPM

Reagan Arthur:
In every way, this book is for you.

PART ONE

OCTOBER

BART

The party is his mother's idea. Bart's birthday is October 31, which is one of the three worst birthdays a person can have, along with Christmas and September 11. It was especially soul crushing when Bart was growing up. Nobody wanted to celebrate a birthday when there was free candy to be had on the street just by dressing up and knocking on doors.

Bart agrees to the party, reluctantly, but he lays down some rules. Mitzi is sitting on the end of Bart's bed in Bart's room with her pen and her legal pad, ready to plan. Does she notice that the room smells strongly of marijuana smoke? She must, though she doesn't comment. Bart figures one reason she wants to throw a party is so Bart will get up out of bed. So he will be social, interact, return to the fun-loving idiot he used to be. He has been back from Afghanistan for ten months, and what Mitzi doesn't seem to understand is that the person Bart used to be...is gone.

"No costumes," Bart says. "Since you're all keen to write things down, start with that."

The corners of Mitzi's mouth droop. Bart doesn't want to make his mother any sadder than she already is, but on this he must hold firm. No costumes.

"Write it down," he says again.

"But...," Mitzi says.

Bart closes his eyes against his frustration. This is Mitzi, he reminds himself. Once she gets an idea, it's nearly impossible to reason with her. Bart tries imagining what a costume party thrown by the Quinn family might look like: His brother Patrick can come wearing an orange jumpsuit and handcuffs, since he spent eighteen months in prison for insider trading while Bart was gone. Bart's brother Kevin can wear a beret and kerchief, and carry a baguette under one arm. Since marrying Isabelle—who was a chambermaid and breakfast cook when Bart left—Kevin has become a regular Charles de Gaulle. Once, when Bart visited Kevin and Isabelle's new house— there had been talk of Bart moving in with them and serving as a manny to their daughter, Genevieve, and brand-new infant son, KJ, but no, sorry, Bart isn't good with children—Bart heard Kevin singing in French to his newborn son.

Singing in French!

Ava can come dressed as a femme fatale in a black dress with a plunging neckline, smoking a cigarette in one of those old-fashioned holders since apparently she has become quite the temptress in the past three years. She tried to explain the trajectory of her love life to Bart—Nathaniel, then Scott, then Nathaniel *and* Scott, then she was, ever so briefly, *engaged* to Nathaniel, then Nathaniel took a job on Block Island, so she was back with Scott. Then Scott got one of the teachers at the high school pregnant, and Ava was left with no one for a matter of months. And somewhere in there— Bart can't remember, his brain has more holes than Swiss cheese now—she met a third person, Potter Lyons, or maybe it's Lyons Potter, who is a professor somewhere in New York City, but according to Ava, Potter Lyons or Lyons Potter is *not* the reason Ava now lives on the Upper East Side of New

York and teaches music at a fancy private school where her students include the grandson of Quincy Jones and two of Harrison Ford's nieces. Ava has grown up. It's a good thing, a natural thing, Bart realizes—but still, he feels resentful. Who is supposed to hold the family together with Ava gone? Certainly not Bart.

And what about a costume for Bart's father, Kelley? Kelley has brain cancer, and after enduring fifteen more rounds of chemo and twenty-eight rounds of radiation, he made an executive decision: no more treatment. For a few months it looked like maybe he had beaten back the disease enough to eke out a few more good years. This past summer he was still able to flip the blueberry cornmeal pancakes and serve the guests breakfast with a smile. He and Mitzi were still walking every day from Fat Ladies Beach to Cisco and back again. But then, in mid-September, while Kelley and Bart were watching the University of Tennessee play Ole Miss—Bart's closest friend in the platoon, Centaur, now dead, had been a huge Vols fan, and Bart had vowed to watch the team since Centaur no longer could—Kelley suffered a seizure and lost sight in his left eye. Now, a mere four weeks later, he is relegated to a wheelchair, and Mitzi has called hospice.

Kelley is beyond the point of dressing up, and that's the real reason Bart doesn't want costumes. Kelley is going to die.

When Bart was on the plane home from Iceland, he swore that he would never let anything bother him again. But returning home to news of his father's cancer had cut Bart out at the knees. Along with profound sadness, he feels cheated. He managed to stay alive and make it home despite untold horrors; it's not fair that Kelley is now dying. Kelley won't be around to see Bart get married or have children. He won't know if Bart makes a success of himself or not. It taps into Bart's oldest resentment: Bart's three older siblings have gotten a lot more of Kelley than Bart has. They've gotten the best of him, and Bart, the sole child from Kelley's marriage to Mitzi, has had to make do with what was left over.

Mitzi winds one of her curls around her finger. "What if we compromise?" she asks. "What if I say 'Costumes optional'? I have an outfit I really want to wear."

Bart closes his eyes. He envisions some guests wearing costumes and some wearing regular clothes. The party will look like a half-eaten sandwich. He debates giving in to Mitzi just to make her happy and to prove himself a nice, reasonable guy—but he can't seem to buck his absolute hatred of Halloween.

"No costumes," he says. "Please, Mom. You can throw the party, I'll go and try to have a good time. But no costumes."

Mitzi sighs, then stands to leave the room. "You could use an air freshener in here," she says.

Bart gives her half a smile, the most he can muster. It's only after Mitzi walks out, closing the door behind her, that he realizes she didn't actually concede.

EDDIE

It's the first invitation he has received since he got out of jail, and Eddie won't lie: he's over the moon. Eddie Pancik, formerly known as Fast Eddie, dutifully served a three-to-five-year sentence (in two years and three months) at MCI–Plymouth for conspiracy and racketeering after confessing to pimping out his crew of Russian cleaning girls to his high-end real estate clients. Eddie's conviction had coincided with his discovery that his wife, Grace, was having an affair with their handsome and handsomely paid landscape architect, Benton Coe—and so when Eddie had first gotten to jail, it had felt like his world was caving in.

If Eddie learned anything while he was incarcerated, it's that human beings are resilient. He won't say he *thrived* during his time at MCI–Plymouth, but it wasn't nearly as awful as he'd expected. In some ways he appreciated the discipline and the hiatus from the rat race. Whereas before, Eddie's focus had always been on drumming up business and the next big deal, jail taught him to be mindful and present. He went to the weight room every day at seven a.m., then to breakfast, then he spent the morning teaching an ersatz real estate class in the prison library. The clientele of the prison was primarily white-collar criminals—embezzlers, credit card scammers, some drug lords but none with violent convictions—and nearly all of them, Eddie found, had a good head for business. Most times Eddie's "classes" turned into roundtable discussions of how good business ideas went awry. Sometimes the line was blurry, they all agreed.

Eddie even managed to sell a house while in lockup—to a man named Forrest Landry, who had hundreds of millions in trust with his wife, Karen. Karen Landry was one of those long-suffering types—Forrest had been unfaithful to her as well as to the law—but prison had made Forrest penitent, and he decided that a house on the platinum stretch of Hulbert Avenue would be just the thing to make amends.

He paid the listing price: $11.5 million.

Eddie's commission was $345,000. Eddie's sister, Barbie, acted as Eddie's proxy, and the windfall was directed to Eddie's wife, Grace, who used the money to pay college tuition for their twin daughters, Hope and Allegra. Hope had gotten into every college she applied to and had opted to go to Bucknell University in the middle of Exactly Nowhere, Pennsylvania. The school is ridiculously expensive, although— as Hope pointed out—*not* as expensive as Duke, USC, or Brown, her other three choices. She is getting straight As and playing the flute in a jazz band. Now in the fall of her sophomore year, she's even pledging a sorority, Alpha Delta Pi, which both Eddie and Grace agreed was a good thing, as Hope had been a bit of a loner in high school.

Allegra didn't get in anywhere except UMass Dartmouth and Plymouth State because of poor test scores and even worse grades. She decided on UMass Dartmouth, with an eye to transferring to the main campus in Amherst her sophomore year—but instead she flunked out. She returned to Nantucket and went to work for her aunt Barbie at Bayberry Properties, a company owned by Barbie's husband, Glenn Daley.

Eddie is secretly okay with the fact that Allegra isn't in college, and not just for the obvious financial reasons. Eddie sees a lot of himself in Allegra. He, too, struggled with traditional book learning. Allegra has common sense, ambition, and enviable social skills. She has started out as the receptionist at Bayberry Properties, but Glenn has been talking about promoting her to office manager sometime in the next year. From there it will only be a matter of time before she pursues her broker's license. The kid is going to be a success; Eddie is sure of it. He has seen her in action at the office—she is polite, professional, and confident way beyond her years. She's even nice on the phone when the odious Rachel McMann calls. Rachel used to work at Bayberry Properties, but while Eddie was in jail, she struck out on her own, and she's had an alarming amount of success, even though she's the worst gossip on the island.

Glenn Daley, once Eddie's biggest rival, offered Eddie a desk at Bayberry Properties at Barbie's insistence. Eddie now sits in the back row against the wall with two other first-year associates, and the three of them split phone duty, although somehow Eddie always ends up getting stuck with the weekend shifts. It's like starting in the business all over again, but Eddie tries to feel grateful. He should be humbled that Glenn Daley has chosen to claim his convicted felon of a brother-in-law and give him a fresh start.

Eddie shows Grace the invitation. "Look," he says. "Bart Quinn's birthday party at the VFW on Halloween!" He tries to tamp down his enthusiasm, but it's difficult. He's thrilled that the Quinns haven't forsaken him. There are others on the island who have either shunned him or given him the stink eye. Philip Meier from Nantucket Bank, for one. Eddie bumped into him at the post office, and Philip walked by Eddie without so much as a hello. And don't get Eddie started on his former office manager, Eloise Coffin. Eddie would love to key Eloise's car, but she drives a twelve-year-old Hyundai, so it would hardly be worth it. When Eddie went to jail, it was Eloise who talked to the press.

"Halloween?" Grace says. She takes the invitation from Eddie and puts on her reading glasses. The reading glasses are new since Eddie went to jail, as is all the gray in the part of her hair. One of the infinite number of things Eddie feels guilty about is causing Grace to look middle aged. "I can't go."

"You can't?" Eddie says. He feels a sense of panic. They've been invited to a party by the Quinns, which may lead to an invitation to the Quinns' annual Christmas Eve party. That would *really* restore Eddie's social credentials. They *have* to go. "Why not?"

"I'm working up the alley," Grace says. "I'm in charge of giving out the candy to the trick-or-treaters. I've been doing it for years."

Doing it for *years?* The phrase "up the alley" annoys Eddie. "Up the alley" means Academy Hill, the former school that is now fixed-income housing for elders. It's a hundred yards from the teensy-tiny cottage Grace bought on Lily Street, up Snake Alley. Grace has been volunteering at Academy Hill since Eddie went away. She may have worked there last Halloween and possibly the Halloween before that, but this hardly qualifies as "doing it for years." However, Eddie holds his tongue. He promised himself in jail that, as far as Grace was concerned, he would be a new man—a kind, patient, and attentive husband. He will not belittle Grace's charity work. He will not ask her to skip it. But what will he do about the party?

"What will I do about the party?" Eddie asks Grace.

Grace sighs and heads into the minuscule kitchen, where she pulls a bottle of wine from the three-quarter-size fridge. The wine is Oyster Bay sauvignon blanc, which retails for twelve bucks at Hatch's. The sight of Grace pouring herself an inexpensive bottle of wine in that pathetic kitchen depresses Eddie, though he knows it's not supposed to. He's supposed to feel grateful that he's a free man, that they have a roof over their heads, that they have money to send to Hope at Bucknell. Gone are the days when Eddie and Grace would drink Screaming Eagle cabernet or, on a random Wednesday afternoon, open a bottle of Veuve Clicquot. The worst part is that Grace doesn't complain; she makes the best of their compromised circumstances. The cottage is barely seven hundred square feet, and a quarter of that is a loft bedroom, which is accessed by a twisty set of stairs. Grace repurposed the back sunroom into a bedroom with a futon, a

TV, and a stackable washer and dryer, leaving the loft for the twins. But once Allegra returned home from her failed year at UMass Dartmouth, she said she preferred the only other sleeping space, a narrow, wood-paneled room with a single bed. The room has a door that closes and a bigger closet. It smells of pine sap and stays cool in the summer. It's kind of like living on a boat, Allegra says.

The house *is* in town and it *does* have a pocket garden out back, which Grace has transformed into a verdant oasis—a postage stamp of lush green lawn that she surrounded with flower beds bursting with hydrangeas, lilies, snapdragons, and rosebushes. People cutting through to town on Snake Alley always stop to admire the garden and to comment on the quaint charm of the cottage. It looks like something from a storybook, they say. It looks like the house where the Three Bears live!

Eddie is bound and determined to earn enough money to buy a bigger house. He won't be able to afford anything as grand as the estate they used to own on Wauwinet Road—they'll never have a home or waterfront acreage like that again—but something with a bigger kitchen, something with more than one bathroom.

Grace takes a sip of her wine. She has grown to like the New Zealand sauvignon blancs, she says. They're bright, grassy.

"Take Allegra to the party," Grace says. "She broke up with Hunter yesterday, and she's been in her room ever since."

"She broke up with Hunter?" Eddie says. Hunter Bloch is a broker at Melville Real Estate; Hunter's father, Hunter Sr., owns the company, and when Allegra and Hunter started dating, Eddie and Barbie and Glenn all got the same gleam in their eye as they fantasized about the two agencies merging, creating the biggest real estate concern on Nantucket. "How come?"

"He was seeing Ina, the Bulgarian receptionist at Two Doors Down, behind Allegra's back," Grace says. She raises an eyebrow and lowers her voice. "Frankly, I think it was good for her to get a taste of her own medicine. After what she did to Brick..."

Eddie holds up a hand. "Stop," he says. "The thing with Brick is ancient history."

"Two and a half years is ancient history?" Grace says. "Well, I'm sure you'd like to think so."

Eddie bows his head; he feels a quarrel coming on. Grace was sweet and steadfast while Eddie was in prison. She sent him carefully curated care packages, and she wrote long, newsy letters. She came to visit every week without fail, often with whichever daughter she could wrangle into joining her. But now that Eddie is back at home, Grace's anger, disappointment, and skepticism float to the surface more often than he would like.

"Brick survived, didn't he?" Eddie says. He knows that Brick Llewellyn, Allegra's former beau and the son of Grace and Eddie's former best friends, Madeline and Trevor, was accepted at Dartmouth, and then he won the Nantucket Golf Club scholarship, which pays his tuition, room, and board for four years. Eddie heard this from Grace, who still talks to Madeline, although their friendship is nothing like it used to be. They used to be closer than sisters. Eddie hasn't seen or spoken to either of the Llewellyns since being released. If Eddie thought they would resume their weekly family dinners, he was apparently mistaken. The Llewellyns, most likely, want nothing to do with Eddie Pancik, making the fact of the Quinn invitation that much more important.

"I'll see if Allegra wants to go to the party," Eddie says.

Grace gives him a tight-lipped smile, swallowing whatever else she wanted to say with the bright, grassy sauvignon blanc. "You can ask her now. She's in her room."

Eddie knocks on the door of the little bedroom, which is no bigger than Allegra's walk-in closet in their old house. "Allegra?" he says. "It's Dad." He nearly says, *It's Eddie,* because *Eddie* is what Allegra calls him at the office, and whereas at first, being addressed that way by his child felt like a bucket of cold salt water to the face, now he has grown used to it.

There's a murmur from the other side of the door that sounds welcoming, but maybe that's too optimistic a word. At home Allegra still displays flashes of her former self. She can be pouty, bitter, self-absorbed. Eddie eases open the door. Allegra is lying on the bed in shorts and a Nantucket Whalers T-shirt with her laptop open on her chest. She barely looks up when Eddie enters, and he wonders what she's so absorbed with. It's probably Facebook, right, or she's bingeing on one of those Internet series that have no boundaries. Troy Steele, a fellow inmate at MCI–Plymouth, made Eddie watch an episode of something called *The Girlfriend Experience,* and it was no better than porn. Eddie wishes that Allegra were on Zillow, memorizing the square footage and floor plans of every property for sale on Nantucket. That's how you get ahead!

"Hi there," Eddie says. Allegra's hair is messy and she's not wearing any makeup. Her eyes are swollen like maybe she's been crying. But she is still beautiful. "In case you're wondering, I think Hunter Bloch is an idiot."

Allegra grants Eddie a patient smile. "That he is," she says.

"I'd like you to do me a favor," Eddie says, and he tosses the invitation onto Allegra's bed. "Go to this party with me?"

Allegra reads the invitation. "Bart Quinn?" she says. "He's hot. I always thought he was hot, but now that he's, like, a war hero, he's *really* hot."

"Hot?" Eddie says, and his spirit flags. Why does Allegra have to be so boy crazy? Why can't she be more like Hope and be obsessed with Emily Dickinson? Why can't she be more like Hope and *act* like Emily Dickinson—locked in her garret room, writing poetry by the light of one flickering candle?

"It's on Halloween," Allegra says. She hands the invitation back to Eddie. "Okay, I'll go."

"You will?" Eddie says. For some reason this answer catches him off guard. He expected a struggle.

Allegra shrugs. "Sure. I was supposed to go to the Chicken Box with Hunter. He was going to sneak me in the back door."

"Oh," Eddie says. He's suddenly relieved Allegra and Hunter broke up. The last thing he wants is for people to see his underage daughter dancing in the front row at the Chicken Box, waving her beer around, making out with Hunter Bloch, or displaying any other inelegant behavior. "Well, this will be much more fun."

"Doubtful," Allegra says. "But it's something to do. Is it a costume party?"

"I assume so?" Eddie says. He searches the invitation for dress code. It says nothing except that it's a birthday party for Bart Quinn at the VFW at 7:00 p.m. on Halloween. Halloween is a Tuesday night, not a usual night for a party, so it must be a Halloween party, which means costumes. Eddie's wheels start turning.

"I don't know about you," Eddie says, "but I'm dressing up."

"I have a Japanese geisha costume," Allegra says. "I'll wear that."

Japanese geisha? Eddie thinks. He supposes it could be worse; at least she'll be fully dressed. "That's my girl," he says.

AVA

She's still struck by the novelty of it: pushing through the turnstiles of the subway and trudging up the stairs, just one of ten million people. She stops by the dry cleaner on the corner of Lexington and Eighty-Second Street and picks up her laundry from Nina Hwang. It's clean, folded, and bagged for fifteen bucks, an urban miracle as far as Ava is concerned. She ducks into the deli next door and gets a bunch of red Gerber daisies, as it's Friday and Ava has made a practice of purchasing fresh flowers every Friday, which is the night Potter comes all the way over from the West Side for dinner at Ava's apartment.

As Ava approaches her building, she fumbles for her keys. Keys, she's still not used to keys. In her life on Nantucket she had only one key, the key to her Jeep, which she always kept on the passenger seat. She never had a key to the inn. It was an inn and therefore always open. Even when it was closed—January, February—it was unlocked. Does a key even exist? If so, Ava has never seen it.

Now her ring jangles with a key to the front door of her building on Eighty-Second Street; two keys to her apartment—doorknob and dead bolt; a key to her mailbox; and three keys to Potter's apartment, which he *insisted* she take at the end of August when she moved, permanently, to Manhattan. Potter had wanted Ava to move in with him on the Upper

West Side from the get-go, and Ava's mother, Margaret, had wanted Ava to either move in with her and Drake on Central Park West or take over Drake's apartment in the West Village. All these offers were tempting, but Ava, at the age of thirty-two, had never lived alone. She had spent her entire adult life living with her father, Mitzi, her brothers, and sixteen rooms filled with virtual strangers. How had she even *considered* marrying Nathaniel or Scott? She would have missed out on this seminal experience: a place all her own.

Ava's one-bedroom apartment is a fifth-floor walk-up, meaning four flights of stairs, but nothing about the climb—even carrying her heavy school bag and a load of laundry—diminishes the joy Ava feels each and every time she walks into her apartment. It is, absolutely, nothing special. The kitchen is the size of a piece of pie, a four-square-foot triangle that features a fridge with a microwave above it on one side and a small stove on the other, a sink in the middle, and enough countertop to either drain dishes or place a cutting board, but not both at the same time. The bathroom floor is made up of tiny hexagonal tiles in black and white, but whole rows of them are missing against the walls. There is exposed brick in the living room, Ava's sole point of pride, as she knows exposed brick to be valued in Manhattan real estate, although she's not sure why, since she can't hang anything on it. The bedroom has two windows, both with bars, and a reasonable closet. Granted, Potter's apartment has cathedral ceilings and a butler's pantry off the kitchen and one and a half baths and original crown molding. Both Margaret's and Drake's apartments fall into the luxury category. Margaret's apartment is a three-bedroom overlooking Central Park—meaning that if you tossed a water balloon, that's where it would land—and Drake's apartment, though smaller, is sleek and modern and filled with actual art that he buys from a dealer in Chelsea. Both Odell Beckham Jr. and Jimmy Fallon live in Drake's building, and there's a pool on the roof and a fondue restaurant on the first floor that is presently the hottest reservation in the city.

But what Ava treasures about her apartment is that everything in it is hers. Her books are lined up on the shelves, her music plays on the wireless speakers—she can play Natalie Merchant whenever she wants, and no one is around to complain—her favorite foods are in the fridge, her twelve pillows dominate the head of the bed. She bought a Persian rug for the living room at the flea market on Columbus Avenue, and she has hung photographs of Nantucket on every available bit of wall space. Set up in the corner is a stepladder that she has decorated with white fairy lights and houseplants. It's not sophisticated, but Ava doesn't care. She loves it because it's hers.

Ava puts the Gerber daisies in her white scallop shell vase and places it in the center of her round white dining table from IKEA (the table is an eyesore; Ava will replace it after she saves up), and she pours herself a glass of white wine. Potter is due at seven. Ava is making tomato soup from scratch, grilled ham and cheese sandwiches, and a green salad with creamy lime dressing. Her past Friday-night endeavors have included roast chicken, pork chops braised in milk, and a gluey mushroom pasta that they decided to throw away after the first bite in favor of pizza from Ray's. Ava takes both her successes and her failures in stride. She isn't cooking to please Potter as much as she is cooking to please herself.

She realizes she may seem solipsistic, but she doesn't care. She is reveling in being her own person.

She needs to go to Gristedes and get started on the soup and the dressing, but an envelope among the pile of mail—a purple envelope?—catches her eye. She recognizes Mitzi's handwriting on the front, and suddenly the purple makes sense. Why settle for a white envelope when you can send purple? That would be Mitzi's logic.

Ava opens the envelope. It's an invitation to Bart's twenty-second birthday party on Halloween at the VFW on Nantucket. *Well,* Ava thinks, *if anyone deserves a party, it's Bart.* He missed his twenty-first birthday. There were no kegs, no streamers or cake, in the prison camp on the barren plains of southern central Afghanistan.

Halloween is a Tuesday this year. There's no way Ava can attend the party, and that's the God's honest truth; she won't feel guilty because her circumstances flow with her personal preference. She doesn't *want* to go. It's not only that she detests Halloween—every teacher in America hates Halloween, with all the kids hyped up the day of and in a sugar coma the day after—it's also that Ava doesn't want to go home. She's afraid that if she sees that her father is sicker than anyone is letting on, and that Bart is clinically depressed, and that Kevin and Isabelle are underwater from the birth of their second baby in two years, and that Mitzi is incapable of holding everyone together—instead of dealing with the real issues, here she is, throwing a party at the VFW—Ava will feel like she has to move back.

Move back! Impossible. She has her apartment; she has a job she adores. Copper Hill is the best place to teach music in the whole country. First of all, music is an elective, so every single one of Ava's seventy-five students—five classes of fifteen—*wants* to be there. Not only do they want to be there, they want to achieve. Ava has singers and piano players and composers and musical history students. And she runs the madrigal group and a club for recording music videos.

Also, Ava has a boyfriend whom she is *healthily* in love with. There's no drama with Potter, no theatrics, no jealousy (not *much* jealousy), no tears, no senseless yearning, no insecurities (or not *much* insecurity, anyway).

Ava is *not* going home, even for a party, even for Bart. She doesn't want to feel guilty.

Halloween is rapidly followed by Thanksgiving, and Thanksgiving is rapidly followed by Christmas. She'll go home for Thanksgiving and Christmas...well, actually, Potter said something about taking a trip to Austria over Christmas—Salzburg and Vienna. Ava nearly shrieked with joy. To visit the birthplace and breeding ground of so many great composers—Mozart, Schubert, Haydn, Mahler, Strauss. She is thirty-two years old and has never been to Europe!

But...she has to wait and see how her father is doing.

Her cell phone rings. It's Potter.

"Hey, baby," Ava says.

"Ava," Potter says. The tone of his voice makes Ava think that something awful has happened. Maybe Gibby, Potter's grandfather, has died. Oh, Gibby!

"What's wrong?" Ava says.

"I have to cancel on dinner tonight," Potter says. "Trish just called. At the last minute she and Harrison decided to fly in from San Fran to attend the Shakespeare symposium at Bard College, so she asked if I could take PJ for the weekend. Of course I said yes."

"Of course you said yes!" Ava says. "This is good news, right? I mean, a bit unexpected and last minute, but still good. I finally get to meet him! Please, bring PJ here for dinner. I was planning on making grilled cheese anyway. Or we can go out. We can go to Serendipity and get foot-long hot dogs and frozen hot chocolates. And then tomorrow we can go to the Museum of Natural History! He's the perfect age for the planetarium, and I think they're having an exhibit on arachnids."

Potter laughs. "You're much more enthusiastic about this than I thought you'd be. You're much more enthusiastic about this than I am."

"You always say you wish you had more time with PJ," Ava says. "You always say you wish he lived closer."

"You're right, you're right," Potter says.

"So do you want to bring him here, or shall we go out?" Ava asks.

"I'll bring him there, I guess," Potter says.

"Or do you want a night with him alone?" Ava asks. "I'm so sorry... I didn't mean to assume..."

"No, no," Potter says. "If I were going to keep him to myself, it would be to avoid inflicting ourselves on you. I've told you, PJ can be kind of difficult. He suffers from only-child-raised-by-bicoastal-academics syndrome."

"I've been teaching for nine years," Ava says. "I've seen my share of difficult children. Maybe not that exact syndrome, but believe me, I can handle it. How many times have I told you about Micah?"

"The two of us will be over at seven," Potter says. "I think we should stay in. Serendipity is noisy and there's always a wait and he'll be tired from traveling."

"Okay, then," Ava says. "I'll set the table for three."

Ava changes into jeans and a crisp white blouse and grabs her bag to go to the store. Her phone pings: it's a text from Margaret. *Drake got a reservation at Le Coucou tomorrow night at nine. Can you and Potter join us?*

Ava's heart sinks just a little. One of the best things about moving to New York has been spending time with her mother. For the twenty-plus years that Ava was growing up on Nantucket with Kelley and Mitzi and her brothers, Margaret often seemed far away, out of reach, and sometimes less than real. Ava most often saw her mother on TV—reporting from Baghdad or Paris or from the CBS studios in New York. Now that they live in the same place, they love doing things together—shopping, movies, museums, and double dates. Margaret is Ava's best friend in the city; Drake and Margaret are Ava and Potter's best couple friends. Last week the four of them had brunch at Le Bilboquet, then took a long walk through Central Park. All four of them have been dying to eat at Le Coucou, but a reservation has eluded them until now.

We can't, Ava texts back. *Potter's son, PJ, is here for the weekend.*

No problem! Margaret responds. *We'll do it another time.*

Then the phone rings and it's Margaret.

"Hi?" Ava says.

"Hi, sweetie," Margaret says. "I just called real quick to see how you're feeling about meeting PJ?"

"I feel excited," Ava says.

"Really?" Margaret says.

"Yes, really," Ava says, and a tinge of impatience creeps into her voice. She knows that Margaret's only "concern" about Potter is that he has a child with someone else, an emotional landscape that Ava is unfamiliar with. Ava pointed out that she has plenty of friends who have children—Shelby and Zack have Xavier, for example—and Ava now has a niece and four nephews. Margaret then suggested that this would be different. More challenging. Ava should be prepared to be patient and make concessions where PJ was concerned. And when she finally met PJ, she should "tread lightly." Those were Margaret's exact words. "I'm excited to meet him. It's been a year since we started dating."

"I know," Margaret says. "You may think you know Potter inside and out, but just remember, you've never seen him be a parent. You may be surprised."

Surprised? Ava thinks. Her mother rarely annoys her, but Margaret is coming dangerously close to doing so now. But before Ava can tactfully inform Margaret that she is perfectly capable of handling herself with PJ and with Potter in the role of father, Margaret says, "Oh, honey, I have to go to wardrobe. Roger is making ugly faces at me from down the hall. Love you, sweetie. We'll miss you tomorrow night. Bye-bye."

"Uh . . . bye," Ava says. She hangs up and heads down the stairs. The phone call was meant to be supportive, she knows, but it leaves her feeling worse. Mostly because Margaret is nearly always right.

Ava has everything ready to go when Potter rings the buzzer: the soup is simmering on the stove, the grilled cheeses are composed, the salad greens are washed and topped with perfectly ripe slices of avocado. (From experience Ava has learned your chances of choosing a perfectly ripe avocado are approximately one in a hundred.) She and Potter don't usually eat dessert, but because PJ is coming, Ava bought whoopie pies at the market, as well as some frightfully expensive organic ice pops. She's playing Wilco—Potter's favorite band—and the table is set for three, with glasses of ice water at two places and a glass of milk at the third.

She hears footsteps on the stairs, then Potter's voice and a child's voice. A *child's* voice. *This is real,* Ava thinks. She's about to meet Potter's son.

She opens the door and stands on the landing wearing what she hopes is a carefree, welcoming smile. She notices tiny pinpricks of red on her white blouse—splatters from the tomato soup.

Oh well, Ava thinks. The blouse is a small sacrifice to make for this suddenly all-important dinner.

"Hi, guys!" Ava says as soon as the top of Potter's head is visible.

Potter turns to give her a warning look. Ava realizes that Potter is pulling seven-year-old PJ up the stairs, and then Ava hears the sobbing. Potter makes it to the landing below Ava's apartment with PJ in tow. When PJ looks up and sees Ava, he lets out an ear-piercing shriek.

Ava puts a finger to her lips. "The neighbors," she says. "Mrs. Simonetta." Mrs. Simonetta is sensitive to noise and has more than once complained about the volume at which Ava plays her Natalie Merchant. PJ's scream will likely spur Mrs. Simonetta to phone in a SWAT team.

Potter picks PJ up, even though he is far too big. "You have to stop, PJ. Ava is nice. Ava is my friend and she wants to be your friend."

PJ shrieks again.

The scene on the landing lasts another sixty seconds or so, with PJ shrieking every time Potter tells him Ava is nice and would PJ please climb the final set of stairs so they can eat supper. Mrs. Simonetta clearly isn't home, because there is no way she would tolerate that kind of commotion outside her door.

Ava resorts immediately to bribery. "If you come upstairs, PJ, I'll give you an ice pop. I have three flavors: cherry, grape, and orange." In truth, the organic flavors are pomegranate, fig, and mango, but they can deal with Ava's deception once they get the child up the stairs.

"I don't *want* an ice pop!" PJ screams.

"I also have whoopie pies," Ava says. She congratulates herself for "treading lightly." Could Margaret Quinn herself be handling this any better?

"What about a whoopie pie, buddy? It's chocolate cake with marshmallow filling."

"No!" PJ screams. "No! No! No!" He looks up at Ava and says, "I hate you! I want my mom!"

Ava draws in a breath. She looks at Potter and sees the expression of helpless agony on his face. "I think he's t-i-r-e-d from traveling," Potter says.

"Okay," Ava says. "Why don't we try this again tomorrow?"

"But—," Potter says.

"I am *not* tired!" PJ screams. "I'm screaming because I hate you! I hate you, lady!"

Ava channels her inner saint. She didn't even know she *had* an inner saint, but apparently she does, because she smiles at Potter and says, "It's fine. Call me later."

"You win, buddy," Potter says to PJ. "We'll go home. But you and I are going to have a serious talk in the taxi."

PJ races down the stairs. Potter mouths *I love you* to Ava, then chases after his son.

Ava closes the door of her apartment, flips the dead bolt, and stares at the table set for three, with the candles flickering and the red Gerber daisies showing their perky, optimistic faces. She inhales the scent of onions, tomato, and basil, and then she starts to cry.

KELLEY

He begged Mitzi to put off calling hospice until things got really bad.

Things are really bad.

Kelley had a seizure while watching a football game with

Bart, and he lost the sight in his left eye. That sight is never coming back, Dr. Cherith said. And he may soon lose sight in his right eye. Then his hearing will go, his sense of smell, his ability to chew and swallow. He feels like the poor chump in the song "Moonshadow."

Kelley is dying and there is nothing he can do to stop it. When Kelley was released from Mass. General after the seizure, he gave Mitzi the okay to call hospice and suspend operation of the inn.

The funny thing was that as soon as the hospice workers started showing up, Kelley felt better, stronger, healthier. He guesses he's the healthiest person ever to use hospice. Today, the twenty-fourth of October, he has enough energy to use his walker all the way down the hall, through the living room, to the kitchen. He wants a cup of tea, and rather than ring his bell, he decides to go in search of the tea himself.

He says to Lara—Lara not Laura, she has corrected him three times, no concessions made for his pronunciation even though he has brain cancer—"Mitzi likes me to drink herbal tea, but would it be okay for me to have a cup of regular Lipton?"

Lara says, "I don't think a cup of regular Lipton will hurt."

Kelley decides to press his luck. He says, "What I'd *really* like is a teaspoon of white sugar in my regular Lipton tea. Not honey, not agave, not raw organic turbinado. Just good old white processed sugar."

"Does Mrs. Quinn keep something as toxic as that in the house?" Lara asks.

"She does," Kelley says. "We keep it on hand for the guests. There are packets of Domino in the breakfront. Might you grab me one...or two?"

Lara disappears into the guest dining room and emerges

shortly thereafter shaking two sugar packets like castanets. Lara is a stickler about her name, but she is wonderfully lenient about other things, Kelley is happy to see.

The next day Kelley is in bed. He can no longer read or watch TV—it puts too much strain on his good eye—and so he listens to books on tape. He considered choosing some classics that he'd always wanted to read, but it turned out there were no classics he'd always wanted to read. He will go rebelliously to his grave never having slogged through *Moby-Dick*. Instead Kelley becomes addicted to the novels of Danielle Steel. Now, *there's* a woman who knows about life: dying billionaires who cut their obnoxious children out of the will, unappreciated housewives who fall into the arms of the children's sailing instructor. And Ms. Steel writes one heck of a sex scene. Today Kelley is listening to *The Mistress*. It's his fourth Danielle Steel book in a row, and he fears he might be falling a little in love with her. But becoming attached to someone new at this stage of the game is probably not a good idea.

Lara comes into the room to do her hospice duties, and Kelley holds up a finger to let her know she should wait until the narrator reaches a break before she takes his lunch order, plumps his pillows, refills his meds, and rubs ointment on his feet.

He pauses his book and says, "Hello, *Lara*."

She smiles. "Hello, Kelley. Are you ready for lunch?"

Kelley grimaces. He fears lunch is spinach soup made without any butter, cream, or salt. Basically, Mitzi boils raw spinach, purées it with some vegetable broth, heats it up, and calls it soup. She serves it with hard little seeded crackers that taste like something she stole from the bird feeder.

"I want a ham and pickle sandwich from the Nantucket

Pharmacy," Kelley says. "On rye bread. With a bag of regular Lay's potato chips and a chocolate frappe."

"That sounds ambitious," Lara says.

It is ambitious. Kelley feels hungry in his mind, but when food is in front of him, he can normally manage only a few bites. But it occurs to him that this might be because he isn't tempted by any of the offerings. If there were something he actually *wanted* to eat, he would devour it. Or eat more than usual. He has lost twenty-nine pounds since he stopped chemo in June.

"Please?" he says.

"I can run out and get it for you now," Lara says.

Kelley's functioning eye widens, and he tries to sit up a little straighter, although doing so hurts. He now has tumors on three of his vertebrae. "You can?"

"I'd like to see you eat," Lara says. "And I'd like to see you happy. It's amazing how indulging a little bit can boost the morale."

"You know," Kelley says. "I used to think Jocelyn was the nice hospice worker and you were the tough one. But you are rapidly gaining ground, Lara. Before you leave, may I inquire: Where is Mrs. Quinn?"

"She left a few minutes ago to meet with the caterers for Bart's birthday party," Lara says.

Yes! Kelley thinks. They have a window! Let the caper begin!

"Go," he says. "Quickly, go!"

The learning curve is steep once you discover you are terminal. Kelley understands so much more about life now than he ever did when he was well. On the one hand, it's frustrating— what good will his newfound knowledge do him once he's six feet under? On the other hand, he's grateful. That's actually the first and last lesson: gratitude for every experience. Gratitude for two packets of sugar in his well-steeped black pekoe tea. How many times in his life did he take something this simple for granted? He feels enormous, tearful gratitude for the first bite of his contraband sandwich: lightly toasted, buttered slices of rye containing luscious ham and pickle salad and crunchy, crisp iceberg lettuce. How many times did Kelley wolf down a similar sandwich while sitting at his desk on Wall Street? He barely tasted those sandwiches, much less reveled in their nuances. If only someone had been there to remind him that his life, someday, would be over and he should pay attention and enjoy while he could.

His next adventure is two Lay's potato chips, one flat, one folded over. Folded-over chips are preferable to flat chips—why is that? It's one of life's ten million mysteries. That has been another lesson. So many things can't be explained; they just are. Love, for example. And illness. Why should Kelley be struck with brain cancer at the youthful age of sixty-four? He had expected to live until ninety. Okay, maybe not ninety, but long enough to make certain all of his kids turned out okay.

And he has done that, hasn't he? Patrick is out of jail and he has some kind of new investment concern going. Jennifer is decorating houses for every *Mayflower* descendant in Beacon Hill, and the three boys are busy with fall lacrosse and fantasy football. (Kelley still doesn't understand fantasy football, and now, he supposes, he never will, a small regret.)

Kevin and Isabelle just ended a wildly successful season at Quinns' on the Beach—the liquor license more than doubled their income, Kevin confided—and Isabelle worked alongside Kevin until three days before she gave birth to Kelley's fourth grandson, Kelley Jacques Quinn, known as KJ. Kelley is honored to have a member of the new genera-

tion named after him; however, he's also glad they decided
to use the nickname KJ, because Kelley can't count the number of times in his life that someone saw his name and
thought he was a girl. Woman. Whatever the proper terminology. (Terminology no longer matters to Kelley, if it ever
did, but pronouncing Lara's name correctly very much
matters.)

Ava has, perhaps, made the greatest strides of all the children. She is living in Manhattan. Kelley initially feared that
she would rent a place in Brooklyn, start wearing vintage
clothes, and get upset about the distinction between *girl* and
woman. But Kelley needn't have worried. Ava settled in the
borough of her youth. She is paying her own rent, working at
a prestigious if elitist private school teaching music, real
music, not just kids banging on wooden blocks. And she's
dating a very nice man, a real man, not one of the boys-
slash-clowns who dominated her life the past three or four
years. Kelley never held a very high opinion of Nathaniel
Oscar; he was far too handsome, and Mitzi enjoyed his company way too much. Scott was better, but ultimately, Kelley
suspected, Ava would have grown tired of him. This new
fellow—at the moment Kelley can't come up with his
name—is a professor at Columbia, and he has a son who
lives in California with the mother. He seems just right for
Ava, or at least right for now. The important thing is that Ava
is finally getting some air under her wings, and she's getting
to see more of her mother, which Kelley knows is something
she missed growing up.

Bart is home safely from Afghanistan after being held
prisoner for nearly two years. Kelley has tried to talk to Bart
about what happened overseas, but Bart is tight lipped, just
as Kelley's own father was silent about what happened during the years he was stationed in the Philippines during

World War II. Kelley talked with Mitzi about getting Bart to a therapist, but Bart flat-out refused. He wants to work through things on his own, he says—meaning, it seems, that he wants to sit in his room and smoke dope. He has reverted to the same behavior he exhibited before he joined the Marines. Has nothing changed? He did go to work for Kevin and Isabelle at Quinns' on the Beach. But the crowds and the fast pace caused Bart to have panic attacks, and after two weeks he quit. There was then talk of Bart working as Kevin and Isabelle's nanny, but that idea got shot down as well. Bart isn't qualified to work for Patrick, even at the entry level. And now there is no business at the inn for him to help out with.

Kelley is worried about Bart.

Mitzi is worried as well, although by necessity her worrying has to be divided between Bart and Kelley. She's putting up a pretty strong front, stronger than Kelley thought possible. Likely, she's in denial. She talks about getting the most out of the time Kelley has left, but she's also praying for a miracle. She prayed for a miracle with Bart—and look what happened! He came home, safe and sound.

Here Kelley would like to point out that there is probably a one-miracle-per-family limit; otherwise, it wouldn't be fair. Kelley knows there won't be a miracle where he's concerned. He feels his body shutting down. He's going to die and he's okay with that. He had a long, elucidating conversation with his old friend Father Paul, and they agreed that Kelley should make his peace with the people he's leaving behind and then have faith that God will take over from there.

Kelley can't share this philosophy with Mitzi, however. She will accuse him of giving up.

Kelley is worried about Mitzi. He doesn't think she can or

should run the inn by herself. She should sell the inn and buy something smaller or move away altogether. Her parents have died; her brother died. Her only family once Kelley is gone will be Bart and Kelley's other kids.

Kelley has had serious conversations with Patrick, Kevin, and Ava: they are not to let Bart and Mitzi fall through the cracks.

We won't, Dad, they said.

Kelley tells himself that he will have a brass-tacks conversation with Mitzi about selling the inn this week.

At that moment Mitzi bursts into the room. What remains of Kelley's sandwich is on the lunch plate before him, along with an untouched dill spear and the half-empty bag of chips.

"You are a very naughty patient," Mitzi says, and she leans in to kiss his greasy, salty lips. She always gives him long, lingering kisses now, and he savors each one. She smells like woodsmoke and fresh air. Her cheeks are pink and her curly hair is windblown. She grows more beautiful each day, at least in Kelley's mind. He feels he's adjusting well to his prognosis, but he won't lie: he experiences fiendish jealousy whenever he thinks of the man Mitzi will fall in love with after Kelley is gone. If he were to voice this thought, Mitzi would throw herself headlong into his arms and vow that she will never meet anyone else. She will remain faithful to Kelley until her own death. And whereas, selfishly, this is exactly what Kelley wants, he knows it is unfair and unrealistic. Mitzi is exactly like one of the heroines in Danielle Steel's novels. Kelley will die and Mitzi will think her own life is over. She will never find love again. She will consider joining an ashram or adopting a cat. But then one day she'll be shopping at Annye's Whole Foods, and she will reach for the last package of flaxseeds—no, kale chips!—at the very same time as a handsome stranger. After deflecting her gentle protests, the stranger will insist Mitzi take the kale chips, and as they're standing in line, he will reveal that his beloved wife of thirty years has just died of MS and he has come to Nantucket to take long walks on the beach and reflect on his loss.

Or…Mitzi will take a trip to Sedona, a place Kelley knows she has long wanted to visit. She will wander into a crystal shop and suddenly feel a hand on her back. It will be the mysterious, bearded owner of the crystal shop, who will ask if Mitzi would like to join him in a cup of matcha. Mitzi will not believe the way the universe provided for her at—literally—her lowest moment.

Mitzi breaks the spell of Kelley's awful reverie. "I just had the best conversation with the caterer! This party is going to be So. Much. Fun."

Party? Kelley thinks. *What party?* He wonders for an instant if Mitzi is already planning his funeral reception. Why else would she need a caterer? Then he remembers Bart's birthday party at the VFW. Kelley tried to discourage Mitzi from planning this party. Why would she take on such an enormous project when her husband was dying and her son was depressed?

She looked at him as though he were a moron, and he realized that was the point. Kelley was dying and Bart was depressed; Mitzi needed a happy distraction. Still, Kelley worries the party will put too much pressure on Bart. He doesn't like being the center of attention. He didn't want any kind of celebration when he came home from Afghanistan, and there he was, a war hero. Kelley himself would have taken the Chamber of Commerce up on their offer of a parade, but Bart said he couldn't stand to be honored when half of his fellow Marines had been killed by the Bely.

Mitzi was inviting *everyone they knew* to the VFW. It would be a Halloween version of their Christmas Eve party. Once Kelley realized that, he turned to Mitzi and said, "Why don't we just throw our Christmas Eve party as usual?"

"But that's so far *away,*" Mitzi said. Before Kelley could chide her for being as impatient as a child, she kissed his forehead and said, "And you're feeling good *now.*"

That was when Kelley understood that Mitzi didn't think Kelley would make it to the holidays. She didn't think he would make it *two more months.* Wow. Well, he would show her! There was no greater motivation for doing anything—including staying alive—than being able to tell your spouse: *I told you so.*

There followed some days, however, when Kelley feared that Mitzi was right. He felt he could barely keep breathing for another hour, much less two more months.

Now he has decided to follow Bart's lead and just nod along when Mitzi talks about the party. It *will* be fun. Sort of. Kelley will have to attend in his wheelchair, but if he takes pain medication, he should be able to stay alert. He won't be out on the dance floor—yes, Mitzi hired a band, some operation called Maxxtone that Kevin recommended—but it'll be fun to see people.

"The caterer suggested a mashed potato bar," Mitzi says. "It's a thing. They make a big pot of mashed potatoes, and then there are dishes of toppings—scallions, cheddar cheese, sour cream, bacon..."

"Bacon?" Kelley says, perking up. "You agreed to bacon?"

"I know it's your favorite," Mitzi says.

"*Was* my favorite," Kelley says. Does he have to remind Mitzi that she forbids him from eating bacon—as well as sausage, ham, pulled pork, hamburger, meatballs of any kind, veal chops, marbled steak, dark-meat chicken, and "fatty" fish such as salmon?

"I've had a talk with Laura—" Mitzi says.

"Lara," Kelley says. "Her name is Lara. Not Laura. You have to pronounce it correctly or she gets upset."

Mitzi nods, though Kelley is certain she didn't process the correction. "Laura seems to think it's fine for you to eat the foods you love. She was very persuasive."

"You mean, you agree with her?" Kelley says.

"Yes," Mitzi says, and she gives Kelley another lovely kiss. "I want you to be happy."

She's given up on me, Kelley thinks. *If she doesn't care if I eat bacon, then I really must be a lost cause.*

Maybe Mitzi has fallen in love with the caterer. Maybe the caterer is one of these hipster types with a man bun.

"There are going to be glass apothecary jars filled with candy," Mitzi says. "Jawbreakers, caramels, Necco wafers, Pixy Stix. It seemed like a natural fit at a Halloween party."

"But it's *not* a Halloween party," Kelley says. "It's a birthday party. We aren't wearing costumes." He pauses. They had better not be wearing costumes! What would he go as? Man Sitting on Death's Door?

"I might wear a costume, since I'm the hostess," Mitzi says. She stands up. "I'd like to wear my gold roller-disco outfit, the one with the matching headband and wristbands. Do you know the one I mean?"

"Um?" Kelley says. He knows exactly the one Mitzi means, because it was this very outfit that Kelley set on fire in their bathtub after Mitzi left Kelley for George Umbrau, the Winter Street Inn Santa Claus, nearly three years earlier.

"You do know the one, right?" Mitzi asks. "I mean, I only had one gold jumpsuit." She opens the door to their closet.

"But I've looked everywhere and I can't find it. Where could it be?"

Kelley is not too sick to recognize the right course of action. He leans back into his pillows, closes his eyes, and pretends to be asleep.

EDDIE

Finally Eddie's job of working the phones pays off!

It's the lowest job on the real estate office totem pole. On a normal day Eddie fields calls, each more inane and frustrating than the last. People call looking to rent a house for the first two weeks of August. They would like it to sleep eight and be on the beach or within short walking distance, and their budget is five thousand dollars. Total. On a good day Eddie responds to such a query with "Do you have any wiggle room with the price? If not, then how about the number of bedrooms or the location? I have a lovely upside-down house in Tom Nevers that sleeps six and rents for forty-five hundred a week. It's a short drive from the beach. It just came on the market for the two weeks you're looking at." On his bad days Eddie says, "The kind of house you're describing, ma'am/sir, would rent for nearly ten times your budgeted amount. Large beachfront rentals in August *start* at twenty thousand dollars a week. That's where they *start*." Eddie then pauses, waiting for the caller to hang up.

Most cold calls are rentals. People who are in the market to sell already have a broker, and if they are no longer on favorable terms with that broker, they hire that broker's worst enemy. (Eddie got plenty of clients this way in his previous life, people defecting from Addison Wheeler and, yes, Glenn Daley.) People in the market to buy are usually referred to a broker by their financial adviser or the guy they play squash with, or they use the broker who helped them when they were merely renters.

It's exceedingly rare that someone cold-calls looking to buy, and buy big, but that's exactly what happens when Eddie picks up the phone.

The woman introduces herself as Masha.

"Masha?" Eddie says. The name sounds vaguely Russian, which unfortunately leads Eddie to think about his crew of call girl housecleaners, who have all been banished back to Kyrgyzstan. "M-a-s-h-a?"

"No, *Masha*," the woman says. "Like, *'Masha, Masha, Masha.'*" Pause. "From *The Brady Bunch.*"

"Oh, *Marcia*," Eddie says. The woman's accent is straight out of Jeremiah Burke High School in Dorchester and Eddie knows not to get his hopes up. People from Dorchester, Jamaica Plain, Brockton, and Fall River don't buy houses on Nantucket. People from those towns generally don't come to Nantucket at all because they don't like paying sixteen dollars for a turkey sandwich, nine dollars for a Bud Light, or five dollars for a gallon of gas. "My name is Eddie, Marcia. Eddie Pancik. What can I help you with today?"

"My husband, Raja, and I..."

Raja sounds vaguely Indian, and Eddie wonders if Raja is a tech millionaire or, possibly, a professor of astrophysics at MIT. But then Eddie calculates in Marcia's muscular accent and realizes the husband's name is Roger.

"Yes?" Eddie says patiently, though he can already tell this woman will be spending her summer vacation at the Shady Rest Motel up-beach in Revere. All is not lost for Marcia and Roger, however; there is an excellent clam shack near the Shady Rest.

"We won Powerball," Marcia says. "The lottery? So now we want to buy a house on Nantucket. We want to look at everything you've got between ten and fifteen million."

Eddie takes a second to clear his throat. "Well, all right, then," he says. His hopes feel like soap bubbles, iridescent and delicate. He waits for them to pop, one by one. Marcia and Roger won Powerball, and out of the twenty-something real estate agencies on Nantucket they have called Bayberry Properties and reached Eddie Pancik on the phone to find them a ten-to-fifteen-million-dollar house. What are the chances? Eddie reminds himself that there are phonies and fakers out there—unsophisticated pranksters and more-nefarious *Talented Mr. Ripley* types. But this Marcia sounds earnest, her accent genuine. Eddie grew up on Purchase Street in New Bedford; he should know. "Let's schedule a day for you to visit, and I'll set up the appointments."

As soon as Eddie hangs up the phone, he Googles the names. Roger and Marcia Christy of East Boston pop up right away in a sidebar of the *Boston Herald*. The couple won $132 million from a lottery ticket that they bought from Lanzilli Groceria in Orient Heights near Constitution Beach.

They're for real! Eddie thinks. A hundred thirty-two million. If they took the payout, they probably ended up with eighty million, and after paying 40 percent in taxes, they're left with forty-eight million. So a ten-to-fifteen-million-dollar investment in real estate seems reasonable. The Christys are coming to Nantucket next Friday for the weekend, and Eddie will set up at least six houses for them to look at. He will take them to lunch someplace charming but modest—either the Nantucket Pharmacy lunch counter or Something Natural. He will chauffeur them around in Barbie's new Escalade, since Eddie and Grace are sharing a sixteen-year-old Jeep Cherokee that has a weird, persistent smell of old popcorn.

Eddie rubs his hands together. If he can sell the Powerball Christys a house, he will officially be *back*.

He tells Allegra he's taking lunch—normally, he works right through it—but he's too excited to eat, so instead he decides to go for a walk. It's a crisp, beautiful fall day on Nantucket. The trees on Main Street are ablaze with color, but the first frost has yet to arrive, so all the chrysanthemums and dahlias in the window boxes are still blooming. If the Christys could see Nantucket right now, today, they would buy in a heartbeat. This is the most charming island in the world, in Eddie's opinion—a whole different planet from East Boston. The homes in town are not just aesthetically pleasing; they're old, they have architectural integrity, they contain stories—stories of the whaling heyday, captains and crews, men lost at sea, men returned safely to loved ones, stories of Quakers and Unitarians, Native Americans and Cape Verdeans, stories of love, betrayal, death, achievement, failure, hope, faith, family. Eddie tears up a little, thinking about how lucky he is to live in so authentic and singular a place. Most people think real estate is a business about property and therefore money, but Eddie would argue that real estate is a business about people.

And about money.

His tears are partially those of relief. If he can split the difference and sell the Christys a house for twelve-five, he'll get a $375,000 commission, a third of which will go to the office, still leaving him with a quarter of a million dollars.

Breathing room. He might even be in a position to start house hunting himself.

He considers walking home to Lily Street to tell Grace the news, but he's torn. On the one hand, he has vowed to be more open and emotionally available to Grace, to share what's going on in his "interior life," and right now what he's feeling is cautiously optimistic. But on the other hand, Eddie is superstitious. He feels that as soon as he discloses the prospect of good news, it will evaporate. The Christys will cancel their trip on Friday, saying they have decided to buy on Martha's Vineyard instead. Or they will have done further exploring on the Internet and decide to go with a different real estate company, most likely Addison Wheeler or, the worst-case scenario, Rachel McMann. There are a million things that can go wrong, Eddie knows. He decides to wait and tell Grace after he spends the day with the Christys.

On his right Eddie passes Winter Street, and he stops. The Winter Street Inn is there at the end of the block, and Eddie wonders if he should stop by to see the Quinns and ask if there is anything he can bring to the party next week. Would it seem rude, popping by unannounced? Grace told Eddie that she was surprised the Quinns were throwing a party because she had heard that Kelley Quinn was quite sick. Prostate cancer or brain cancer, she couldn't recall which. Eddie chided Grace for repeating rumors. The gossip on this island was toxic. Hadn't they learned that much?

Eddie strolls down Winter Street, deciding that he will pop in to say hello, not least of all because he's feeling a bit peckish, and the inn is famous for serving homemade snacks like warm cheddar tartlets and sweet-and-spicy pecans throughout the day.

Eddie steps up to the front door and uses the knocker.

A long moment passes with no answer, long enough for Eddie to think that nobody is home. But is that likely? At an inn? But then the door swings open and Mitzi is standing before him, her cheeks rosy, her hair mussed. She smiles, but he can tell she doesn't quite recognize him. Can he blame her? He hasn't seen her in a number of years. The last Christmas Eve party Eddie attended here at the inn, Mitzi was mysteriously absent, and there were rumors about *that,* to be sure, something about Mitzi having an affair with Santa Claus, too weird and fantastical to believe.

"Hi, Mitzi," Eddie says. "It's Eddie, Eddie Pancik."

She still looks uncertain, and so Eddie resorts to use of his loathsome nickname. "Fast Eddie."

He watches this click into place. Her face lights up with recognition, if not with actual joy. "Eddie!" she says. "I'm so sorry! You must think me dreadfully rude. It's just . . . well, I wasn't expecting anyone, least of all you. You're home, then? Back on Nantucket? For good?" She seems to be scrambling for the proper way to ask if Eddie has been released from jail. He has found the best way to deal with people is to be straightforward.

"Back home," he says. "I served my time. I'm a new man."

"Well, that's good to hear," Mitzi says. "Not that there was anything wrong with you before. Listen, if anyone knows about losing one's way for a while, it's me—as I'm sure you've heard."

Eddie isn't sure what to say. Maybe the rumors about Mitzi running away with the inn's Santa Claus are true, then. And yet, here she is, answering the door, looking as pretty and fresh as ever. Still with the long skirts and the dangly earrings, like she just returned from a Peter, Paul and Mary concert.

"Grace and I got your invitation," Eddie says. "Unfortunately, Grace has volunteer duties she can't escape from, but I will be attending your party with my daughter Allegra."

"How lovely!" Mitzi says. She holds the door open a little wider. "Please, come in for a minute, won't you?"

"Well, I don't see why not," Eddie says, motivated by the

possibility of a few warm cheddar tartlets. "Although I really just stopped by to give you my RSVP in person and to see if I can bring anything."

"Now, remind me, Eddie," Mitzi says as she leads Eddie through the inn's living and dining rooms to the spacious, airy country kitchen. Eddie scans the counter for tartlets or nuts or muffins, but all he sees is an open bag of kale chips. He feels like maybe he's made a mistake in dropping by. If he remembers correctly, Mitzi is a talker. He might be held hostage for the remainder of the afternoon. "I lose track of other people's children so quickly. Are the twins still in high school?"

"They graduated in 2016," Eddie says. "So right now Hope is a sophomore at Bucknell. And Allegra is living at home with Grace and me. Turns out, college wasn't for her. She's working with me at Bayberry Properties right now, trying to figure out her next step."

"College isn't for everyone, Eddie," Mitzi says. "And there's no reason to be ashamed. Until recently Kelley and I had three out of our four adult children living at home. Now, thankfully, Kevin has a place of his own, and Ava has moved to New York. So we only have Bart. He's also trying to figure out his next step. He's been trying for ten months."

"He's a war hero," Eddie says.

"This is true," Mitzi says. "But he still has his entire life ahead of him. All he does is . . . sit in his room." She looks at Eddie and her eyes fill with tears. "I don't know what to do. He won't see a therapist. I'm throwing this party mostly to get him out of the house, to get him out among the living again."

Eddie nods and arranges his face to appear sympathetic, although he feels uneasy. As his wife, Grace, will gladly tell you: Eddie is unqualified to be anyone's therapist. "How's Kelley doing?" he asks, hoping to change the subject.

At this, the tears fall. "He's dying," Mitzi says. "His doctor says two, maybe three, months at the most. He has an inoperable tumor on the brain that is rapidly encroaching on his basic functions. He lost sight in his left eye. He has tumors on three of his vertebrae. And you know what? He's as cheerful as I've ever seen him. He doesn't seem to mind that he disappears a little more each day. He doesn't seem to care that he's leaving us behind. I mean, what am I going to do?" Mitzi tilts her head toward the ceiling, tears streaming down her face, and Eddie feels genuinely awful. Poor Mitzi! Her son has some form of PTSD, most likely, and her husband is dying. By comparison, Eddie's problems seem very small indeed. He has to answer the phones—so what? His house is only seven hundred square feet—boohoo! At least Grace and the girls are healthy. All the hardships Eddie is enduring right now he has brought upon himself. He needs to remember that.

He wants to reach out to Mitzi. Should he hug her? He thinks not. That's how affairs get started. Not that Mitzi would ever be interested in *him,* although he does think he's a sight better looking than Santa Claus.

"What can I do?" he asks. "How can I help?"

Mitzi wipes the tears from her face with a dish towel. "You can sell the inn for me."

"Really?" Eddie says.

"I can't run it anymore," Mitzi says. "I won't be able to run it without Kelley, even if Bart helps."

"Are you sure?" Eddie says. Obviously, he would love to take on the inn as a listing, but he doesn't want Mitzi to make any snap decisions while she's emotional.

"I could probably make it work for a little while," Mitzi says. "But I don't want to. Kelley and I were getting burned out on it a few years ago, which is part of the reason why . . ."

Here she stops and waves a hand in front of her face, as if clearing away a cloud of gnats or a bad smell. "Why we had all of our issues. I think Kelley approached you about selling the inn a few years ago, didn't he?"

"He may have mentioned something about it," Eddie says. He remembers that at the last Christmas Eve party Eddie attended, Kelley was quite keen to sell the inn. But Eddie never heard anything further, so he assumed it was a dead end, like so many others.

"You're the only broker Kelley likes," Mitzi says. "He thinks you're a hustler." She blinks. "In a good sense. You hustle. You work hard, nose to the grindstone. You get results."

"I understand," Eddie says. He surveys the kitchen for any snacks he may have missed. He's starving. "I've always loved this inn."

"We've made some capital improvements," Mitzi says. "Kelley's ex-wife, Margaret Quinn? The news anchor? She lent Kelley some money—gave him some money, really—that he then poured back into the building."

"I would be happy to sell the place for you," Eddie says. "And I could get you a wonderful price, I'm sure." Without seeing upstairs, he's thinking of listing at seven and a half million, and settling on six-five or seven. If he has the listing and the buyer, he will be looking at a payday of over four hundred grand. "But why don't we wait until you're absolutely sure."

"I am absolutely sure," Mitzi says, and her voice takes on an affronted tone that Eddie recognizes from Grace. The tone says: *Are you not taking me seriously because I'm a woman?*

"Okay, then," Eddie says. "Let's get together sometime after the party, and we'll write up a listing sheet."

Mitzi exhales in a long stream of relief. "Thank you," she says.

"It's my job," Eddie says. He rubs his hands together; his stomach is now seriously rumbling. "I should go."

Mitzi sees Eddie to the door and waves as he strides down Winter Street. "See you Tuesday," she says. "With Allegra."

Eddie waves back. He is so stunned at his good fortune that he's already back on Main Street before he realizes that he forgot to ask about costumes.

JENNIFER

In theory, Jennifer is too busy to be unhappy. She's finishing up a project she adores—an 1827 single-family home on Garden Street in Beacon Hill—and she is about to start a from-scratch job on a penthouse suite in the brand-new luxury building Millennium Tower, on the site of the original Filene's in Downtown Crossing.

The two projects couldn't be more different. The Garden Street house is owned by one of the most wonderful couples Jennifer has ever known—Leanne and Derek Clinton—who have moved back to the city from the suburbs now that their four children are out of the house. Derek is the head of the actuarial department at John Hancock, and Leanne works part-time as a pro bono civil rights attorney. They are gracious, evolved people who want to restore the house to the glory of its former heyday, but with modern conveniences and decorating vignettes in each room, which Leanne calls "moments of joy." Jennifer blends classic paint colors and carefully curated antiques with her signature whimsy—a zebra-print rug, a feathered chandelier, a mirror in the powder room decoupaged with pages from Derek's and Leanne's old passports.

The penthouse, on the other hand, is owned by a man named Grayson Coker, who goes by the nickname Coke. He's the fifty-four-year-old, thrice-divorced CEO of Boston Bank. (Jennifer has tried calling him Mr. Coker, but she gets reprimanded every time. "Coke, please, Jen," he says. He is so insistent on this informality that Jennifer doesn't have the heart to tell him that she loathes being called Jen.) Coke isn't particular about how Jennifer decorates his apartment as long as the space is "sleek," "modern," and "intimidating."

"Intimidating?" Jennifer asks, thinking she's misunderstood. "You want your apartment to frighten people?" She has been decorating for twelve years, and this is the first time she has received this instruction.

"Not frighten, exactly," Coke says. "But I'd like to put my visitors on edge. I'd like the space to make a statement. I'd like it to convey power."

"Power," Jennifer says. She's already longing for Leanne with her offers of homemade maple-ginger scones.

"I'm thinking sharp angles, bold art. Nothing fussy. Nothing feminine."

Jennifer nods. She is so far out of her comfort zone that she considers turning the project down. How did Coke end up finding Jennifer in the first place? She decides to ask him point-blank.

"A friend of a friend recommended you," Coke says. "She told me you're the best in Boston."

Jennifer resists the flattery (the "friend of a friend" is likely one of Coke's lovers; there are many, Jennifer is sure), but she decides to stick with the job because the payday is too phenomenal to ignore. Patrick has launched a new hedge fund, but it's taking him longer to raise the capital than he initially anticipated. He works around the clock for little or no monetary gain.

Jennifer also hopes that by taking on a project so foreign to her nature she might beat back some of the *cravings* she's been experiencing lately.

The cravings have become more frequent and more and more pronounced recently. Jennifer will be perusing fabric samples or making chicken salad for the boys' lunches, and she'll think: *Something is missing.* This niggling thought irritates her further. She has everything she could ever want: her husband is back, her children are healthy, her career is booming. But then Jennifer watches Leanne Clinton move through the world with such ease, such contentment and clarity of purpose; it's like she's keeping a wonderful secret, the secret of happiness. Aside from her part-time work on behalf of the commonwealth's underdogs, Leanne goes to barre class six days a week and to Mass every Sunday.

Does Jennifer need more exercise? Does she need religion?

She misses the pills. There, she's said it.

Once the house on Garden Street is finally finished, when there is nothing else she can purchase, tweak, or fluff, Jennifer fills with a sense of mournful good-bye like it's the last day of summer camp. It's time to get serious about the penthouse project. Before she makes her first big purchase for Coke, she sets up a meeting; the last thing she wants is to order eighty thousand dollars' worth of furniture only to discover that he hates it all.

Coke works preposterous hours, and he says that the only time he can meet with Jennifer in the space is at eight thirty on Thursday night. Eight thirty is smack in the middle of the hour that Jennifer cherishes the most. It's after dinner, the boys are doing their homework (or, more likely, playing Minecraft and Snapchatting), Jennifer is well into her third and final glass of wine of the evening as she cleans up dinner and makes the lunches. She is usually wearing her yoga pants and her Patriots T-shirt. The prospect of getting dressed up and going out at that hour is exhausting—but what choice does Jennifer have?

She decides to make the best of it. She encourages Paddy to take the boys out for barbecue at Sweet Cheeks for some father-son quality time. Meanwhile, Jennifer puts on a skirt and boots and takes herself out for a cocktail at Carrie Nation, next to the State House. She gets a few appreciative looks from the businessmen having drinks at the bar, which cheers her up. Why doesn't she do this more often? She could meet one of her divorced-mom friends for drinks. She could even meet Leanne. But then Jennifer comes to her senses. She doesn't frequent the Beacon Hill bars because she is busy running a business, raising three boys, and being happily married.

Coke is at the space when Jennifer arrives. She notices a bottle of scotch and two highball glasses on the black porphyry bar. An acoustic version of Bruce Springsteen singing "Fire" plays over the sound system. All the lights are out.

Coke is standing in front of the floor-to-ceiling windows looking northeast over the financial district and the seaport. To the west is Boston Common, the Boston Public Garden, and Back Bay. This penthouse has been designed to make the owner feel like the king of Boston.

"The views are much better at night with the lights off," Coke says. "Can I fix you a drink?"

Jennifer is about to ask if he has any wine, but she doesn't want to come off as fussy. She has never tasted scotch, although Patrick drinks it occasionally, so how bad can it be?

"Sure," she says.

He pours them each a drink and they clink glasses. Coke says, "Not only the best interior decorator in Boston, but certainly the most beautiful. Do people ever tell you you look like Selma Blair?"

"All the time," Jennifer says, because they do, and this gets a big laugh out of Coke. Jennifer laughs right along and takes a sip of her whiskey. It's bitter firewater, but Jennifer savors the burn.

Jennifer pulls out her laptop, but Coke waves it away. "I don't need to see the pictures," he says. "I trust you."

"Are you sure?" Jennifer says. These are the words every decorator wants to hear, but she's wary. Most of the things she picked out are severe, but some are softer, such as two Kelly Wearstler soufflé chairs. The chairs verge on feminine, but Jennifer's thought is that they will make the room seem inviting to women. She has also picked a selection of antique banks to line the accent shelf in the living space, since all she knows about Coke, really, is that he's a banker. She also knows he's a philanthropist to Boston charities—the Jimmy Fund, the MFA, Boston Ballet. And he's something of a notorious bachelor, photographed with a different woman on the social pages of nearly every issue of *Boston Common*.

"I'm sure," Coke says. "I did my research."

"You looked at my designs online?" Jennifer asks.

"Some," Coke says. "I learned what I could about you as a professional and as a person. You grew up in San Francisco, you attended Stanford, you worked for six years at Christie's, you're married to Patrick Quinn, formerly of Everlast Investments, and stood by his side while he served time for insider trading. You live on Beacon Street in the house that has the Christmas tree in the bay window, the one all the tourists take pictures of."

"Wow," Jennifer says. "I'm flattered. And also a little frightened."

"Well, I figure if I'm going to be paying someone north of half a million dollars and entrusting her with a budget that's four or five times that, then I'd better know who I'm dealing with."

Jennifer nods slowly and takes a closer look at Coke. He's six feet tall, has salt-and-pepper hair. He's reasonably well built, but he's not overtly handsome. And yet he has something. He's a conqueror. His confidence is the biggest thing in the room. It's impossible not to notice, difficult not to admire. He heads one of the biggest banks in Boston, but what that entails Jennifer isn't sure. Probably it entails being decisive, strong, and...intimidating.

"Did you learn anything else about me?" Jennifer asks.

He throws back his scotch and gives her a laser stare. His eyes are green, which gives him a touch of humanity somehow. "Is there something else you want to tell me?"

Jennifer imagines divulging her dark secret—her addiction—and then the even darker news that she still thinks about the pills all the time. But she would never want Coke to know about her weakness. She would sooner take a dive off the wraparound balcony.

"No," she says. "You can learn as we go along." She worries it sounds like she's flirting. Coke's eyes are resting on her throat, and then they travel down the front of her body.

"There is something I want to ask you about the master bath," Coke says. "I have a friendly enemy, a competitor of mine over at Bank of America, who told me that his master bath has an accent wall of lunar rocks."

"*Lunar* rocks?" Jennifer asks. "Rocks from the moon? The actual moon?"

"Come, let's look at it," Coke says. His hand lands on the

exposed bare skin of Jennifer's back. The halter blouse she's wearing is one she bought specifically to please Patrick upon his return from prison. Coke leads Jennifer into the next room, the bedroom, which is empty save for a California king platform bed and a black lacquered dresser. The master bath is on the far side of the bedroom, but Coke stops Jennifer in front of the south-facing window, from which one can see Washington Street, the theater district, Chinatown.

Jennifer is now very, very sorry she agreed to this meeting and even sorrier that she wore such a seductive outfit. The music changes to John Mayer singing the world's sexiest song. It's then Jennifer realizes that Coke intentionally laid a trap and Jennifer has fallen right into it.

She clears her throat and says, "Well, there's no arguing with the view—" But before her words are fully out, Coke is pulling her toward him for a kiss. His hand runs down her spine.

She can't believe this is happening. When his lips meet hers, she panics. What should she do? She pushes against the front of Coke's beautifully tailored shirt.

"No," she says. "I'm sorry, Coke, I can't. I'm happily married."

There is one instant when Jennifer thinks things might still be okay. Coke can laugh it off, apologize, blame his forwardness on the alcohol. He can promise to behave himself from here on out so that they can have a drama-free working relationship, and Jennifer can collect her half a million in fees and be the decorator for the most prestigious project in Boston.

But instead Coke pulls Jennifer in even closer and places his mouth on the sensitive skin just below her ear. He bites her lightly and says, "Come on, Jen. We both know you aren't *that* happy."

"*What?*" Jennifer says. Coke's voice is that of her inner demons. She's *not* that happy. But sleeping with Grayson Coker isn't going to help; it's going to make things far, far worse. Jennifer struggles to disentangle herself without actually striking out at him, but he won't loosen his grip. She can still feel his breath on her neck. "Please," she says. "Let me go. Let me go right this instant."

He pushes her away and she stumbles in her boots, but thankfully doesn't fall. She steadies herself and hurries into the other room, where she pulls on her coat. She should never have taken it off! She should never have worn this blouse! What was she *thinking!* She snatches up her bag.

"I'm leaving, Mr. Coker," she says. "I'm sorry, but I don't think this job will work out for me."

Coke stands in the doorway, shaking his head as though she's a disappointing child. "It's your loss, Jen."

"Jennifer," she says. "My name is Jennifer Quinn." With this, she storms from the apartment onto the elevator and prays he won't follow her.

Walking home, Jennifer is shaking, addled, confused. How did that meeting go off the rails so quickly? Was it her fault for agreeing to the late hour, to the empty apartment, to the drink? She had worn the wrong outfit, and she should never have gone for a cocktail at Carrie Nation. She shouldn't have worn makeup or perfume, a skirt or high-heeled boots.

Then Jennifer stops herself. It wasn't her fault. Coke misinterpreted her body language or her nonverbal cues, maybe even the tone of her voice. Jennifer asked him nicely to stop; she was firm and clear, and still he persisted. He was in the wrong. Jennifer's only choice was to walk away from Grayson Coker and his fabulous project and all his money.

It's your loss, Jen.

She can't help feeling he's right. She and Paddy needed that money. Needed it badly.

Jennifer arrives home a few minutes before Paddy and the boys, which gives her enough time to change out of the cursed outfit into her yoga pants and Patriots T-shirt. Paddy looks happier than he has in weeks, maybe months; the time alone with the kids cheered him up. He has barbecue sauce on his cheek. Jennifer wipes it off, and he kisses her.

"How was the meeting?" he asks.

She hears the boys happily roughhousing out in the hallway. "Fine," she says.

Patrick leans farther in and kisses nearly the exact spot by Jennifer's ear that Coke bit. Jennifer tries not to cringe. She likes to tell Patrick everything—or nearly everything—but she knows there is no way to share this story without ruining the night and creating a scene. It will be beyond a scene, as two issues are at stake: Jennifer's honor, for one, and the lost money, for another. Jennifer can easily imagine Patrick deciding to walk over to Millennium Tower with a baseball bat, prepared to threaten Grayson Coker. And what if Jennifer takes partial responsibility? What if she shows Patrick what she was wearing?

"I Googled the guy," Patrick says. "He's the sixth-richest man in Boston."

"I'm not sure it's the right project for me," Jennifer says.

"I thought we went over this," Patrick says. "If you don't stretch, you won't grow. It'll be good for you to try something different."

Jennifer can't find the words to refute him, and so she hugs Patrick close and nods against his chest. She's going to have to tell him the job is gone, but she won't do it tonight.

"I'm going downstairs," she says. "I need to make the lunches."

*   *   *

The next morning, despite a slight hangover from the scotch, Jennifer decides to meet Leanne at barre class. She needs to pulse out her anxiety. She thinks she might even tell Leanne what happened with Grayson Coker and ask her advice about how to handle it with Patrick. What Jennifer needs is a friend, a confidante.

What she needs, she thinks, is an Ativan.

She's crossing the Public Garden when her phone pings. She gets a funny feeling and thinks: *It's Grayson Coker, apologizing.* But when she sees the alert, she stops in her tracks.

It's a text from Norah Vale.

It's as if Norah Vale has read her mind or sensed that this morning of all mornings is when Jennifer is at her most vulnerable.

Jennifer plops down on the nearest park bench. She should delete the text without reading it, she thinks. Because what could it possibly say?

Well, Jennifer reasons, it doesn't automatically have to be about drugs. Jennifer hasn't seen or heard from Norah since the previous Christmas, when Norah kindly switched ferry tickets with Jennifer so that Jennifer, Paddy, and the boys could get to Nantucket in time for Kevin's wedding. Kevin's *second* wedding—because Kevin's first wedding had been to Norah herself. Norah Vale should have been the last person to offer to help, but she did so anyway.

Curiosity gets the best of Jennifer. She opens the text. It says: *Something I want to talk to u about. Will u be on Nantucket anytime soon?*

Jennifer freezes and scans her surroundings, as though she's worried Norah is somewhere in the Public Garden watching her.

Something I want to talk to u about.

Wait! Jennifer thinks. Norah asked her for a letter of recommendation last year because she was applying to business school. So maybe Norah wants to use Jennifer's interior decorating business as one of her case studies. There's no reason why Jennifer should automatically assume the worst. Norah is a person who has made authentic changes in her life.

Will u be on Nantucket anytime soon?

This seems odd, right? Because if Norah merely wanted to talk, they could do so over the phone. Very few topics require an in-person conversation...unless it's something too sensitive for the phone.

Such as the pills.

Jennifer's legs are shaky when she stands up. She needs to get a grip; she needs to get to barre class. She needs to put her eyes on Leanne's placid face and hear about Leanne and Derek's latest heavenly dinner at Giulia.

As Jennifer walks down the footpath in the middle of Comm. Ave., she realizes that she *will* be on Nantucket soon—next week, for Bart's birthday party. It's on a Tuesday and therefore wildly inconvenient, but Patrick's former secretary, Alyssa, volunteered to stay overnight with the boys and even take Pierce and Jaime trick-or-treating. Both Jennifer and Patrick realize how important it is to Mitzi that they attend.

Has Norah somehow found out about the party? Is this text just her angling for an invite? Jennifer knows that Norah harbors some regret about no longer being a part of the Quinn family. Jennifer doesn't think she longs for Kevin, exactly; it's more that she wants to be included in—or perhaps forgiven by—the larger family.

As Jennifer turns left onto Clarendon, she sees Leanne

waiting for her outside the barre studio, and her anxiety diminishes just a little. Jennifer waves.

Be present, she tells herself. She will think about Grayson Coker and Norah Vale later.

AVA

She stands at the entrance of the Museum of Natural History at five minutes to eleven, waiting for Potter and PJ to emerge from the subway. Potter called the night before, saying that PJ had fallen asleep in the taxi. "I think his overreaction was due to exhaustion," Potter said. "It's harder to fly east than fly west."

"Is it?" Ava said.

"Jet lag is a real thing!" Potter said defensively.

Potter's plan today was to let PJ sleep in, then take him for a big breakfast at Tom's Restaurant, and then they would fulfill PJ's fervent wish to ride the subway. PJ's enthusiasm to ride the subway has been fueled in part by Potter's ex-wife, Trish, who said that under no circumstances was PJ to ride the subway.

Ava takes a deep breath of crisp October air. They will spend the afternoon at the museum, capping off their visit with the Hayden Planetarium, and then they will go for a late lunch. There's a great banh mi shop down the street, or if PJ is amenable, they can sit outside at Cafe Luxembourg, where Ava and Potter can split a bottle of Sancerre and PJ can eat *frites* out of a paper cone.

And then tonight...what will they do tonight? An IMAX movie? A trip to the top of the Empire State Building? The ghost tour of Greenwich Village? The possibilities are endless.

Ava loves New York!

Ava's reverie is disrupted by the sight of Potter's head. They are so connected that Ava sometimes feels his presence before she actually sees him. A few seconds later PJ appears. Potter has PJ by one hand, but in PJ's other hand is a device that has captured his attention. At least he's not resisting, shrieking, or throwing a tantrum.

Ava waves to Potter, and he waves back and cuts a diagonal across the street, pulling PJ along.

"Hey there," Potter says. His demeanor is unruffled. Ava decides to proceed as though last night never happened.

"Hey there yourself," Ava says. She refrains from kissing Potter in front of PJ, although it's difficult. *Tread lightly,* she thinks. They can act as though they're friends who have randomly met up on the street. "Hey there, PJ. I'm Ava."

PJ doesn't respond. He doesn't even look up. He's absorbed in his game. He's playing it on an iPhone 7, which is a nicer phone than either Ava or Potter has. Where did he get it? Does it belong to Trish? Certainly it's not his—he's only seven years old.

"Put the phone down, buddy, and say hello to Ava," Potter says.

PJ doesn't respond. His fingers are skating across the screen.

"What game are you playing?" Ava asks.

PJ doesn't answer.

"Minecraft," Potter says.

Ah, Minecraft. Ava has long listened to the people she knows with children complain about Minecraft. Apparently, it's the bane of every parent's existence. Even Ava's sister-in-law

Jennifer complains about it. But now Ava wishes she had been paying closer attention about what Minecraft *is* exactly. If she knew the details, she might be able to bond with PJ over the mines or the crafts.

"Shall we go in?" Ava asks. She leads the way through the entrance and waits while Potter gets tickets for the three of them, then they glide into the museum.

Ava hasn't set foot in this museum since she was a child herself, but all the memories come rushing back. She recalls school field trips—brown bag lunches, the buddy system, worksheets to fill out in each wing—as well as the rainy weekends after her parents split. Ava and Patrick and Kevin used to spend the week with Margaret in the brownstone on East Eighty-Eighth Street, and the weekends with Kelley in his sleek, new high-rise down in the financial district. Kelley was a lost soul in those days. Ava wasn't old enough to understand it then, though it's clear to her now. Kelley's brother, Avery, was dying of AIDS down in Greenwich Village, and so Kelley was adamant about spending his weekends with the kids uptown. Patrick and Kevin were teenagers, so they had friends and sports to use as excuses to escape the sad, desperate weekends with Kelley. But Ava was stuck. In clement weather she and Kelley went to Central Park, where they watched the roller skaters or threw stones in the Lake. When it was cold or raining, they came here.

There were things about this museum that Ava loved: the big elephant, the squid and the whale, the gemstones. She has bad memories of the dinosaurs and even worse memories of the Hall of Indigenous Peoples. She was sick to her stomach one Sunday and threw up in her father's hands in front of the diorama of the Maoris.

"Where shall we start?" Ava asks. She has the map in her

hand and is filled with optimism. The offerings in this day and age are almost overwhelming. There's the Butterfly Conservatory, an exhibition on the Arctic, an exhibit on bats, an exhibit on the city of Petra, and one on the jewelry of Native Americans. There's the planetarium, which they'll save for last. There are the fossil halls, the dinosaurs, the mammals, the gems and minerals—they'll have to stroll through there for old times' sake—the Hall of Human Origins, and...the Discovery Room! Ava forgot about the Discovery Room, but she can vividly recall whiling away the hours there while Kelley read the Week in Review section of the *Times* on a bench. He didn't realize that *quality time* meant he should get down on his hands and knees and marvel with Ava over the drawer filled with cowrie and turret shells.

But Kelley made up for it later. He was a wonderful father. He is *still* a wonderful father, Ava thinks. She fights to keep composed, but neither Potter nor PJ is paying attention to her anyway. PJ is staring at the phone, and Potter is looking around the museum, clearly at a loss.

"Dinosaurs," Ava says. "Let's start with dinosaurs."

"Dinosaurs," Potter says. He's clearly relieved that Ava has taken charge. "You like dinosaurs, right, bud?"

PJ is too engrossed with his game to answer, and Ava looks up at Potter. *Take it away from him!* she thinks. *We are in a museum!* Surely, there are plenty of interactive screens here now, many more than twenty-five years ago. She can't believe Potter is allowing him to willfully ignore his surroundings.

"PJ...," Potter says, but he stops. He looks helpless. What can Ava do but reflect back on Margaret's words: *You may think you know Potter inside and out, but just remember, you've never seen him be a parent. You may be surprised.*

Potter is the most intelligent, evolved, kind, sexy, charming, and fun-loving man Ava has ever met. He's everything she could dream of wanting. And yet as a parent... well, the most flattering word Ava can come up with right now is *ineffectual*. But she, for one, isn't going to let PJ miss the wonders of this museum.

She crouches down. She realizes she hasn't seen the color of PJ's eyes. Are they blue like Potter's?

"Hey," she says. "PJ, we're in a museum, and the museum has a lot of cool things in it, like dinosaurs and bats. Bats echolocate. Do you know what that means?"

PJ doesn't flinch, or even blink. He is intent on his game, moving a finger with a sad, chewed-up nail over the screen. It's like he's hypnotized. Ava puts one hand on his arm, and with her other hand she reaches for the phone.

"Bad touch!" PJ screams. "Bad touch! Bad touch!"

Ava recoils. She stands up, her cheeks blazing. "I'm sorry," she says.

Potter says, "Buddy, put down the phone. Here, I'll take it." He reaches out a hand, which PJ ignores.

Just take it from him! Ava thinks. But PJ is not her child. She needs to tread lightly.

Potter retracts his hand and shrugs. He offers Ava a lame smile. "Shall we go see the dinosaurs?" he asks.

They wander through the museum, two adults feigning enthusiasm for arachnids and the rings of Jupiter, while PJ tags along, playing Minecraft. Ava hardly sees the point of all this. At the threshold to each new hall, she wants to tell Potter she's going home. She will leave them alone for the rest of the weekend; she will join Drake and Margaret at Le Coucou tonight. But if she tells Potter this, he'll be upset, maybe even angry. He'll say she's abandoning ship... then she'll tell *him* he's a piss-poor skipper...and then they will become one of *those* couples—a couple who bickers in public places.

So instead Ava plays along, and at one point, in the lush, steamy greenhouse that is the Butterfly Conservatory, Potter reaches for her hand and gives it a tight squeeze. And for just a moment everything is okay.

When they leave the museum, Ava is starving. She and Potter have been so busy trying to find an exhibit that would snatch PJ from the grasp of his device that they forgot all about lunch.

"Should we try for a table at Cafe Luxembourg?" Ava asks Potter once they are out in the mellow sunshine of the street.

He shakes his head. "Subway home," he says.

"All right," Ava says. "I'll say good-bye now, then."

"No!" Potter says, so loudly that PJ actually stutter-steps and looks up. "Please come back with us. I'll order you the shrimp tebsi from Massawa."

Ava does indeed love the shrimp tebsi from Massawa, but she also feels that what Potter and PJ need is time alone, time to bond, time to connect without interference from Ava. To tread lightly means to now make a graceful exit.

But when she looks up into Potter's eyes, she sees fear. He's afraid to be left alone with his own son.

"Okay," she says. "Subway home, shrimp tebsi."

Either the novelty of the subway wore off on the ride downtown or PJ was never really into it to begin with, because the wait, embarkation, ride, and disembarkation are all marked by the pinging and bleeping of PJ's game. Ava begins to worry about the child's eyesight and the unnatural bend to his young neck. She yearns to grab the phone and throw it at the third rail, where it will explode in a burst of blue electronic flame.

The doorman in Potter's building, Keith, is a student at Columbia Journalism School. Ava has befriended him, and she enjoys talking with him about politics, but today his face is pained, stressed even, and Ava wonders if it's midterm time already.

"Professor Lyons?" he says. "You have guests waiting outside your apartment."

"Guests?" Potter says.

Keith shows Potter the IDs. "I told them you were out, but they said they wanted to wait. She said—"

"Yes, I know what she said." Potter is suddenly abrupt.

"What is it?" Ava asks. She's thinking it's a disgruntled student, because Potter has this problem occasionally. He teaches plenty of kids who got used to coasting by with automatic As in high school only to arrive at the Ivy League and realize life isn't always so easy.

Potter shakes his head and presses his lips closed as they enter the elevator.

When they step off on the seventh floor, Ava sees shadowy figures lurking outside Potter's apartment door. Ava sees it's a couple—a man with dark, curly hair wearing a gray flannel scarf wound artfully around his neck, and a woman wearing horn-rimmed glasses. The woman has a long braid trailing down one shoulder, and she's wearing an adorable short white boiled-wool belted coat over a houndstooth skirt and boots. They look too old and too sophisticated to be students. Are they colleagues, maybe?

And then Ava gets it.

PJ drops his phone onto the carpeted hallway and sprints toward the couple.

It's Potter's ex-wife, Trish, and Trish's boyfriend, Harrison. Ava remembers Harrison's name because Harrison is British and Ava thinks of George Harrison, the Beatle.

Ava stands up a little straighter and runs a tongue across her teeth. She bemoans her own outfit: jeans and a J.Crew turtleneck in forest green, topped by her ancient brown corduroy jacket. The jacket is her security blanket, and she intentionally wore it hoping it would serve as a shield or armor against any insults or injuries inflicted by PJ. But now that she is faced with Trish in her supercute belted coat and fabulous suede stiletto boots, she wishes she'd worn something chicer.

When Ava said that she doesn't feel (much) insecurity, she should have added an asterisk that said *except where Trish York is concerned*. What does Ava know about Trish? That she's a brilliant Shakespearean scholar, that she is a full professor at Stanford, that she comes from an aristocratic family (she grew up in one of the houses on Rainbow Row in Charleston, a city that Potter thinks is the most charming in the world). Trish grew up sailing and that is how she met Potter; they were both crew members on boats during Antigua Sailing Week.

Ava studies Trish now. She's pretty in a sneaky way. The glasses are meant to obscure her clear eyes and impeccable skin. But Ava has learned by now—hasn't she?—that beauty is as beauty does. She has wasted too much of her life fretting over supposedly beautiful women like Kirsten Cabot and Roxanne Oliveria, neither of whom proved to be a threat.

Potter says, "What are you doing here, Trish?"

Harrison steps forward, offering a hand. "Good to see you, Potter." He has a very posh accent. "Potter" comes out as "Pawtah." "We heard there was a bit of trouble, so we left that new fellow Simpson lecturing on Trump as King Lear and came straightaway."

"Trouble?" Potter says.

Trump as King Lear? Ava thinks. She suspects most Shakespeare scholars have run out of things to talk about now, four hundred years later.

"PJ texted me about a 'bad touch,'" Trish says. Her voice too holds a tinge of British accent, which comes across as an affectation to Ava. She expected a Southern belle. "You took him to the museum? Did someone fondle him?"

PJ buries his face in his mother's coat. He's clinging to her like a life buoy.

"The bad touch was me," Ava blurts out. She cannot *believe* this is happening. She cannot believe that PJ, a seven-year-old without any discernible social skills, has manipulated four adults this way. She tries a smile. "I'm Ava, by the way. Ava Quinn."

"That's right," Harrison says, returning her smile in spades. "You're the daughter of Margaret Quinn. I think she's brilliant, by the way. But I hear she's retiring?"

"Next month," Ava says. She is grateful to Harrison for the kindness, but she doesn't want to veer off topic. "Anyway, I did touch PJ's arm. I was trying to encourage him to lift his eyes from the game. He was really preoccupied."

"That blasted game," Harrison says.

"He only plays it when he feels uncomfortable," Trish says.

"That's bollocks and you know it, darling," Harrison says. "He'll play it nonstop if you let him."

"Are you trying to say he feels uncomfortable around me?" Potter says.

"It's not surprising," Trish says. "He barely knows you."

"Because you won't let him see me," Potter says.

"You're welcome to come to California whenever you'd like," Trish says.

"Right," Potter says. "Because I'm free to just fly to California every weekend."

"Not every weekend," Trish says. "We agreed on one weekend a month. That lasted...what? One month? Two? But I understand you have plenty of time to jet off to Anguilla." She cuts a glance at Ava. "And Nantucket."

"Traveling down this road again, I see," Harrison says. He holds his arms open to PJ, who jumps into them like a spider monkey. "I'll take this chap down to the lobby so he doesn't have to endure the parental quarrel." He winks at Ava. "Care to join me, Miss Quinn?"

Ava doesn't have much of a choice. Clearly Potter and Trish need to settle things privately. Ava follows Harrison and PJ into the elevator.

"Why is *she* coming?" PJ asks Harrison.

"'She' is Ava, PJ," Harrison says. "I know you're enough of a gentleman to address a lady properly, and when we reach the lobby, you'll let Ava step off the elevator first. That's what gentlemen do."

"I don't like her," PJ says.

"What?" Harrison says. "You don't like Ava? Well, I like Ava quite a lot myself. She's a beautiful woman."

"No, she isn't," PJ says.

"I'm standing right here," Ava says with a smile. "I can hear you."

"Maybe you're not old enough to appreciate Ava's beauty," Harrison says. "And that is all well and good. You're only seven years old, after all. Barely out of short pants."

This gets a giggle from both Ava and PJ. The elevator doors open, and the gentlemen big and small wait for Ava to exit first.

"Why don't you like Ava, PJ?" Harrison asks. "Did she lock you in a closet, feed you snakes, and then go and get her nails done?"

"No," PJ says.

"Then tell me why you don't like her."

"Because," PJ says.

"Because isn't a reason," Harrison says. "We've been over this a few thousand times, have we not?"

Reluctantly PJ nods. Ava is impressed with how deftly Harrison handles PJ. She likes to think she has solid skills in relating to children, but she was never this good.

"Don't worry about it," Harrison whispers to Ava. "He'll come around."

"Do you think?" Ava says. She wants to pepper Harrison with questions: How did Harrison first bond with PJ? What are a few of his favorite things, other than Minecraft? What is Ava's best strategy for getting PJ's guard down?

Harrison says, "I have an idea, actually. Why don't you give me your cell number?"

"Okay?" Ava says, though she's a bit taken aback. Why on earth would Harrison need her cell phone number? Still, she rattles it off and Harrison programs it into his phone.

A few seconds later Trish comes clipping through the lobby with a suitcase and a small backpack. She grabs PJ by the hand and says to Harrison, "We're going."

"Okay?" Harrison says. He smiles ruefully at Ava. "Cheerio, then, Ava. Lovely to meet you."

"And you," Ava says. She tries to catch Trish's eye. They're all adults; there's no reason why they can't be civil. But Trish storms through the revolving door to the street without a word or look in Ava's direction.

"Bye, PJ!" Ava calls out, but it's too late. He doesn't hear her.

Ava fills with sadness and—she's not going to lie—with relief. Meeting PJ was an unmitigated disaster, but at least now it's over.

For the time being. If she's going to have a future with Potter, she will need to find a way to relate to Potter's child.

Ava waves at Keith, the doorman, who has his nose in a book, studiously trying to appear uninterested in the drama.

Sometime tomorrow Ava will have to call her mother, tell her what transpired, and ask her advice.

But wait—no. Margaret knows nothing about being a stepmother, or even a father's girlfriend. Drake doesn't have children, and to Ava's knowledge, Margaret never dated anyone else with children, or at least young children.

The realization dawns on Ava that she *does* know someone who has been through this. She does know a woman who had no choice but to parent a child not her own. Three children, in fact.

Mitzi. Ava needs to talk to Mitzi.

She could call, she supposes, but the conversation she wants to have would be far better broached in person. As Ava pushes the button for the seventh floor, she makes a decision. She will go home on Tuesday, home to Nantucket. She will go to Bart's birthday party.

BART

The party has three saving graces. One is there will be plentiful alcohol; it is a Quinn party, after all. Two is there will be meat: tenderloin sandwiches, crumbled bacon at the mashed potato bar, passed pigs in a blanket, and *more* bacon wrapped around Nantucket bay scallops. Bart isn't immune to the allure of good food. He has been living at the inn along with Mitzi and Kelley; he has been subjected to the watery spinach soup and the kale–egg white soufflé.

The third saving grace is that his siblings are attending. Patrick and Jennifer are leaving the kids behind in Boston so that they can enjoy an adult evening, and Ava is taking a half day off Tuesday and a personal day on Wednesday so that she can attend. Bart knows his siblings love him, but this party is wholly Mitzi's idea, and ... well, sometimes the elder Quinn children resist Mitzi's ideas.

It does feel good to wake up on the thirty-first and be met with a purpose. It feels good to take a long shower, to shave, and to put on some nice clothes. Bart is wearing jeans, a white button-down shirt, a navy fleece vest, and his good Chucks, the black ones that Mitzi bought him for Christmas. She bought them without even knowing if Bart was alive or not.

He asks his mother if there is anything he can do to help. He is, after all, an able-bodied twenty-two-year-old Marine, still in pretty formidable shape despite everything. Both his parents treat him like a cracked vessel that must be handled gently or it will break in two.

And aren't they right, in a way?

The only injury Bart sustained overseas was a puncture wound to his right cheek; he was attacked when he was trying to save Centaur's life. "Take me, not him!" Bart had cried out. He had tried to pull Centaur from the grip of two Bely, the ones the Marines had nicknamed Grim and Reaper; one of them fought him off with a sharpened piece of rebar, which he caught just under his eye. It knocked him out cold, and when he came to, Centaur was gone.

The only other damage done was to Bart's psyche. He rode high for about six weeks after his return to America. Everything was a cause for celebration: He was free! He was on Nantucket, with his family! Once he'd been captured, he'd lost hope of ever seeing Sankaty Head Light again, of seeing his mother's eyes again, of seeing the Civil War monument at the top of Main Street or his childhood bedroom or the Atlantic Ocean again.

But then once the holidays passed and civilian life on Nantucket became his new normal, Bart started having nightmares about the Pit. His nightmares were followed by panic attacks during the day. There were times when he became convinced that Centaur was alive, as long as Bart... what? That was the terrifying thing: Bart didn't know what he had to do to keep Centaur alive. He would lose control of his breathing to the point of hyperventilation. He would sweat, his vision would splotch, he would feel like he was about to pass out. Then reality would intercede. Centaur was dead. Grim and Reaper had marched him off to the Pit.

Bart shakes his head to clear it. See how easy it is to get trapped in the black grip of his mind?

"I don't want you to see the space before tonight," Mitzi says. "I want you to be surprised. So I'm going to leave now to take care of last-minute details. You can keep your father company."

Okay, good idea. Bart has been meaning to have a conversation with Kelley, but his mother is always, always around, and now there are also hospice workers, two placid women who float around with nearly holy authority, like nuns. Bart is afraid of the hospice workers. They seem to know something about death that he doesn't, and he knows a lot about death.

He knocks on his father's door and peers in. His father is in bed, of course, listening to something on earphones. When Kelley sees Bart, he pulls an earbud out.

"Happy birthday, son," he says. "I meant to tackle you and give you twenty-two noogies, but I think my tackling and noogie days are on hold for now."

Bart breathes, blinks. He loves his father for keeping faith that the tackling and noogie days might return. "What are you listening to? Shouldn't you be sleeping? Getting rested for tonight?"

"It's a Danielle Steel novel," Kelley says. "This one is called *The Mistress*. Want to have a listen?"

"Not really," Bart says, but Kelley ignores him. He pulls the earphone jack out, and a man's melodious, British-accented voice starts describing so-and-so's sweeping desire.

Kelley pats the bed, indicating Bart should sit down, and Bart does so reluctantly. He doesn't think he can tolerate Danielle Steel, even if it were narrated by John Cleese or Daniel Craig.

"There's something I want to talk to you about," Bart says. "Something serious."

Kelley smiles benignly, his eyes at half-mast. Bart knows his father is heavily medicated, but Bart also sees this as his only chance. Kelley isn't going to get any better. His ability to comprehend isn't getting any sharper. Bart reaches over and pauses the book.

This gets Kelley's attention. "What's wrong?" He jerks his head, and Bart remembers that Kelley can see him out of only one eye.

"I want to talk to you, Dad," Bart says.

Kelley sinks back into his pillows and closes his eyes. "Of course, son. I'm sorry."

"I just wanted to let you know that I've made a decision about my future." Bart pauses. He hates the drama of the moment. He hates the circumstances—it's his birthday, Kelley is dying—but he needs to say this. *Say it!*

"I'm going back to active duty. I'm going back to the Marines."

Bart feels a thousand times better now that it's out, but he also braces himself for Kelley's inevitable rebuttal. If Bart goes back on active duty, who will take care of Mitzi? That's the issue. Bart wants to go back to active duty because it's the only thing in his life that he's proven to be good at. He loves the discipline, he craves the camaraderie. He needs to be regimented; otherwise, he falls apart. He started going to the gym on a regular basis after Christmas, but it was a means to no end. Why work out if there is no mission, no goal? Bart thought he would be able to work at Kevin's beach shack, at least through the summer, but the endless line of people flustered him, and he found the general sense of triviality—beachgoers losing their temper over how long it took to get their fish tacos and Coronas—off-putting. Didn't these people realize how privileged they sounded? Did they not realize that people had died—and were dying still—in order to safeguard their freedom? Real things, serious things, were happening in the world. The U.S. was engaged in a war against ISIS, and there were flesh-and-blood soldiers out there fighting it. While Bart and the rest of his platoon had been held prisoner, people in America had been at the beach. While Bart's fellow soldiers had been randomly selected and marched to the Pit, civilians at home had been going to brunch, then Snapchatting photos of their avocado toast. Bart knows it's unrealistic of him to think that the entire nation would have hit the pause button on their happy, productive lives and waited with bated breath to find out what had happened to the servicemen gone missing outside of Sangin, Afghanistan, or even that the DoD would have dedicated every cent of its budget to locating the platoon. It was 2014—people went missing but didn't stay missing. But Bart and the rest of his platoon had been marched off the grid and stayed off the grid for nearly two years.

Kelley hasn't spoken, but Bart can tell he understands what Bart is telling him.

"I need to go back, Dad," Bart says.

Kelley opens his mouth to speak. Bart knows what he's going to say. *What about your mother?* Bart has to stay on Nantucket and take care of Mitzi. There will be no one else.

Kelley reaches out to squeeze Bart's hand. "It's okay," he says.

What's okay? It's okay if Bart returns to active duty? Or maybe Kelley meant that Mitzi will be okay. This is what Bart wants so badly to believe: that his mother is stronger than anyone imagines, that Mitzi will not fold, crumple, or flail. She will bounce back—resilient, strong, capable. If she wants to run the inn, she will hire competent help. If the inn is too much, she'll sell it and buy a smaller house, maybe even a house on the beach.

Kelley's eyes close and Bart feels a hand on his shoulder. It's one of the hospice workers. Laura, he thinks her name is.

"Your father needs to sleep before the party," she says.

Bart nods in agreement and stands to leave.

"Your brother and sister-in-law are in the kitchen," Lara says. "They're anxious to see you."

Bart heads to the kitchen expecting to see Kevin and Isabelle, a prospect that doesn't exactly excite him. Growing up, Bart always sensed that Kevin resented him—loved him, of course, because they were brothers, but maybe didn't *like* him. Bart, after all, had turned Kevin into more of a middle child than he already was. Since Bart has gotten home, Kevin alone has been tough on him. What are Bart's plans for the future? What is he going to *do* with his life? Does he plan on making a career out of sitting in his room and smoking dope? This feels hypocritical coming from Kevin, because back when Bart enlisted, that's what Kevin was doing. He was living at the inn, managing the Bar, licking his wounds from his disastrous marriage to Norah Vale, doing pretty much nothing productive or worthwhile—and he was far older then than Bart is now. Among the biggest surprises for Bart upon returning home was discovering that Kevin had gotten married, sired a child, moved into a rental cottage, and started a successful business that had nothing to do with the inn.

Probably, Kevin and Isabelle come bearing gifts, and Bart feels slightly more eager. Isabelle is French; she always chooses good presents. For Christmas she gave Bart a sterling silver shaving kit, which he never uses but is happy to have.

When Bart pushes through the French doors into the kitchen, he sees his brother Patrick and his sister-in-law Jennifer. Patrick has two beers in front of him, and Jennifer is pouring herself a glass of wine. When they see him, they start singing "Happy Birthday" in two-part harmony, and Bart smiles in spite of himself. These two are the perfect couple. They may have flaws as individuals, but you can't beat them together.

When they finish, Jennifer hands Bart a card.

"Aw, guys," Bart says. "The song was enough. I said no gifts." He opens the envelope. It's a $150 gift certificate to Fifty-Six Union, a restaurant here on Nantucket that Patrick and Jennifer love. "Thank you!" he says, trying to muster enthusiasm. What is he supposed to do with *this?*

"Figured you could take a girl out on a date," Patrick says.

"Girl?" Bart says. "It's October, man. There aren't any girls on Nantucket."

"What about Savannah Steppen?" Jennifer asks. "She was cute."

Bart looks at Patrick. "I hope that other beer is for me."

"It is, man," Patrick says. "Happy birthday. And thank you for giving us a chance to get away from our kids for the night."

"What was wrong with Savannah?" Jennifer asks. "She *was* cute."

"She was my prom date," Bart says. "My junior prom date. And she's in college. She went to, like, Cornell." Bart takes a sip of his beer. Savannah Steppen was cute, no argument, but she is stuck firmly in Bart's past. *High school.* Which might as well have taken place a few millenniums earlier, so irrelevant is it to who Bart is now. All of his friends from high school are now in college—or, hell, *out* of college—and those who stayed here to work, Bart has no interest in fraternizing with. Which is the other reason he needs to go back into the Marines.

Bart is saved from having to explain this—which he would have done badly, especially since both Patrick and Jennifer believe Bart should apply to college himself—by the side door to the kitchen slamming. They all turn to see Ava walk in. She's wearing jeans, an ivory cable-knit sweater, and her old brown corduroy jacket.

"Ava!" Bart says. He rushes to hug her. God, he's missed her and that familiar ugly jacket.

She squeezes him tight, and when she pulls away, her eyes are shining with tears. "I can't believe I thought about skipping this," she says. "Also, I can't believe you let Mitzi throw you a party. You *hate* your birthday."

"Please," Bart says. "Do you think I had a choice?"

"No," Ava, Patrick, and Jennifer all say at the same time.

Ava takes off her jacket and slips it over one of the stools at the counter. She drops her overnight bag to the floor and pulls an envelope out of her purse. "For you," she says. "Happy birthday."

It's two round-trip Acela tickets from Boston to New York.

"I left the dates open," Ava says. "Figured you could

either come twice by yourself and stay with me, or you could bring a date and stay at Drake's apartment, which is a three-million-dollar piece of real estate sitting empty."

A *date?* Bart thinks. Why are his siblings suddenly so keen to set him up with a girl? Girls are the farthest thing from Bart's mind. Still, the idea of going down to New York appeals, sometime before he goes back on active duty.

He'll have to pass a battery of tests before he's allowed to reenlist. The physical ones he'll pass. The psychological ones...?

"Thanks, Sis," Bart says. He studies the train tickets. First class! "This is a great idea."

Kevin and Isabelle walk in the side door next. "Look," Kevin says. "It's a party."

"Want a beer?" Patrick asks.

"Pope, funny hat," Kevin says.

"Ava, Isabelle, wine?" Jennifer asks.

"Isabelle is nursing," Kevin says.

"Une biere, s'il vous plait," Isabelle says. She hands Bart a garment bag. *"Pour toi. Bon anniversaire!"*

"Thanks, Isabelle," Bart says. The garment bag is from Saks Fifth Avenue, which means it's *not* a navy blazer from Murray's. Bart has no fewer than eight such blazers in ascending sizes hanging in his closet. Mitzi won't let Bart take them to the thrift shop. They're a record of his growing up, she says.

Bart unzips the garment bag to find a slate-blue cashmere jacket, the cut and beauty of which Bart cannot believe. It's the most beautiful article of clothing he has ever seen, certainly more sophisticated than anything he owns. It's an adult jacket, an adult civilian jacket. Still, Bart feels a thrill as he slips it on. It fits perfectly.

Patrick whistles. "Looks great, bro." To Kevin he says, "What'd that run you, six bills?"

Kevin says, "Isabelle got it and she's too elegant to disclose the price."

Jennifer swats Patrick. "How much it costs doesn't matter. What matters is that you look gorgeous in it, Bart."

Ava claps her hands. "You can wear it to New York City."

"Tu peux le porter ce soir," Isabelle says.

"Ce soir?" Bart says.

"A la soirée," Isabelle says.

Bart shoots his cuffs. Maybe he will wear it to the party tonight. Why not? He looks around the kitchen at his siblings and he raises his beer.

"Thanks, you guys," he says, but he is too overcome with emotion to say anything more. He doesn't even need to go to the party, he thinks. The real party is right here.

EDDIE

Allegra is ready to go—she has been ready for nearly twenty minutes, despite the two-hour preparation to do her hair and makeup and to get into her kimono, obi, and silk slippers. The costume looks authentic...and very, very expensive.

Meanwhile, Eddie is torn.

He has two ideas for costumes and he can't decide between them. His first idea is to go dressed as a pimp—fur coat, wide-brimmed hat, sunglasses, diamond rings. It's outrageous because, technically, Eddie used to *be* a pimp. Dressing as a stereotypical one now would be Eddie poking fun at himself. Everyone would be talking about him and his costume—but would the other partygoers think the costume was hysterical, brave, and appropriately self-effacing, or would they think it was in atrocious taste? Eddie would like to believe the former, but he fears the latter. It's probably too soon to go dressed as a pimp. Next year enough time will have passed that absolutely everyone will think it's funny.

And so Eddie defaults to his second idea: he will go dressed as Fast Eddie. What this means is that he will dress as his former self—in a beige linen suit and a Panama hat.

When he emerges from the bedroom, Allegra gives him a sharp look. Or maybe that's just her makeup.

"Really, Dad?" she says. "The hat?"

"It's my trademark," Eddie says.

"*Was* your trademark," Allegra says. "Back when you were breaking the law."

Eddie is very glad he didn't pursue the fur coat option. "Let's go," he says.

They head out to the Cherokee. Allegra, whose range of motion is constricted by her costume, needs help getting in.

"Are you going to be able to dance in that getup?" Eddie asks.

"If I feel like dancing, I'll take the kimono off," Allegra says.

"But you do have something on underneath, right?" Eddie says.

"Yes, Dad," Allegra says. "What kind of woman do you think I am?"

Eddie lets that question slide as rhetorical. As they head out of town, he realizes he has the next twelve minutes alone with his daughter, a rare opportunity.

"How are you feeling about the breakup?" Eddie asks.

Allegra shrugs.

Okay, Eddie thinks. He tries another avenue. "Do you miss your sister?"

"A lot more than I thought I would," Allegra says. "I feel...I don't know, *abandoned* almost. She's off at school, meeting people, creating a network of friends and connections that will last her the rest of her life. And I'm stuck at home in a dead-end job."

"It's not a dead-end job," Eddie says. "You're the face of the company."

"Glenn is the face of the company," Allegra says.

"You're the first person people see when they walk through the door," Eddie says. "And you're doing a terrific job. In no time you'll be a sales associate, and then once you take the requisite courses, you'll be a broker like me."

"I don't expect you to understand," Allegra says.

"Understand what?" Eddie says.

"You and Aunt Barbie grew up in New Bedford," Allegra says. "So for you guys, coming to Nantucket was a big step forward. But I grew up here. And here I remain."

"Well, I'll point out," Eddie says, "you could be stuck somewhere worse. There aren't many places better than here."

"I always saw myself someplace more glamorous," Allegra says. "New York City, London..."

"Tokyo!" Eddie says, but Allegra doesn't even crack a smile. He understands what she means, but at the same time, he feels hurt. He worked his ass off to be able to raise the twins here—and until his recent misfortunes, their lives had been pretty darn blessed. He'd given them whatever they asked for—fancy Italian leather jackets, three-hundred-dollar jeans, riding lessons, a Jeep, and the expensive college-prep classes that Allegra chose to skip.

There's no time to bemoan his daughters' squandered privilege, because now he and Allegra are pulling into the parking lot at the VFW, which is already jam-packed with cars. Eddie feels a surge of excitement. Finally he's back in the swing of things; he's where the action is. When he told Glenn and Barbie that he'd been invited to Bart Quinn's birthday, they were envious. He saw it on their faces.

"Here we are," Eddie says. "Let's get this party started."

It takes Eddie about half a second to realize that he and Allegra are the only ones at the party wearing costumes. Eddie first sees their error in the faces of Mitzi and Bart, who are standing at the entrance to the party greeting the guests. When Mitzi sees Eddie and Allegra, her mouth falls open, then she quickly transitions to a smile. Bart cocks an eyebrow. Eddie feels humiliated, primarily on Allegra's behalf. He has only dressed as himself. Allegra, on the other hand, looks like she stepped out of *Shōgun*. Eddie decides he will offer to run Allegra right home so that she can change, but he turns to see her shuffling in tiny steps toward Bart and then executing a deep bow with her hands at prayer in front of her chest.

"Happy birthday," she says when she rises. Then she holds out a hand. "I don't know if you remember me. I'm Allegra Pancik. I was a freshman when you were a senior."

"I think I do remember you," Bart says. "And that's a dynamite outfit. But you know this isn't a costume party, right?"

"Right," Allegra says. "However, I always dress up on Halloween."

Eddie is extremely impressed by the confidence of this answer. Hope may be at Bucknell paving a golden road into her future, but Hope would not be able to finesse a situation as awkward as this and work it to her advantage. Of the twins, Allegra has been blessed with the superior survival skills.

"Come with me, Allegra," Bart says. "I'll show you where the bar is."

They disappear inside before Eddie can remind Allegra that she's only nineteen years old and also that Ed Kapenash, chief of police, will likely be in attendance tonight. Eddie sighs, then offers his hand to Mitzi. "Sorry, we thought it was a costume party."

Mitzi says, "I wanted a costume party, but Bart put his foot down."

"Well, I came dressed as myself, or my former self, but I doubt anyone will notice," Eddie says.

"I'd like to meet with you before the end of the week about that thing we discussed," Mitzi says. "Are you free Friday?"

"I have clients coming from off-island to look at houses on Friday," Eddie says. "How about Thursday?"

"Thursday works for me," Mitzi says.

"Okay, let's say Thursday at ten. I'll come to you, we can do a walk-through and write up a listing sheet. We'll get you your asking price, I promise."

Mitzi opens her mouth to speak, but she clams up when Kelley rolls over in a wheelchair pushed by a woman with a stethoscope around her neck and a blood pressure cuff hanging out of her jacket pocket. *Costume?* Eddie wonders. He takes one look at Kelley and decides the answer is no. That's a real nurse. Kelley's complexion is gray, his face is gaunt and sunken; he has a patch over one eye.

But when Kelley sees Eddie, the corners of his mouth turn up. "Eddie," he says. "Welcome."

Eddie is rendered speechless. He knew Kelley was sick, of course, but Kelley doesn't look like he'll last until tomorrow.

However, Eddie is good at nothing so much as ignoring

unpleasant realities, especially those right in front of him, and so Eddie reaches out to shake Kelley's hand as though everything is just fine, as though Kelley has merely come dressed as someone in a wheelchair—FDR, or Tom Cruise in *Born on the Fourth of July*.

"Kelley," Eddie says. "Looking good, man!"

Kelley barely nods. His hand, in Eddie's, feels like a bunch of brittle sticks. Eddie isn't sure what else to say. He won't mention the sale of the inn because clearly it's a measure Mitzi is taking after Kelley's death.

"Sounds like a great party already," Eddie says.

"Go in and get yourself a drink!" Mitzi suggests.

"Yes," Eddie says. "Yes, I think I'll do that."

Eddie weaves and wends his way through the crowd toward the bar. There are some faces he recognizes from the Quinn family—he sees one of the Quinn sons with a pretty blond woman, then he sees the Quinn daughter. Once upon a time, she was the girls' music teacher. Eddie sees Kai, the woman who owns the new crystal store in town; she used to be Eddie's neighbor out in Wauwinet. He sees Chief Kapenash with his wife, Andrea. The chief has been friendly since Eddie's release—he calls every once in a while to "check in"—but now Ed just raises his glass in front of his face, as if to say, *Don't come over here.* And really, can Eddie blame him? The last thing the chief wants is to be seen talking to a convicted felon, the most renowned criminal Nantucket has seen in recent history.

Standing at the bar in front of Eddie is Hunter Bloch Sr., which makes Eddie wonder where Allegra has gotten to. He scans the party. He doesn't see a geisha girl or anyone else in costume. Eddie can't help but feel miffed and misled. If you're throwing a party on Halloween and it's not a costume party, this should be explicitly mentioned. *No costumes.* Eddie realizes he's still wearing his Panama hat, but he's hesitant to take it off because what if he loses it? God knows they aren't cheap.

Hunter Bloch Sr. turns around holding two cocktails— million bucks says he's come to the party with his broker Rosemary Whelden. He's always seen in public with Rosemary, never his wife, Kathleen. All of Nantucket seems to accept this without comment. How is it, Eddie wonders, that some people can get away with whatever they want?

Hunter gives Eddie the once-over. "Linen suit, Eddie? Don't you know it's almost November?"

Eddie won't bite. So he's unseasonal—sue him. "Heard your son stepped out on my daughter," Eddie says. "Allegra is taking it pretty hard."

"Is she?" Hunter Bloch Sr. says. "She can't be taking it too hard, because I just saw her following the guest of honor out the side door, and they had a bottle of tequila with them." Hunter Bloch Sr. winks at Eddie, a gesture Eddie finds patronizing. "She'll bounce back. Like father, like daughter. Now, I've got to go deliver this drink."

"Yes," Eddie says. "Give Rosemary my best."

Eddie shakes his head. Why was he so anxious to attend this party? He doesn't like anyone here. And if what Hunter Bloch Sr. says is true, then Eddie has just lost his date. Eddie wonders if he should try to find Allegra. Maybe he should just call her.

He does neither. It's his turn at the bar finally. He'll order a drink.

"Vodka martini, please," Eddie says.

As the bartender is shaking it up, Eddie feels a poke-poke-poke in his left shoulder. He turns and barely stifles a groan. It's Rachel McMann.

"Hey, Rachel," Eddie says. Rachel McMann is a social butterfly. She must know nearly everyone here, so why is she bothering to talk to Eddie? "Happy Halloween." He's surprised that Rachel didn't come in costume. He can easily picture her dressed as Carmen Miranda, with a big basket of fruit on her head.

"Eddie," Rachel says.

Eddie sees Rachel's husband, Dr. Andy McMann, standing a few yards away. Dr. Andy used to be Eddie's dentist, so Eddie can't exactly ignore him. Eddie waves halfheartedly; Dr. Andy hoists his drink much like Chief Kapenash just did, his body language saying, *I'm acknowledging you, but a more in-depth conversation is not necessary.*

"Eddie," Rachel says again. She has positioned herself under his chin; she's as persistent as a housefly.

"Yes, Rachel," Eddie says. "What can I do for you?"

"I heard you have the Powerball people coming this week," Rachel says. "Congratulations."

"Who told you that?" Eddie asks. He tries to recall whom he told about the Powerball people. Glenn Daley knows, and Barbie, and Grace. And Addison Wheeler, who wants to show the Christys two high-end properties off Polpis Road (one of the properties has its own vineyard, which will likely scare the Christys off).

So actually, there are a couple of ways Rachel could have found out.

"I have a listing in Monomoy," Rachel says. "I think you should show it to them."

"How much is it?" Eddie asks.

"Twenty-nine million," Rachel says.

Eddie fights to keep his poker face. Rachel McMann has a twenty-nine-million-dollar listing. How does that happen? Anyone who owns such a valuable piece of property should have the good sense to use a broker with experience and with more... gravitas. Rachel is about as intellectually substantial as a balloon on a parade float.

"Too high," Eddie says. "Their max is fifteen."

"My buyer would settle for twenty-five," Rachel says. She winces. "Divorce."

"Still too high," Eddie says. "Sorry. Thanks for thinking of me." *And stay away from my buyers,* he thinks.

Rachel sighs. "Well, I have other properties. Cheaper. One on Medouie Creek Road. I'll call you tomorrow."

Don't bother, Eddie thinks. The bartender empties the cold elixir into a martini glass and rubs a lemon twist around the rim. *Here,* Eddie thinks as he takes the first sip, *is the antidote to Rachel McMann.* "Please do," he says.

This is Rachel's cue to drift away and either find someone else to foist her business on—Hunter Bloch Sr. would do, he always has a stable of millionaires and billionaires on his client list—or go talk to her husband, although Eddie has always found something vaguely pathetic about husband and wife conversing together at parties. But is it any more pathetic than showing up at a party with your daughter— who ditched him at the first possible opportunity, he notes— instead of your wife?

It hardly matters because Rachel remains in front of Eddie, her face upturned and expectant, as though she's waiting for Eddie to kiss her. Rachel, too, has a son in college. Calgary. (What kind of name is that? Eddie has always wondered. It would really only be acceptable as a name if one grew up in Alberta or if it was a family name, but Eddie gets the feeling that if he asks Rachel, she'll confide that she just "liked the sound of it.") Calgary attends... UC Berkeley, where he's studying Japanese. Possibly Rachel wants to brag about Calgary or ask about Hope or comment on Allegra's geisha costume. Eddie can't predict, but one thing is for certain—he isn't walking around this party with Rachel McMann stuck to him like a burr on his sweater.

He takes another sustaining sip of his drink. "Was there something else?"

"Sort of?" Rachel says. "I'm not sure if I should mention it? I'm not sure if you care?"

Eddie looks down: Is his fly open?

"What is it, Rachel?" he asks. She's not sure if she should mention it, which means she damn well better mention it. And immediately.

"Benton Coe is here," Rachel says. "By 'here' I mean at this party—he came as a guest of Edith Allemand, who has that gorgeous property at the top of Main Street—but I also mean 'here' as in here on Nantucket. Back on Nantucket. For good. He's finished in Detroit. He's moving back here and he's even spending the winter."

"Well, you were right to wonder," Eddie says. "Because I don't care."

Rachel shrugs. "Okay."

But the fact of the matter is: Eddie does care. He cares very much. Benton Coe, Eddie and Grace's former landscape architect, Grace's former lover, is back on Nantucket for good. He's going to spend the winter here, instead of going wherever he used to go.

Eddie quickly throws back the rest of his martini, then returns to the bar for another one. He should eat something. He's starving and there's a lavish buffet, but his first order of business now has to be putting his eyes on Benton Coe.

With his second cocktail in hand, Eddie peruses the crowd. A few people see Eddie looking and wave. Eddie waves back, despite not being quite sure whom he's waving at. It's a bad habit—but he can't be expected to curb his indiscriminate waving when he's so stressed out.

Benton Coe is here. Here at this party. Here on Nantucket. For good. What are the chances that Rachel is mistaken? Eddie wonders. But no sooner does he entertain this soothing notion than he sees Benton Coe two tables over. The reason Eddie didn't pick him out right away is because he's wearing a Groucho Marx glasses-nose-and-mustache combo. It's horrifically ironic that the only other person at the party in a costume of sorts is Benton Coe. Benton is with Edith Allemand, a spry woman of eighty or so. She is fearsomely WASPy, notoriously old-school Nantucket, persnickety about not only her home and gardens but the historical integrity of Main Street in particular and the island in general. Edith Allemand doesn't know Eddie Pancik, but if she did, she would not approve of him. She would consider him a wash-ashore, even though he's been here over twenty years. He's a real estate broker, and therefore, to Mrs. Allemand, he would represent everything that's wrong with Nantucket—and that's before finding out about his recent escapades.

Benton removes his nose and mustache and sets it on the table so that he can dig into a pile of mashed potatoes. Benton looks older, Eddie notes with satisfaction. There's some gray in his red hair and he has wrinkled up a bit, probably thanks to so many hours in the sun. Sun…in Detroit? Isn't that where Benton Coe has been? Jump-starting gentrification and greening up the most dangerous city in America? Well, Detroit has done Benton Coe no favors.

Eddie approaches the table. He's not sure what he's going to say. Maybe he won't say anything. Maybe he'll just stand there until Benton Coe notices him, excuses himself from

Edith Allemand, and steps with Eddie outside, where they can have words privately.

Eddie steps up. Benton raises his face, sees Eddie, awards him a curt nod, then continues his conversation with Mrs. Allemand.

Eddie throws back the second martini in one long gulp. He will *not* be dismissed by the man who slept with his wife. He steps right up to Benton's chair and taps one of his very broad shoulders. He feels brave, but he doesn't want this to escalate into a physical confrontation, because Eddie will lose. Benton has him by six inches and forty pounds. At least.

And so Eddie tries to manufacture conviviality. "Benton Coe, is that you? I thought that was you, but then I thought, 'No, my pal Benton lives in Detroit now.' I figured you'd still be there, hanging out with Justin Verlander and Kid Rock."

"Eddie," Benton says. He takes a deep breath, then moves his napkin from his knee to the table and stands up to offer Eddie his hand. They shake. Benton's grip is firmer than it needs to be, Eddie thinks. Maybe he's trying to send Eddie a nonverbal warning. "Eddie Pancik, please meet my friend Edith Allemand. Edith, this is Eddie Pancik."

Edith gives him a tight smile. "Charmed," she says. She stands, but it's not to shake Eddie's hand. "I'm going to excuse myself for a moment, gentlemen. Thank you."

Eddie is relieved to see her go. He says, "So I hear you're back?"

"I'm back," Benton confirms.

"For good?"

"For good," Benton says. "I may take on projects else-where down the road, but for the foreseeable future I have more than enough work here to keep me busy."

"How was Detroit? Did you meet a girl? Get married?

Have a baby?" Eddie is shooting from the hip here, but maybe these questions aren't so far-fetched. Maybe the reason Benton looks so old and tired is because he's been up nights warming a bottle for a newborn! Or maybe he married someone much younger who wears him out in the bedroom.

"Detroit was work," Benton says. Then, perhaps realizing how abrupt he sounds, he adds, "And the occasional Lions game."

"Ah, I would have pegged you for a baseball fan," Eddie says.

"I hate baseball," Benton says. "Too slow."

Hating baseball is un-American, Eddie thinks. But he refrains from saying anything uncharitable. He refrains from responding at all, which leaves him and Benton to swim in a sea of awkward silence. Eddie is waiting for Benton to ask how he, Eddie, is doing. And Benton—well, Benton is probably fighting the urge to do so. Or possibly, Benton is waiting for Eddie to tell him to stay away from Grace. But Eddie is going to let that particular elephant remain in the room for a while longer. He says, "I came to this party with my daughter Allegra. Hope is in college. She's a sophomore at Bucknell."

"Yes," Benton says. "I'm aware."

"You're *aware?*" Eddie says. How could Benton Coe possibly be aware? Did Grace tell him? Are they still in contact? Did Grace send Benton the annual Christmas card? Or did Benton merely see Hope's choice of college mentioned in the *Inquirer and Mirror*?

"Good for her," Benton says. "She's a smart kid. And now, Eddie, I have to excuse myself as well. I'm sure I'll see you around." With that, Benton Coe moves to the next table, where he stops to shake hands and chat with Hunter Bloch Sr.

Wait a minute, Eddie thinks. *I'm not finished!* But Benton, apparently, is. There will be no détente, then, no gentleman's agreement that Benton will stay away from Grace. For all Eddie knows, Grace is planning to leave him for Benton tomorrow.

Eddie senses that Benton Coe and Hunter Bloch Sr. are talking about him. Hunter Sr. tosses his white lion's mane of hair back and laughs. Laughing at Eddie's expense?

Thank God he didn't wear the fur coat!

Speaking of costumes, *where* is Allegra? Eddie pulls his phone out, which serves the additional purpose of making it seem as though he has a call to take that is far more important than this party.

His call goes right to Allegra's voice mail.

Eddie hangs up without leaving a message and goes back to the bar.

JENNIFER

Jennifer decides to wait and tell Patrick what happened with Grayson Coker when they're out of the house, on their way to Nantucket. This way they will be alone, in the safe cocoon of the car, and there will be no chance the kids will overhear. It's a solid plan, but Jennifer still feels anxious. She doesn't want to downplay what happened, because then Patrick will accuse her of making much ado about nothing. But if she explains it exactly as it happened, a confrontation between Patrick and Coke will be inevitable, giving Coke the chance to say that Jennifer was the instigator. Jennifer tries to reassure herself that Patrick is a supportive spouse. He will see it through Jennifer's eyes. He will understand.

When they climb into the BMW and head out of the city, Patrick lets out a cowboy whoop.

"I can't believe how great this feels!" Patrick says. He glances over at Jennifer. "Hey, are you okay?"

"Huh?" she says. "Yeah, of course." *Tell him!* she thinks. He's noticed the tension around her eyes. *Tell him!*

"I really appreciate you agreeing to do this when you're so busy," Patrick says. "I feel like you're always making sacrifices for me."

"Going to see your family is *not* a sacrifice," Jennifer says.

"It's not just this," Patrick says. "You've been so patient with me getting the fund up and running. You took on a project you don't necessarily want to do…"

"About that…," Jennifer says.

"That money is critical," Patrick says. "I hate to say it, but we couldn't make it through the holidays without it. But by spring I should be throwing fastballs and you can take a much-deserved rest." He taps his hands against the steering wheel as Jennifer sinks back in her seat. She can only assume that Coke has not yet received the refund of his hundred-thousand-dollar retainer; Jennifer mailed it back to him on Friday. He will likely get it today, and that chunk of cash will vanish as magically as it appeared.

Patrick turns up the radio—Joe Cocker sings "Feeling Alright"—and Jennifer closes her eyes. She is beyond tired. She is exhausted—because she has been up the past five nights worrying about the conversation that she is supposed to be having with Patrick right now.

That money is critical. That money *is* critical, so critical that Jennifer considers calling up Grayson Coker to recant. Yes, she *is* that desperate. She can say she is sorry there was a misunderstanding and might they start again fresh?

What if he says no? What if he informs her that he has already hired another decorator? What if that decorator is Mandy Pell, Jennifer's archnemesis? Of course it will be Mandy Pell. She will decorate the penthouse in a creatively formidable, evil way, and it will be featured in a six-page spread in *Domino,* and the next thing Jennifer knows, Mandy Pell will be credited with giving birth to the intimidation movement in decorating.

And what about Jennifer's self-respect? If anyone should be apologizing and asking for a fresh start, it should be Grayson Coker!

With this thought, Jennifer falls fast asleep...and awakens when Paddy pulls into the parking lot at the Hyannis airport.

"We're here," Patrick says. "How was your nap?"

It's probably best that Jennifer didn't tell Patrick about Grayson Coker, because then the entire trip to Nantucket would be ruined. Instead everything unfolds seamlessly. Patrick and Jennifer have only five minutes to wait before their Cape Air flight to Nantucket boards. They are the only two people on the flight aside from the pilot, and the day is crisp and clear. The flight across the blue glass of Nantucket Sound is like a magic carpet ride.

Jennifer will wait and tell Patrick later. She will tell him on their way home.

Jennifer and Patrick take a taxi to the inn, where a bottle of Jennifer's favorite chardonnay is chilling in the fridge. Jennifer and Patrick repair to their room upstairs to enjoy some much-needed alone time. Afterward they shower and get dressed, then go back down to the kitchen, where they forage for some unhealthy, nonorganic snacks. Jennifer comes up with a box of Bremner wafers, a hunk of Brie, and a can of Spanish peanuts. Bingo! As she lays out the feast, the kitchen fills with Quinns: Bart first, then Ava, then Kevin and Isabelle.

Jennifer is reminded of just how fortunate she is. She's an only child, and since her father's death, her "family" has consisted of just her and her mother, Beverly. But she and Patrick have been together for so long that Jennifer truly feels like Patrick's family is her family, and she realizes that they feel the same way about her.

This bubble of happiness is all but popped when Jennifer goes upstairs to put on her makeup but Patrick stays downstairs because Mitzi wants to "chat" with him "real quick" before they head out to the VFW.

When Patrick comes back to the room, he looks like he's about to cry.

"What?" Jennifer says. "Is it your father?" She agrees that Kelley looks very sick, but everyone's expectations have been adjusted. Hospice has been called. Kelley has a month left, maybe two if they're lucky.

"It's Mitzi," Patrick says. "She's going to sell the inn."

Jennifer nods slowly. On the one hand, she thinks selling the inn is a good idea. It's too much for Mitzi to handle alone, and Kevin and Isabelle now have their business to run and their children to raise. Bart could help if he were at all interested, but that doesn't seem to be the case. On the other hand, the idea of selling the inn worries Jennifer. At some point over the summer when Kelley's health took a turn for the worse, Mitzi talked to Jennifer about what she might do next, if the unthinkable happened and Kelley didn't get better.

"I'd love to do what you do," Mitzi said. "Become an interior designer. Maybe we can go into business together."

Jennifer murmured some vague encouragements in response,

but she would never, ever, *ever* go into business with Mitzi. She thought about how kitschy-country charming Mitzi's taste is. She thought about the Byers' Choice carolers Mitzi sets out at Christmas. She tried not to shudder.

"It might not be a bad idea," Jennifer says to Patrick.

"What?" Patrick says. He's genuinely agitated; the tips of his ears are turning red. "Do you know what that would mean? It would mean we would have no place to stay here on Nantucket. We would no longer be Nantucketers."

"Oh," Jennifer says. "Won't Mitzi buy something else?"

"She says she hasn't decided," Patrick says. "But she also said she might buy a condo in Sherburne Commons."

"Sherburne Commons?" Jennifer says. "But she's only . . . what? Forty-nine? Fifty?"

"Whatever she buys won't be big enough for all of us to come visit," Patrick says. "And Kevin and Isabelle don't have room for us."

"So we'll rent," Jennifer says.

Patrick sits on the edge of the bed and drops his head into his hands. "We should have bought when we had the chance."

Jennifer decides not to point out that when they "had the chance" was back when their accounts were fat with illegally gotten funds. "Please," she says. "Let's not ruin tonight by fretting about money. You need to get your business up and running, then we can worry about Nantucket."

"I don't expect you to understand," Patrick says. "I'm losing my father and I'm losing my home."

Jennifer is glad she didn't break her news to Patrick on the way here—but is it going to be any easier on the way home? She blithely suggested they could rent, but without the penthouse project, they'll never be able to afford it.

She needs another project—and fast. A big client. *Who*

are the five people in Boston richer than Grayson Coker?
she wonders.

She takes a deep breath. "Stand up," she says. "People are
waiting for us."

As they're driving out to the VFW, Jennifer's phone pings.
She checks the display, expecting it to be a report from the
babysitter, but she sees it's a text from Norah Vale. Kevin is
driving, Patrick is sitting shotgun, and Isabelle is seated next
to Jennifer in the backseat. Jennifer feels a wave of guilt that
she is receiving a message from Kevin's ex-wife. Why is she
the only person among the Quinns who is still tethered to
Norah?

Well, she knows why. The drugs.

The drugs, even the flicker of the possibility of drugs in
Jennifer's future, are too much to resist. Maybe if she stays
away from the oxy . . . maybe if she just sticks to the Ativan . . .
then at least she will be able to sleep.

She opens the text. It says: *I'm assuming you're on island
for Bart's party? Any chance you can meet me tomorrow for
coffee? I'd really like to talk to you about something.*

Jennifer knows she should delete the message. Or not
respond. She should *definitely* not respond with two glasses
of wine sitting on top of her anxiety.

Jennifer gives Isabelle a sidelong glance, then she types
back: *I may have some time early tomorrow. Where for
coffee?*

Her phone pings a second later: *Hub at 8:30?*

Okay, Jennifer responds. *See you then.*

BART

He knows his mother won't like it, but oh well. He lifts a bottle of Patrón and two Coronas from the bar and leads Allegra Pancik out the side door of the VFW, where there is, conveniently, a small porch with a table and two chairs over-looking the scrub pines of the state forest.

"But it's your party," Allegra says.

"We'll be back before anyone misses us," Bart says. "My presence isn't really required. This is a party my mother threw to make *herself* feel better."

"Parents," Allegra says.

Bart isn't sure what happened, but when he saw Allegra Pancik all dolled up like a geisha, he thought: *My siblings are right. I do need a girlfriend.*

And.

There.

She.

Is.

She was a freshman at Nantucket High School when he was a senior. So maybe he still has upperclassman allure? She's not too young for him. At nineteen, she's an adult, although not old enough to drink.

Legally.

"We'll each do three shots," Bart says. "Chased by these beers. Then we'll go back inside."

"I'm in," Allegra says.

Tequila shot #1:

Bart says, "Why are you still on Nantucket? Did you not go to college?"

"Wow," Allegra says. "Tough questions right off the bat."

Bart cocks an eyebrow, a trick Centaur taught him while they were still in basic training.

"I went to UMass Dartmouth last year," Allegra says. "Flunked out. Too much partying."

"So let me guess," Bart says. "This wasn't your first shot of tequila?"

In lieu of answering, Allegra takes a little bow. "Now let me ask you something."

Bart nods.

"Why are *you* still on Nantucket? You're a war hero. Doesn't the government give you a million dollars and a mansion in Beverly Hills?"

"Hardly," Bart says. He takes a long draft of his beer. Then he wants to belch, but he holds back, as he is in the presence of a lady. "I'm here on Nantucket for two reasons. One, my father is dying. Two, I don't know what else to do." He looks at Allegra. "And by the way, I'm *not* a war hero."

Allegra tilts her head, and Bart sees the chopsticks securing her dark bun. "No?"

I let them take my best friend to the Pit, Bart thinks. *I tried to save him, but I failed.*

"Time for another shot," he says.

Tequila shot #2:

"Tell me about your family," Bart says.

"Well," Allegra says, taking a ladylike sip of her beer. "I have a twin sister."

"You mean there are two girls on Nantucket as beautiful as you?" Bart asks.

"Hope goes to Bucknell," Allegra says. "She's the smart one, I'm the pretty one."

"But you're identical?" Bart says.

"Yes," Allegra says. "I only say that I'm the pretty one to

make myself feel better. Hope is at college, and I'm working as a receptionist at my aunt and uncle's real estate agency. Bayberry Properties, on Main Street."

Bayberry Properties, on Main Street. Bart makes a mental note. That's what one is supposed to do with women—notice the little things. Maybe later this week he'll stop by to see if Allegra wants to have lunch. Maybe he'll send flowers.

"What about your parents?" Bart asks. "That was your dad you came in with, right?"

"My parents are kind of a sore topic," Allegra says. "Until three years ago they were normal, boring parents. We lived out on Wauwinet Road in a big house that overlooked Polpis Harbor. My father used to own his own real estate company, and my mother had this enormous garden where she raised chickens."

"Chickens?" Bart says. His stomach lurches. He can't talk about chickens.

"My mother was annoying at times, and my father used to complain about how much money we were costing him. But then, over the course of one summer, my mother started having an affair with our landscaper, and my father ran a prostitution ring out in Sconset. He went to jail. He just got out in July. We lost the house in Wauwinet, and now we all live in this tiny cottage in town."

Bart nods. Affair. Prostitution ring. Jail. He knows he should be shocked, but if anyone has a family with weirder stories than Allegra, it's Bart Quinn.

"But your parents are still together?" Bart asks. "They survived?"

"They are," Allegra says. "They did. My mom didn't come tonight because she's volunteering at Academy Hill. Handing out candy."

"My parents are still together too," Bart says. "And my

mother had an affair." Here he shakes his head. He eyes the bottle of tequila but drinks his beer instead. "With this guy named George who came to our inn every year to play Santa Claus."

This makes Allegra laugh. As it should. Because it's absurd. Apparently, while Bart was away, Kelley and Mitzi *separated*. Mitzi moved with George to Lenox, Massachusetts. And Kelley entertained thoughts of getting back together with Margaret, his first wife. But love won out in the end—that's what Mitzi said when she explained it all to Bart. She said she wanted to tell Bart everything so that there were no secrets in the family. But honestly, Bart feels like he wouldn't have minded if Kelley and Mitzi had kept all of that a secret forever. Mitzi and George—ick! And it had been going on all the years that Bart was growing up, even back when Bart believed that George *was* Santa Claus.

"My siblings are fine," Bart concedes. "They're my half siblings, the children of my father and Margaret Quinn, the news anchor."

Allegra nods like she gets it, but she may be too young to know who Margaret Quinn is. Only old people watch the news on TV.

"Patrick and Kevin are married with kids," Bart says. He thinks about informing Allegra that Patrick has also been to jail recently, but why not save some surprises for the second date? "Ava teaches music in New York City. She's still single, but she's dating some guy. A professor."

"Your sister was my music teacher in fifth grade," Allegra says.

Bart laughs. "She was?" he says. "Too bad for you."

Tequila shot #3:

He's trying to decide if Allegra might be a person to

whom he can confide everything. She has good listening skills, and she seems to have a fair amount of emotional depth, more than one would expect from a beautiful nineteen-year-old. Girls who look like Allegra have life unfold easily. They get what they want. They don't hit roadblocks. Allegra seems to have a few demons of her own, although they are nothing compared with Bart's. She's never been out of the Commonwealth of Massachusetts. She is, in essence, *him* before he joined the Marines.

"Do you have a boyfriend?" Bart asks. Here he is, all but proposing to the girl, and he hasn't even checked if she's available. Girls as pretty as Allegra always have boyfriends, he reasons. But then again, if she had a boyfriend, would she have agreed to come outside with him?

"Had," she says. "Until recently. Hunter Bloch. You know him?"

"Ugh," Bart says. "Yes." Hunter Bloch was two years ahead of Bart in high school. He was a hockey player and his father had money, two factors that made Bart steer clear of the guy. "Until *how* recently?"

"We dated for four months," Allegra says. "I found out a couple of days ago that he was cheating on me."

Bart whistles. "Idiot."

Allegra executes her cute little bow again.

"Maybe his stupid mistake is my good fortune?" Bart says.

Allegra tilts her head. "Maybe."

Is it the tequila taking control of his brain, or is she actually the most desirable woman he has ever laid eyes on? "I haven't dated anyone since high school," he says. "I mean, before I deployed, there were girls...one-night stands."

Allegra says, "I would expect nothing less."

"Then I was held prisoner for two years," Bart says. "I watched half of my buddies..."

"Bart," she says. She steps closer to him and takes his hand.

Kiss her, he thinks. Does he remember how? He leans in. His lips meet hers, softly, so softly.

Yes, he remembers how.

KELLEY

Mitzi is a social butterfly. A *papillon*. Kelley watches her from his wheelchair. He and Lara are stationed at one of the central tables, where he can feel like part of the action without having to do much. Mitzi gave up her fanciful notion of wearing the gold roller-disco jumpsuit—thank heavens, as it no longer exists—and instead chose a flowing purple gown with diaphanous sleeves that look like wings. Her wild, curly hair frames her face. Her cheeks are pink with excitement. She flits from group to group, grasping hands, leaning in to ask questions about this person's new job, that person's aging mother. *How does she keep track of it all?* Kelley wonders. One of the things that has come to him with age is a narrowing of the periscope; he cares, now, only about his family. But Mitzi, of course, is young and healthy, she thrives on interaction, and since they closed the inn, her world has shrunken considerably.

Kelley wonders if, perhaps, she is anxious for him to hurry up and depart already, so she can get on with her life.

What a maudlin thought! And unfounded! Whenever Mitzi moves from group to group, she seeks out Kelley's eyes, waves, and blows a kiss.

*   *   *

Kelley tries to take inventory of the rest of his family. The band has started playing, and Kevin and Isabelle are the first ones out to dance. They're good, too, fluid and elegant, like the dancers in one of those movies Kelley's mother used to love. Frances Quinn was a sucker for Fred Astaire and Gene Kelly, and for the large-scale productions of *Show Boat* and *Silk Stockings.* She loved a man in a white dinner jacket. When Kelley got married to Margaret, Kelley and his brother, Avery, and all the groomsmen wore white dinner jackets to the rehearsal dinner as a surprise for Frances. The photographer took a picture of all of them surrounding Frances. If Kelley is remembering correctly, that was the happiest Frances had ever looked.

Frances Quinn would have loved Isabelle, Kelley is certain. She is classing up the Quinn bloodline. Even at two years old, Genevieve babbles in French; she can count to ten and recite the days of the week. She calls Kelley Grand-père and Mitzi Grand-mère. Margaret is Mimi.

Where is Margaret? Kelley wonders. He doesn't see her.

Ava is standing at the bar talking to Mrs. Gabler, Bart's kindergarten teacher. Ava is a saint.

Paddy and Jennifer are sitting and eating, although Paddy is on his phone and Jennifer has a faraway, distracted look on her face. *Are they okay?* Kelley wonders. They have weathered a couple of big storms recently—Patrick's incarceration, Jennifer's addiction to pills—but Kelley thought the ship had righted itself. They don't look *miserable,* just not as happy and carefree as Kevin and Isabelle.

Where is Bart, the guest of honor? Come to think of it, Kelley hasn't seen Bart all night. But since Mitzi doesn't seem to be worried, Kelley isn't worried. Although it must be nearly time to cut the cake—ice cream cake from the Juice Bar, a tradition—so Bart had better turn up. Just as Kelley thinks this, the side door opens and Bart walks into the party, holding hands with a Japanese geisha girl.

Dear Lord, Kelley thinks. *Is this girl a...? Did Mitzi arrange for a...? Did Kevin and Patrick, maybe, as a joke, hire a...stripper dressed as a geisha?*

Mitzi sees Bart and the geisha, swoops them up in her purple wings, and ushers them toward Kelley. No, not toward Kelley, toward the round table that holds the ice cream cake festooned with twenty-two candles, plus eighteen extra candles, one for each of the soldiers in Bart's platoon who perished. That was at Bart's request, his insistence.

Lara turns Kelley in his chair so he has a good view of the cake. Jennifer and Patrick stand up, Ava breaks away from Mrs. Gabler, and the band finishes its song. Kevin leads Isabelle off the dance floor. Mitzi lights the candles, and Ava clinks a spoon against a glass. The crowd quiets and people gather around the table in a loose ring.

Bart is still holding hands with the geisha. Kelley is confused. Who is it?

"Who is that?" Kelley asks Lara, but his voice is drowned out when the band launches into "Happy Birthday," and Lara wouldn't know anyway, would she? Lara lays a hand on Kelley's shoulder as everyone starts to sing.

"Happy birthday to you."

It's the worst song ever written, in Kelley's opinion. Nobody sings it well. One person, maybe, in history. The woman in the white dress. What was her name?

"Happy birthday to you."

Kelley will not live until his next birthday, which means he will not have to sit like a dumb mute while people sing to him terribly off-key. Another small point of gratitude. He cried when he was small and his assembled friends sang to him in Perrysburg, Ohio. Frances snapped a picture of little Kelley in tears with the white cake from Wixey Bakery; she relished showing this photo to the girls Kelley brought home. She showed it to Margaret.

Where is Margaret? Kelley wonders again. Then he remembers that she declined the invite. She is retiring from broadcasting next month, so there are no more vacation days. He will see her at Thanksgiving. Hopefully.

"Happy birthday, dear Bart."

Bartholomew James Quinn, born at 4:30 a.m., October 31, 1995, weighing eight pounds eleven ounces, measuring twenty-three inches long. Mitzi had pushed for ninety minutes without drugs. Without any drugs! She wanted to be present for every instant of the experience, and Kelley remembers the expression on her face when Bart was out, whole and healthy, wailing on her chest. She was radiant, exhilarated.

"Happy birthday to you!"

Bart takes a deep breath, then he turns his gaze to the geisha and blows the candles—all forty of them—out in one breath. The crowd erupts in applause and whistles.

Kelley closes his eyes. *Let the kid have his wish,* he prays. *Please, whatever it is, let that wish come true.*

AVA

Potter offers to cancel his Tuesday-afternoon seminar on the nautical novel and come with Ava to Nantucket, but she tells him she thinks it will be best if she goes alone. Potter is hurt, she can tell, and every sentence she utters as an explanation—"My whole family will be there," "My father is sick," "It will be an emotionally fraught time"—serves to make things worse.

"Isn't that why you have a partner?" Potter asks. "So there's someone to share the emotionally fraught times? So you have support? I like your family, and if you'll forgive my hubris, I think they like me, too."

"They do like you," Ava says. And it's true: they do. They like Potter so much that Potter could go to the party and Ava could stay in New York and everyone would be just as happy, if not more so.

"So why don't you tell me what's really going on?" Potter says.

Because she *can't,* that's why!

She has felt a shift since PJ's visit. Maybe it's a blip or maybe it's something more substantial; Ava can't tell. She feels like she failed. PJ *hated* her. What's harder to admit is that Ava also feels that Potter failed. His parenting was rusty, she knows that, but he came across as weak and ineffectual, two words she never dreamed she would pin to his name.

Ava had thought—and not unreasonably—that Potter was the real thing. The man she would marry. Meeting PJ was, in essence, the last frontier to conquer before they moved the relationship forward into lifelong commitment.

But it all went so horribly, horribly wrong. The only bright spot was Ava's unexpected rapprochement with Harrison, Trish's boyfriend, an unlikely ally if ever there was one. Ava was too shy to tell Potter about her conversation with Harrison. After Harrison and Trish left with PJ, Ava went back upstairs to see Potter, who seemed relieved that PJ was gone. Relieved that his only child, whom he never saw, had been unceremoniously removed from his care. He squeezed Ava and said, "I don't want you to dwell on what happened. None of this was your fault."

Of course it wasn't Ava's fault! She had barely interacted with the kid. PJ had seemed turned against Ava from the get-go. Maybe Trish had spoken ill of Ava, which hardly seemed fair, as the two had never met. Maybe PJ harbors hurt or angry feelings because Potter is never around. But he seems a little young to resent that. Trish took him to California when he was two, so he would have no memory of Potter and Trish together—and he seems to have bonded wonderfully with Harrison.

You need to spend more time with PJ, Ava wants to tell Potter. *Visit him more. Get to know him one-on-one. Forge a father-son relationship.* Potter acted like an incompetent babysitter.

And as for Ava, a concrete step she can take is to have a candid one-on-one conversation with the person she believes will best understand her predicament: Mitzi. The conversation is Ava's main motivation for traveling all the way to Nantucket for Bart's party.

Once she has arrived at home, she realizes there are other benefits. She gets to spend time with her siblings, and she gets to see her father—who looks a little better than Ava expected. She gets to hug Bart after he blows out the candles and meet the girl suddenly attached to Bart's side. The girl has come dressed in an exquisite geisha costume. Ava so admires it that she makes a mental note to find a similar one for herself for next year.

Imagine her surprise when she discovers the girl at Bart's side is Allegra Pancik, her former student. Ava had Allegra and her twin sister, Hope, in her first year of teaching; they were in the fifth grade. Allegra was unremarkable, but Hope showed enormous promise as a musician and went on to play the flute all through high school.

"Hi, Miss Quinn," Allegra says. She offers Ava her hand.

"Allegra, good to see you!" Ava says. "How old are you now?"

"Nineteen," Allegra says.

Nineteen. Ava can't believe her students are now old enough for Bart to date.

The real payoff for Ava happens after the party. She stays until the end because Mitzi stays until the end, even though Kelley leaves with his hospice nurse, Patrick, and Jennifer shortly after cake is served. Isabelle and Kevin head home to relieve their babysitter, and Bart disappears with Allegra Pancik. Hence, it's just Mitzi, Ava, and the last few party stragglers.

"Do you need me to help you clean up?" Ava asks Mitzi.

"The caterers will do it," Mitzi says. "Come on outside. I want to have a cigarette while we wait for the cab."

"Ohhh . . . kay," Ava says. She knows Mitzi started smoking when she left Kelley to live with George the Santa Claus, but she thought she'd quit. Now, apparently, she's back at it. Ava can't really blame her, can she? Watching Kelley's health deteriorate must be tough.

They stand out in front of the VFW in the crisp fall air, and Mitzi lights up.

"Only late at night," she tells Ava. "After your father is asleep. Or after I've been drinking."

Ava holds up her hands. "No judgment here."

"Thank you," Mitzi says with a relieved smile. "It's too bad Potter couldn't get away."

"He could get away," Ava says. "He wanted to come, but I asked him not to."

"Oh no!" Mitzi says. "Trouble in paradise?" She laughs. "Forgive me for saying that. I'm too old to believe that *anyone's* relationship is paradise."

"We had a challenging weekend," Ava says. "His ex-wife

and her boyfriend were in New York for a Shakespeare conference, and they left PJ, Potter's son, with us. Well, with Potter. And Potter wanted to introduce PJ to me."

"Naturally," Mitzi says. "How'd it go?"

"On a scale of one to ten it was a negative thirty," Ava says. She tells Mitzi about PJ screaming Friday night, about the video game on Saturday at the Museum of Natural History, about PJ texting his mother to say that Ava had touched him inappropriately.

"Good heavens," Mitzi says. "What a nightmare!"

"Nightmare," Ava concurs. She takes a deep breath and inhales some of Mitzi's secondhand smoke, which isn't unpleasant or unwelcome. "How did *you* do it, handling the three of us?"

"Ha!" Mitzi says. "The worst year of my life was my first year married to Kelley. Do you not remember?"

"Not really," Ava says. "Bits and pieces." She tries to hearken back. She was ten when they moved to Nantucket with Kelley. The boys were teenagers. Patrick was fine in Ava's memory, Kevin less so—until he met Norah Vale. But what memories does Ava have of herself?

"You were afraid of the dark, do you remember that?" Mitzi asks. "You were fine going to sleep on your own, but then during the night you would come into our room and demand to sleep with your father. I had to go to sleep in your room. You wouldn't sleep in the bed with me, you hated me, and Kelley never said no to you because he felt so guilty."

Guilty, Ava thinks. Kelley felt guilty because he'd gotten divorced, then met someone new, then quit his high-paying job as a trader and moved the kids out of New York all the way up to Nantucket, which had been a favorite place of theirs in the summer. But living year-round on the island was another story entirely. *Does* Ava remember being scared of the dark? Not really. She remembers missing her mother. She remembers Kelley taking her to South Station in Boston and putting her on the train to New York by herself. She remembers crying when Margaret took her back to the train to send her home. She remembers coloring books, paper dolls, and then finally an electric keyboard with headphones to pass the four-hour ride.

What does she remember about Mitzi? A standoff over a brown rice casserole. Ava's refusal to let Mitzi take her shopping for her first bra. *You're not my mother.* Ava said that a lot.

"I was awful to you," Ava says. "How did you deal with it?"

"I cried," Mitzi says. "I even called Margaret."

"You did?"

"I called her without telling your father. I asked her what I could do to make you like me. To make you acknowledge me."

"And what did Mom say?" Ava says.

"She wasn't quite the wonderful woman she is today," Mitzi says. "I can see now that your mother felt guilty as well. She had chosen her career, and Kelley had taken her children away, which she had fought at first, then reluctantly agreed to. She didn't *want* you to like me or acknowledge me, but she did tell me to hold my ground, to be myself, not to spoil you or flatter you or ingratiate myself to you. She said you'd come around."

"And I did," Ava says. "Right?"

"You were always the hardest on me," Mitzi says. "You were enamored with Bart, so I had that in my favor, but I always felt like you resented my presence in your life, in the family. And now look! You're in a similar situation and you've come to me for advice. I have to say, I find poetic justice in that."

"I'm sure," Ava says. "And you have my wholehearted apology."

"I don't need an apology," Mitzi says. "You were a child."

"You also have my gratitude," Ava says. "For sticking it out. Not only when we were kids, but two years ago. Thank you for coming back to Dad."

Mitzi takes a long drag of her cigarette. "When Bart was lost, I was lost," she says. "Thank *you* for forgiving me."

"I love you, Mitzi," Ava says. A lump presents in her throat. Has she ever told Mitzi this before? "You're our... well, you're not our biological mother, but you've been another mother, one we didn't always appreciate like we should have."

"That's nice to hear," Mitzi says. "I love you and your brothers. I always have. Even when we were battling, I always loved you like you were my own."

Ava sees headlights coming down New South Road; the taxi is approaching. "So what should I do about PJ?"

"In the words of Bob Dylan," Mitzi says, "'Keep on keepin' on.' Be yourself. Don't spoil him or flatter him. Just treat him with love and respect and kindness. Let him feel that he can trust you. Let him understand that you're not going anywhere, that you're his ally even when he treats you like an enemy. You have a great advantage."

"I do?" Ava says.

"Yes," Mitzi says. "You're the adult." She smiles as the taxi pulls up. "And who knows, maybe twenty or twenty-five years from now, PJ will be asking *your* advice."

"Maybe," Ava says. The idea of twenty-seven-year-old PJ coming to Ava for advice is preposterous—but not impossible. Mitzi holds the door to the taxi open, and Ava slides in.

She smiles at the taxi driver. She feels much better. She *is* the adult! She, like Mitzi, will keep on keepin' on.

"Winter Street, please," she says.

PART TWO

NOVEMBER

JENNIFER

To meet Norah for coffee, Jennifer had to lie to Patrick. Meaning she has to continue to lie to Patrick.

She said, "I need to go to the Nantucket Sewing Center when it opens tomorrow. They carry a fabric I want to use..." She nearly said *in Grayson Coker's penthouse,* but she stopped short of that treachery. Patrick will assume it's for the penthouse, however, because what else would it be for?

"Cool," Patrick said. "What time does it open?"

Jennifer swallowed. "Eight thirty. I should be back in an hour."

"Great," Patrick said. "That'll give me time to visit with Dad before we leave."

He's not suspicious at all, Jennifer thinks. Somehow, the fact that he wholeheartedly believes her makes her feel worse. He thinks her addiction is a thing of the past. He believes she's honest, forthcoming, transparent. His faith in her is almost more than Jennifer can bear.

Norah is at the Hub waiting for Jennifer, which is a relief, but what is *not* a relief is that Norah isn't alone. There's a man with her, a man about Jennifer's age with tattoos on his neck and his forearms. He has jet-black hair, longish though not unkempt, and he's wearing jeans, a gray cashmere sweater pushed up on his arms to display the aforementioned tattoos, and a pair of white Converse high-tops. Is he a hipster or a drug lord? Jennifer can't tell.

Jennifer checks his wrist for a watch. He's not wearing a watch, but he sports some fairly nice bracelets—John Hardy silver bangles, if Jennifer had to guess, and one black cord bracelet with a silver and rhinestone skull. He looks at Jennifer and smiles. His teeth are straight and white. He looks friendly. There's something about his face that's familiar. Does she know this guy?

"Jennifer, hey!" Norah says. Norah, too, looks hip and stylish. She's in a black turtleneck, skinny jeans, and Black Watch plaid ballet flats, and she's wearing a fabulous pair of shoulder dusters that are a cascade of intertwining gold circles. Norah's hair is cut in an asymmetrical bob, and her makeup is subtle. Norah Vale has never looked so good.

"Norah, hi," Jennifer says. She isn't sure how to greet her former sister-in-law–slash–drug dealer. A handshake seems too formal, a hug too intimate. Jennifer settles on an air kiss.

"Can I get you a latte?" Norah asks.

"I'm drinking a matcha," the man with the bracelets says.

Latte? Matcha? Jennifer gets the distinct feeling that this meeting is not what she expected, and she feels a piercing disappointment. Ativan, she needs Ativan!

"Uh…just coffee," Jennifer says, feeling suddenly middle aged and fuddy-duddy. "Regular American coffee."

Norah orders while Jennifer sneaks another look at the man who's with Norah. Maybe this is Norah's boyfriend?

The man catches Jennifer's eye and offers his hand. "You might not remember me? I'm Danko Vale, Norah's brother.

We met...oh, I don't know...at one of the Quinn family functions years ago."

"Okay, wait," Jennifer says, because now that she is looking at the guy full-on, she nearly has it, a memory with him attached. Norah's brother Danko. Norah, Jennifer recalls, grew up in a bizarre family situation. Lots of brothers, only one of them her full biological brother, and not the one everyone expected. Jennifer tugs at the memory like it's a stubborn knot. Danko Vale. He's the tattoo artist, the one who talked Norah into the godforsaken python on her neck. Yes! And... he's the oldest brother, Norah's full brother, because the mother reunited with Danko's father after having three boys by other men, and she got pregnant with Norah.

And...wait! Yes! Jennifer *has* met Danko before, but not at a Quinn family function. Jennifer and Patrick were up at Great Point in the Land Rover they owned before they bought the BMW, and Patrick got the Rover stuck in the sand. Danko Vale rolled up in a black Jeep. He was brown from the sun, wearing black swim trunks and a red bandana over his head, and with all the tattoos, he resembled nothing so much as a pirate. Patrick was wary at his approach, but then Danko introduced himself and there was an aha moment as Patrick realized he was Norah's brother, the one who had given Norah away when Norah and Kevin got married. It was a tad awkward, since Norah and Kevin were at that point in a period of split-up-but-still-kind-of-together—however, Danko was a perfect gentleman, not to mention a lifesaver, as he produced a towrope and freed the Land Rover from the soft sand. Patrick, Jennifer remembers, offered Danko forty bucks, but Danko waved the money away, saying, "Nah, man, anything for family."

"You pulled my husband and me out of the sand!" Jennifer says now. "In our Land Rover, I mean. Up at Great Point."

Danko snaps his fingers. "That's right! I told Norah I'd met you, but I thought it was only at the wedding."

Norah turns around and hands Jennifer her coffee. "I'm glad you guys are hitting it off. Shall we go sit on the bench outside so we can talk?"

Bench outside? Jennifer thinks. *So we can talk?* The "bench outside" that Norah means is a bench that faces Main Street. It's the most public place on the entire island. Jennifer does *not* want to sit on the bench with Norah and Danko, but what choice does she have?

It's a beautiful morning on Main Street, however, unseasonably mild for the first of November, and so Jennifer takes a seat and raises her face to the sunshine. *Just a few Ativan,* she thinks. A few meaning twenty. Or thirty. Danko and Norah must be in business together, which is weird, and awful, but who is Jennifer to judge? They are both well dressed; they exude success. They are dealing pharmaceuticals to the top 1 percent; they have an image to uphold now, Jennifer supposes.

"So," Norah says. "We have a proposition for you. An exciting proposition."

They want her to sell, Jennifer thinks. It only makes sense; she lives in an elite neighborhood populated by unhappy housewives. The pathetic thing—the *truly pathetic thing*—is that she will consider it. She *has* to consider it—she needs the money!

But the terms will have to be favorable. In fact, they will have to be *her* terms. She will keep a percentage of sales, and there needs to be safeguards in place. She can't get caught. The kids managed to survive their father being imprisoned for financial shenanigans, but they won't survive their mother being imprisoned for drug dealing.

"Oh really?" Jennifer says with cheerful naiveté. "What is it?"

"Danko is a TV producer," Norah says. "With SinTV."

"Really?" Jennifer says. She feels a bit starstruck. She would never in a million years know what SinTV is except that Leanne, Jennifer's beloved client, is addicted to not one but two shows on SinTV. The first is called *Swing Set,* a reality show about six couples living in Fishers, Indiana, who start swinging, as in sleeping with one another's spouses. It sounds awful to Jennifer, but Leanne can't get enough of it; she's greatly anticipating the spin-offs set in Traverse City, Michigan, and Sebastopol, California. Soon, Jennifer supposes, every small town in America will be swinging. Leanne also watches a cooking show called *Fatso,* where every recipe starts with two sticks of butter and ends with an extra side of mayonnaise. Again, it sounds repugnant to Jennifer, and yet this is where Leanne got the insanely delicious recipe for her fried chicken club sandwiches with lime pickle relish and bacon aioli, which Derek affectionately refers to as a Heart Attack on Brioche.

"I worked at Vice for three years and for TMZ before that," Danko says. "SinTV was the natural next step."

"They've put him in charge of developing a home-improvement show," Norah says. "They want something that will be competitive with *Rehab Addict,*" Danko says. "And *Flip or Flop.*"

"I always thought *Flip or Flop* was a flop," Jennifer says, though that's likely her envy talking.

"The divorce was the best thing that ever happened to that show," Danko says. "Their ratings are through the roof now."

"Viewers love to know the real-life stories behind a show's host," Norah says. "Which brings us to our idea."

"Your idea?" Jennifer says.

"We want you to host a show on SinTV," Danko says.

"Me?" Jennifer says. She would be lying if she said the

thought had never crossed her mind. She tries *not* to watch HGTV, just like she's sure novelists try not to pore over the *New York Times Book Review*. Jennifer suffers from professional envy, for certain, but she also doesn't want to inadvertently copy what other decorators are doing.

"You're beautiful, you're smart, you're poised," Norah says.

"The network wants a show set in Boston," Danko says. "They feel the demographic up there is underexploited."

"The show Danko has created is called *Real-Life Rehab*," Norah says. "They have a couple of townhouses they're looking at in Dorchester."

"Dorchester?" Jennifer says.

"Part of the hook is that we'll be renovating homes in transitioning neighborhoods," Danko says. "Buying teardowns, essentially, and then affordably and sustainably remodeling them in an attempt to jump-start gentrification."

"That's what happened in the South End," Norah says.

"Yes, well, Dorchester is hardly the South End," Jennifer says. She thinks of her clients Peter and Ken and their divine home on Washington Street. But didn't Ken tell Jennifer that they'd bought the property in 1992, when the neighborhood was a wasteland? There's no reason why Dorchester can't rise up. And Jennifer could be a part of it. "But I like the concept. It's design as altruism, in a way."

"Exactly," Danko says. "SinTV has a reputation for being a little bit of a bad-boy network. This would be our way of showing we have a heart."

"And there's another hook," Norah says. "You. You, Jennifer Quinn, as a recovering addict. You are your own real-life rehab story."

"I pitched it to the network executives," Danko says. "They went *crazy*. They are giving this show an enormous budget. So if you agree, you'll be very well compensated."

"Wait a minute," Jennifer says. She hears the phrase *very well compensated* and a cheer goes up in the back of her mind, but she has gotten snagged on what Norah said. "So people will *know* I had…" She can't even find words to express what she's thinking. "A problem with pills? We'll tell them?"

"We'll tell them," Norah says. "I think seeing you and learning what you've overcome will help a lot of people who are going through the same thing."

"Okay, but…" The only word Jennifer can come up with is *no*. No, she is not going on television and admitting she was addicted to pills! Her family knows—her mother, Kelley and Mitzi, Margaret, even the boys know a little bit—but that's a very small circle compared with…well, the *entire country*. Or the portion of the country who watch shelter programs on SinTV.

Leanne will find out. And Grayson Coker. And all the mothers from the kids' school. And Mandy Pell. And the women who organize the Beacon Hill Holiday House Tour. And all the people Jennifer went to high school with and her classmates from Stanford. It's not random strangers—Megan Hoffman from wherever—that concern Jennifer; it's the people she knows, the people who *thought* they knew her.

"We know it seems scary," Danko says. "It takes a really brave, really strong person to admit she has fallen prey like that. Believe me, I know. I've been in AA for fifteen years."

Why don't you *do the show then?* Jennifer nearly asks. When she looks at Danko, she sees kindness in his eyes. Empathy. He gets it—maybe.

"I can't," Jennifer says. "I just…can't."

"Why don't you take some time and think about it?" Norah says. She puts a hand on Jennifer's leg and leans in. "You would be *so* great. A role model, a *real* role model, someone who has been through a rough patch and then come out the other side."

But I'm still in *the rough patch!* Jennifer thinks. She came here this morning hoping to score some Ativan!

"Just so you know, the show will pay you thirty-five thousand dollars an episode for the first twelve episodes, with the option to negotiate for the second season," Danko says. "And I'll point out that there are also endorsement opportunities, and that any host who broadcasts nationally sees a spike in her own personal design business."

"Meaning you'll be the most sought-after designer in Boston," Norah says. "Tom and Gisele will be hunting you down to redo their kids' playroom."

Jennifer smiles—she does have a file at home filled with creative playroom ideas—and at the same time, she's trying to calculate: thirty-five thousand times twelve. It's four hundred twenty grand, which is nearly what she lost by giving up Grayson Coker. Plus endorsements. Plus business rolling in, more business than she can handle.

But she has to tell the world she was addicted to pills. *The struggle is real,* she imagines herself saying into the camera. *And it is constant.* Could she bring herself to be that honest?

"I need to think about it," Jennifer says.

"We have some time," Danko says. "Can you give us an answer before Thanksgiving?"

"Yes," Jennifer says. "I'll let you know by the Friday before Thanksgiving. The seventeenth."

They all stand up, and Norah gives Jennifer a sisterly squeeze. "Just so you know, I don't get a finder's fee or anything. When Danko told me about this project, I automatically thought of you. You would be so great on TV."

"Real-life rehab," Jennifer says wryly. "That's me."

She shakes hands with Danko, who gives her an encouraging smile. "You'd be perfect," he says. He holds up his hands. "But no pressure. Stay in touch."

"I will," Jennifer says as he and Norah walk away.

She sits back down on the bench for a second and picks up her cup of coffee, which she has all but ignored. It's then that she sees the blond woman with the baby carriage across the street staring her down.

It takes Jennifer a second to realize who the woman is, and another second for her to register the appropriate amount of horror. It's Isabelle, out for a walk with the baby. Isabelle must have seen Jennifer talking to Norah Vale. Isabelle must have seen Jennifer *hugging* Norah Vale.

This is bad. For so many reasons.

"Isabelle!" Jennifer calls out. "Isabelle!" She waves at her sister-in-law, but Isabelle pretends not to notice. She turns the carriage around and walks away.

EDDIE

He tries not to let his hopes deflate when he sees the Christys step off the ferry. Masha —for Eddie can think of Marcia Christy only as Masha—told Eddie to look for a woman with yellow hair and a purple coat. Eddie assumed he would be looking for a blond. But in fact, the very first person off the boat is a woman in a puffy purple parka, and she has *yellow* hair. Yellow, the color of marshmallow Peeps.

"Masha?" Eddie says.

She immediately envelops Eddie in a puffy purple hug. She's wearing a sharp-smelling perfume, reminiscent of the cheap drugstore brands Eddie's sister, Barbie, used to wear in high school.

Eddie will not judge Masha. Masha has won Powerball. Masha has more money than 90 percent of the folks who come to Nantucket looking to buy.

"Eddie," Masha says. "Please meet my husband, Raja."

"Nice to meet you, Raja," Eddie says, extending a hand. He doesn't bother correcting his pronunciation, and neither Masha nor Raja seems to mind or notice. Raja is magnificently ordinary—white, pudgy, balding, bespectacled. He's wearing a plaid shirt, flat-front Dockers, a red Windbreaker, some comfortable-looking loafers—Hush Puppies, maybe.

Raja's handshake is a baggie of warm pudding. No surprises there.

"Welcome to Nantucket, both of you," Eddie says. "My car is parked in the lot. We have six properties to look at, so we'd better get cracking."

Masha lets out a whoop. "I like you already, Eddie. Ha! I'm a poet and I didn't know it."

"Right this way," Eddie says.

Masha is a talker. Between the parking lot and the top of Main Street, Eddie learns the following: Masha is a hairdresser, grew up in Lynn, Massachusetts, and attended Empire Beauty School in Malden. Raja is also from Lynn. Both Masha and Raja attended Lynn Classical, but Raja was three years ahead, plus he was one of the smarties in the chess club, and Masha—*as you can probably guess, Eddie*— was a cheerleader who hung out with the real popular kids. Raja is an engineer with National Grid, and for fun he plays chess online. They have a West Highland terrier named Jack, who is "basically our child," Masha says. Jack went with Masha to buy the Powerball ticket from Lanzilli's, and three of the numbers Masha picked were the components of Jack's birthday. So Jack is really the person responsible for the Christys' good fortune, Masha says.

"Jack isn't a person." Raja speaks up from the back.

Masha swats Eddie's arm. "That's an engineer for you," she says. "Hung up on details."

Eddie laughs, then hopes that Raja doesn't think Eddie is laughing at his expense.

"I know what you're thinking," Masha says. "I never shut up. It's true. I'm a chatty Kathy. Raja is a man of few words, so I talk for both of us."

Eddie can hold his own with pretty much anyone, but after being in the car with Masha for five minutes, he needs a break. He pulls onto Winter Street.

"I just have to make a quick stop," Eddie says. "Drop off a listing sheet for some other clients who are putting their house on the market. Won't take a minute." He double-parks in front of the inn and slowly approaches the front door, savoring the moment of quiet. Eddie uses the knocker, and a few seconds later Bart Quinn opens the door. He's holding a large bouquet of flowers.

"Hi?" Bart says.

"Bart, hi. Eddie Pancik," Eddie says. He holds out the plain white envelope that contains the listing sheet. "Would you give this to your mother, please? Only your mother. It's something she specifically requested."

Bart takes the envelope, but he seems to be studying Eddie. "Eddie *Pancik?* You're Allegra's father, right?"

"Guilty as charged," Eddie says.

"Is she at work right now?" Bart asks.

"As far as I know," Eddie says.

"Great," Bart says. "These flowers are for her, actually. I'm going to surprise her."

"Well!" Eddie says. "I'm sure she'll be thrilled. And you'll give that envelope to your mom? Put it in her hands?"

"You bet," Bart says. "Thanks for stopping by, Mr. Pancik."

Eddie heads back to the car, buoyed by the interaction. Bart Quinn is a polite young man, a war hero, and thoughtful! What woman doesn't want to get flowers? Eddie should bring Grace flowers tonight, for no reason other than that he loves and appreciates her. If it goes well with the Christys, he'll get the flowers; otherwise, he can't really justify the expense.

Eddie hasn't mentioned anything to Grace about seeing Benton Coe. He has given it thought and has decided it's best if Grace doesn't know that Eddie knows that Benton has returned. He's going to watch for changes in Grace's behavior; you'd better bet he's going to watch!

When he climbs back into the car, Masha is holding the second copy of the Winter Street Inn listing sheet.

"I want it," Masha says.

"Excuse me?" Eddie says.

"This inn, it's for sale, right? And I want to buy it. I've always wanted to run an inn. Haven't I always wanted to run an inn, Raja?"

"This is the first I've heard of it," Raja says.

"Probably because you tune out ninety percent of what I say." Masha turns to Eddie. "If I'm not talking about dinner, he doesn't hear me."

"You've never once said you wanted to run an inn," Raja says.

"Maybe I never said it because I never thought it was possible," Masha says. "But now, with the money, *anything* is possible." She swats Eddie's arm again. "For us, a couple of kids from Lynn."

Eddie says, "Running an inn is a lot of work. More than you probably realize."

"I'm no stranger to hard work," Masha says. "And I like meeting new people."

"Well, we have some other exciting properties for you to look at," Eddie says.

"I want the inn," Masha says.

"Honey," Raja says.

"Can't we look at the inn?" Masha says. "You said it's on the market."

"It's going on the market," Eddie says. "It's not on the market yet. We can't look at it today. But I have some other exciting properties to show you."

"But...," Masha says.

"Let the man do his job, Masha," Raja says.

Eddie starts with the three houses close to town because they are all Bayberry Properties listings. All three are Glenn's, but Glenn told Eddie to "have at it," meaning Eddie will be the only broker present. On the one hand, this is good because Eddie will get a chance to bond with the Christys. On the other hand, it's bad because Eddie suspects that Glenn Daley doesn't consider the Christys real, viable clients.

"Lottery money," Glenn says. "Always iffy."

The first house is on Hulbert Avenue, listed at $11.2 million. It's on the "wrong" side of Hulbert, meaning across the street from the water, but that's what makes it affordable. Houses on the "right" side of the street go for double that price tag, but it's a moot point because those houses come on the market only once in a lifetime.

When Masha walks into the house on Hulbert, she says, "Is it just me, or does this house smell like mice?"

"I'm not sure what mice smell like," Eddie says, although he does agree the house has a funny smell. "This is an older house, in need of some TLC." The furnishings are worn and tired, the prints of the sofa and chairs have been bled of their colors, the coffee table is marred with white rings. Eddie can see that Masha is underwhelmed.

"I can't believe they're charging eleven point two million for this," she says.

"What you're paying for here is the address," Eddie says. "Hulbert Avenue is very prestigious, and it's close to town."

"But it's not *in* town," Masha says, smiling. She has a very pretty smile, Eddie sees. "The inn is in town!"

"Let's look upstairs," Eddie says. "There are four bedrooms."

The upstairs of the house proves to be just as disappointing as the downstairs. The two bedrooms that have water views are small, and they share an outdated Jack-and-Jill bathroom with pocket doors that stutter on their runners. The two bedrooms in the back of the house are bigger, but they look out over scrubby wetlands. And as everyone knows, wetlands breed mosquitoes. Eddie can't believe the price tag on this pile either; it's basically a teardown. But that's what Nantucket has come to these days. Land is at such a premium that an empty lot on the wrong side of the right street will cost you eight figures.

Eddie nearly decides to skip the two houses he has on Lincoln Circle. They, like the Hulbert Avenue house, are older homes in need of serious updating. Eddie has shown both of the Lincoln Circle homes before. They have a certain charm; they're quintessential Nantucket summer cottages, nothing flashy or newfangled about them. Masha won't be impressed . . . but Eddie will show them anyway, if only for a comparison to the bigger estates he has in store for the Christys out in Wau-winet, Squam, and Shimmo.

The first Lincoln Circle home has a screened-in porch with a fireplace, a charming feature that Eddie shows off right away.

"Nice," Masha agrees. However, she sniffs at the kitchen with its particle-board cabinets and drop-in stainless steel sink. "Our kitchen in East Boston is nicer than this," she says. "How much did you say this house costs?"

"Twelve point three million," Eddie says. "Again, you're paying for the address. And this house has full water views from the second floor."

"It feels like a rip-off," Masha says.

"Okay," Eddie says. He decides to cut his losses and skip the second listing on Lincoln Circle. He should have realized that the Christys would want a house with all the bells and whistles, a house that feels like it's worth twelve million dollars. "Time for something different. I can assure you, the next house I show you will be much, much more to your liking."

"I liked the inn," Masha says.

Raja puts a hand on Eddie's shoulder and gives him a silent shake of the head. The meaning is unmistakable: they are *not* buying an inn.

As Eddie drives along Polpis Road, he chastises himself for not doing a better job of reading the Christys. He should have skipped the old-school summer homes. Those will eventually sell to someone who grew up summering on Nantucket and always dreamed of owning a house on Hulbert Avenue or Lincoln Circle. To appreciate the pedigree and charm of those cottages, one needs to have an affinity for under-statement and reserve.

Eddie is so consumed with disappointment and doubt in

himself—*What if I blow this sale? I can't blow it! I'm count-ing on the commission!*—that he almost doesn't notice Grace pedaling down the bike path. Eddie hits the brakes and swivels his head. That's Grace, all right, head hunched over the handlebars like Dennis Quaid in *Breaking Away.* She's headed toward town.

"My wife!" Eddie says. He realizes he's cutting Masha off; she's in the middle of a long-winded story about a cruise she and Raja took to the Bahamas. Their luggage was lost and not returned to them until the very end of the trip. How did they even get on that topic? Eddie wonders. He follows the thread backward and thinks, *Oh yes. The last time Masha and Raja were on an island.* "I'm sorry," Eddie says. "It's just that that was my wife back there, riding her bike on the path. We just passed her."

"Funny," Masha says. "That happened to us once. Raja stopped at Lanzilli's after work to buy some cheeseburger-flavored Pringles, which he loves but I refuse to buy, and I was at Lanzilli's because we'd completely run out of toilet paper. I've never been so surprised to see anyone in my life, and I'll tell you what, neither was Raja. He thought he was getting away with something."

Eddie can't come up with a response to that; he's too busy checking the rearview mirror for another glimpse of Grace. It was her—she was wearing her new favorite hat, the dark-green one with the faux-mink pom-pom on top, and she had on Allegra's old navy Whalers hoodie, which she favors because it makes her feel young.

"Is your wife a big biker?" Masha asks. "Neither Raja nor I exercise, except when we walk Jack."

"And I walk to the T station," Raja says.

"We both walk to the T station," Masha says. "But it's only half a block away, so it doesn't count for much."

Eddie knows that Grace took to riding her mountain bike while Eddie was in jail, but she hasn't, to his knowledge, ridden it since he's been back.

Why today? he wonders. It isn't as though she has to go to the bank or the grocery store. She's all the way out here on Polpis Road. It's not raining or even very cold, but neither is it sunny and mild like it was on Wednesday.

Why today?

And then Eddie notices a big black truck barreling toward him. He freezes. Is it Benton Coe's truck? He looks at the man driving, while at the same time trying to memorize the license plate—M23 . . .—but he can't do both at once. He got half the plate and a split-second glimpse of the driver, who was wearing a hat and sunglasses. Impossible to tell if it was Benton Coe or not, and half a license plate is useless. Benton Coe *does* drive a black truck, or he used to before he left for Detroit. But then again, half the contractors on Nantucket drive black trucks. That could have been anyone. Eddie can't let his wild imagination get the best of him.

He has missed the last three or four paragraphs of Masha's ongoing monologue. Now she's talking about a recipe for s'mores you can make under the broiler, which makes you feel like you're beside a campfire even when you're sitting in an apartment in East Boston.

Eddie's phone pings. He's distracted and nearly misses the turn for Medouie Creek Road. They are now out in Wauwinet, not far from the house where Eddie and Grace used to live. He wonders if Grace decided to bike out here to look upon their house and maybe even wander through their old gardens. The people who bought the house, the Pattons, live in Dubai and are on Nantucket only in August, so there would be no danger of interrupting anyone at home.

Somehow the thought of Grace pedaling out to set her

eyes on their old life makes Eddie even more depressed than thinking of her rendezvousing with Benton Coe. Eddie failed her, failed her badly. He lost everything they had—and still she has stayed with him.

He will make it up to her. He will sell the Christys a house, this house on Medouie Creek Road, listed at thirteen and a half million, and he will invest every cent into Grace's future happiness.

But first he has to get his head back in the game!

The nice thing about Masha is she doesn't require anyone else's participation in the conversation; she just prattles along happily by herself.

Eddie pulls into the driveway. "Here we are," he says. It takes a second to recall that this is Rachel McMann's listing; her turquoise Mini Cooper is parked in front of the garage.

"Now that's what I'm talking about!" Masha says, interrupting herself when she sees the house, the pool, the pool house, the trimmed boxwood hedges and manicured lawn, the hydrangea bushes neatly bundled in burlap for the winter, and the view of the harbor spread out before them like a painting.

Rachel is standing in the doorway, wearing a dress that would look right at home on Marion Cunningham from *Happy Days*. She has an apron on over the dress, and she's holding out a plate of freshly baked chocolate chip cookies; Eddie can smell them from the front walk.

So this is how she does it, he thinks.

He might as well be invisible. From the second the Christys walk through the door, Rachel takes over. She has made cookies, and she has classical music playing and a fire burning in each of the six fireplaces. She has staged every single room. There are fresh flowers in the common areas, including an arrangement of fresh lilies in the vestibule that towers over Eddie's head. There are French milled soaps in the bathrooms and stacks of novels on each of the nightstands. The house has every amenity known to man: six bedrooms, each with its own bath, and a deep Jacuzzi tub in the master; a cathedral-ceilinged gourmet kitchen; a library; and in the basement, a home theater, a billiards room, and a wine cellar.

Masha is speechless.

Raja eats four cookies in rapid succession, then takes a fifth, which he carries around with him as they head outside to look at the pool and the pool house, which also features a steam sauna and a fully equipped gym, the answer to the Christys' lack of exercise. Then they all meander out to the end of the deep-water dock.

"Do you two have a boat?" Rachel asks.

"Not yet," Masha says. "But we might soon, right, Raj?"

Rachel leads them back to the house to warm up by the fire. Masha says she needs to use the little girls' room.

"Powder room down the hall on the left," Rachel says. "I'm just going to box up these cookies for you to take home. Feel free to wander. Jump on the beds if you want to, shoot a game of pool. I want you to feel at home."

Masha disappears into the powder room, and Raja stands up, seemingly at a loss without her.

"Want to go back upstairs?" Eddie asks.

"There's a built-in cigar humidor in one of the master closets," Rachel says. "I may have forgotten to point that out."

"A built-in cigar humidor?" Raja says. He seems nervous, almost intimidated. It *is* a lot of house, Eddie agrees. Maybe it's too much house for the Christys; they're both acting sheepish, like this house is a museum where they're not allowed to touch anything.

"Let's go take a look," Eddie says.

"Let Roger go by himself," Rachel says. "He's going to be the man of the house, after all. You stay here, Eddie, and keep me company."

Keeping Rachel company is the last thing Eddie wants to do, but he complies. Rachel McMann has proven to be a master at the art of selling a house.

"So what do you think?" Rachel says. She abandons the dishes in the kitchen sink, links her arm through Eddie's, and leads him to the front room, which has an enormous picture window that looks out over the garden and the harbor. "Are they for real?"

"Yes," Eddie says. "I mean, I think so. Hulbert and Lincoln Circle were a bust. They don't understand the old-money thing."

"No, I wouldn't think so," Rachel says.

"To be honest, *I* don't understand the old-money thing," Eddie says. "That heap on Hulbert is listed at eleven mil."

"It'll go for ten," Rachel says. "The lot alone." She points out the window at a bench in the garden. "Do you know where that bench originally came from? The Tuileries in Paris."

"What?" Eddie says. At his former house down the way a bit, *they* had a bench that originally came from the Tuileries in Paris. It was one of Benton Coe's big coups, finding Grace that bench. It was one of a hundred ways he seduced her. "Are these Benton Coe–designed gardens?"

"They are," Rachel says. "I didn't mention it because I didn't think his name would mean much to the Christys."

"It wouldn't," Eddie says. It does, however, mean something to him. "Was Benton here a little while ago?"

Rachel shakes her head. "Not to my knowledge. I haven't seen Benton since the party Tuesday night."

"Oh," Eddie says.

"Why do you ask?" Rachel says.

Eddie shakes his head. Benton wasn't here. He was, likely, checking on one of his other estates out this way—if that was even Benton in the truck. And Grace was just out for a bike ride to get fresh air and exercise before winter descends.

Or is Eddie being naive?

Eddie and the Christys wave good-bye to Rachel—who hands Raja a white bakery box of cookies tied with ribbon—and they pile into the Cherokee.

"So," Eddie says. "What did you think?"

Raja shocks Eddie by speaking first. "That house was something else."

Something else: What does that mean? Eddie decides not to press. He can't remember where they're headed next. He checks his phone and remembers the text that came in while he was driving.

It's from Addison Wheeler, canceling the other two houses.

Eddie blows out a stream of frustrated air. He gets the distinct feeling that nobody else in the world of Nantucket real estate is taking his buyers seriously. But Eddie takes them seriously.

"You can be honest with me," Eddie says. "Did that feel like too much house? Could you see yourself living there? We do have other options, but I just got word from the listing broker that he's no longer available to show us the other two houses today. So if you still want to look around, I suggest we plan a return trip for you. Maybe over Christmas Stroll weekend?"

"I'd like to put an offer in on the house we just saw," Raja says.

Eddie's heart sings.

"I want the inn," Masha says.

MARGARET

She doesn't begin the countdown until the final week. Five broadcasts left, then four, then three. She's in denial, she supposes. Lee Kramer, head of the network, has been running around like Chicken Little since August 1, which was the day that Margaret announced she was retiring.

"But *why?*" Lee said. "Is it money? You're already the highest-paid anchor in the business. You make as much as Rather did at the end." He said this as if Margaret should be thanking him.

"Nothing to do with money," Margaret said, although a part of her was curious to see how high she could get Lee to go. But no amount of money would make her change her mind. "I'm needed elsewhere."

"You signed a noncompete!" Lee said.

"My kids need me," Margaret said. "Kelley's cancer is back. He's dying, Lee."

Lee blinked. "That's awful, Margaret. I like Kelley, hell of a guy." Lee took his glasses off and rubbed the bridge of his nose. "But aren't your kids grown?"

"My last day will be November tenth," Margaret says. "Friday."

"November tenth is only three months from now!" Lee said. "How can I possibly replace the most iconic news anchor the world has ever known in three short months?"

"Flattery won't work, Lee," Margaret said as she turned and walked out of the office.

"Does this have anything to do with politics?" Lee called after her.

Margaret's retirement has nothing to do with politics or the polarization of America or the increasingly dire content of the news Margaret has to report. It has to do with Kelley. Their three kids *are* grown; they are independent, fully functioning adults. They don't need their mother. But Kelley's diagnosis—he's terminal—has brought certain things into focus for Margaret. There is a long list of things she still wants to do. She wants to travel with Drake. She wants to visit her grandbabies. She wants to practice yoga, grow an herb garden; she wants to read.

For all of Margaret's adult life, the news has been a drug. Her broadcasting career started small. She reported car accidents, fires, robberies, strikes. Her big "break"—and she is loath to call it that—came during her coverage on September 11. She was reporting on that tragic day for NY1, and something about her screen presence caught the attention of the executives at CBS. By the end of that unforgettable week, she had been offered a seat at the evening news desk, and a year later she was the sole anchor.

Since then Margaret has covered the war with Iraq, the death of Saddam Hussein, the tsunami in Southeast Asia, Hurricane Katrina, the election of not one but two new popes, the war against terror, the rise of ISIS, the election of Barack Obama, the legalization of gay marriage, the eradication of Osama bin Laden by U.S. Navy SEAL Team 6, and countless gun massacres—Sandy Hook Elementary, San Bernardino, and Aurora, Colorado. Margaret has announced the deaths of Robin Williams, Whitney Houston, Prince,

Philip Seymour Hoffman, James Gandolfini, Heath Ledger, Carrie Fisher, David Bowie, and Michael Jackson. She has covered Darfur, Boko Haram, the war against Ukraine, the civil war in Syria, the earthquakes in Haiti and the Philippines.

Margaret has had a good run. She does her job faithfully to the very best of her ability each and every night. But now she's both tired and energized: tired of being tethered to the news cycle, energized by the prospect of joining the civilian world.

Lee had a hard time finding Margaret's replacement. The network wanted another woman, preferably a woman of color. Lee enlisted Margaret to help him watch the clips, and even she had to admit, none of them seemed ready. The top two contenders were Stephanie Kane, an anchor with the CBS affiliate in Anchorage, Alaska, of all places, and Catherine Bingham, who currently anchored the evening edition of ESPN's *SportsCenter.* Margaret leaned toward Catherine. Somehow professional sports seemed closer in tone and tenor to the news of the world than anything happening in the happy, peaceful Pacific Northwest. Although Stephanie did have the advantage of being half Inupiat.

And Stephanie it was! Lee made the announcement, and Margaret rallied behind his decision. "It doesn't matter if she isn't ready. I wasn't ready. She'll grow into the job."

Two broadcasts left. Roger in wardrobe asks Margaret what she wants to wear for her final broadcast.

"Black," Margaret says. She hasn't ever been allowed to wear black, but Margaret feels it's fitting for her final broadcast.

"Oh, please," Roger says. "How funereal. How somber

and depressing. I thought for sure you would go with purple. Or silver and gold sequins. Or a T-shirt that says *Cash Me Outside How Bah Dat.*"

"Black," Margaret says. It's a color that will make a statement, it has gravitas, it indicates finality.

"Black it is," Roger says. "Let's hope they don't complain upstairs."

"What are they going to do?" Margaret asks. "Fire me?"

One broadcast left. On Friday afternoon when Raoul drives Margaret to the studio, she's nervous. Nervous about *what?* she wonders. Despite her insistence that she did not want *any fuss made,* she knows that the producers have assembled photos for a ninety-second montage to end the broadcast. This will follow the sixty seconds they have allotted so that she can say something meaningful to leave with her viewers.

Something meaningful.

It's in Margaret's nature to be overprepared, but every time she has sat down to figure out what this *something meaningful* should be, she has drawn a blank. She doesn't want to make too big a deal out of her departure. After all, she only reports the news; she's not a pediatric brain surgeon like Drake, saving lives every single day.

She hopes that inspiration will come before airtime. She doesn't want to be sentimental; she can't grow weepy. The fact is, she has a hard time believing this is her last broadcast. If something were to happen at four forty-five in the afternoon on Friday, November 10—if the president declared war on North Korea, if suicide bombers infiltrated Disney World, if Prince George and Princess Charlotte were kidnapped from Kensington Palace—then Margaret would stay planted in her chair for weeks. But then the next story would break, and the next. The news is as relentless as the ocean.

There will never be a quiet, uneventful time to exit. She has to do it tonight, no matter what.

Was there any doubt? Roger has chosen perfectly. Margaret is to wear a black silk Diane von Furstenberg wrap dress. It's simple and elegant yet has no shortage of sex appeal. Margaret loves Diane as a person and counts her as a friend. One of the privileges of Margaret's career has been all of the legends she has met.

As far as jewelry goes, Margaret opts for only pearl earrings—and the Cartier tank watch that was a long-ago present from Kelley. She has worn it for every single national broadcast. Part of the reason is pragmatic (she needs to know the exact time), part is style (the watch became a Margaret Quinn fashion statement), and part is symbolism. She means to honor Kelley by wearing the watch, even as she knows that pursuing her career was what undid their marriage.

She knows Kelley will be watching her tonight from home—along with Mitzi, Kevin, Isabelle, and the kids. Patrick and Jennifer will be watching in Boston with the three boys. Barrett, Pierce, and Jaime will have no interest in watching Mimi deliver the news; they'll fidget and excuse themselves for the bathroom, where they will sneak in a few minutes of Minecraft. This makes her smile and relax. There's nothing like grandchildren to keep one humble.

The network is expecting to double their ratings. Normally, Margaret garners four to five million viewers; Lee is hoping for ten million tonight. It's not the idea of five million extra anonymous viewers that makes Margaret nervous. It's only knowing that the people she cares about are watching.

Especially Kelley.

She wants to do a good job for Kelley.

* * *

When she's ten minutes out, she stops by the greenroom. Drake is there, chilling a Rehoboam of Dom Pérignon. It's equal to six bottles of champagne and costs as much as a vacation in Hawaii but he insisted it was either the champagne or a surprise party, and Margaret opted for the champagne.

"Where's Ava?" Margaret asks. She wants to kiss Drake, but she can't smudge her lipstick. She wants to hug Drake, but she can't wrinkle her dress. Instead she squeezes the heck out of his hand.

"She and Potter are on their way," Drake says. "They had last-minute surprise visitors, and I guess these visitors are coming to the studio as well."

"Oh dear," Margaret says. She wonders if the surprise visitors are Patrick and Kevin. As lovely as that would be, it's unnecessary. Margaret does not want this to be a big deal!

"It'll be fine," Drake says. "Oh, look, here they are now."

Margaret turns to see Ava and Potter enter the greenroom. Behind Ava is a young woman Margaret is sure she doesn't know, and behind the young woman is . . . well, for a second Margaret's heart stops.

It's . . . it's . . . Kelley. No, it can't be. But it looks for all the world like a young Kelley Quinn, Kelley when Margaret first saw him, standing by the Angel Tree at the Metropolitan Museum of Art. It's Kelley, forty years ago.

"Look, Mom," Ava says. "Bart is here!"

Bart! Margaret thinks. Her heart resumes its regular activity. Margaret hasn't seen Bart since the previous Christmas, right after he got back from Afghanistan. Now his hair has grown out and he's gained back all the weight he lost.

"Bart," Margaret says, gathering him up in a hug despite

the inevitable dress wrinkles. "You gave me a fright. You look . . . exactly like your father did when he was your age. I had a bit of a senior moment. I thought you were him."

"Time to retire!" Drake says.

Margaret takes another moment to look at Bart. He's the spitting image of Kelley—it's *uncanny*—whereas Patrick and Kevin both favor Margaret's side of the family. "I'm so happy you're here. I'm honored you came."

"Thank you for having us," Bart says. He ushers the young woman forward. "Margaret, this is my girlfriend, Allegra."

A girlfriend! Margaret thinks. Kelley and Mitzi must be overjoyed.

Margaret takes Allegra's hand. "Allegra is one of my favorite names. I've loved it ever since I read 'The Children's Hour,' by Longfellow."

" 'Grave Alice, and laughing Allegra,' " Allegra quotes. "It's my mother's favorite poem."

"Two minutes, Margaret," Mickey, the producer, calls out.

Margaret blows everyone in the greenroom a kiss. "Off to work," she says.

One last time.

Margaret greets the world with a smile and says, "It's Friday, November tenth, two thousand seventeen. From the CBS studios in New York City, I'm Margaret Quinn."

The news is serious as always—the president, Congress, Syria, Russia—but there is nothing earth-shattering. No surprises. Margaret feels the minutes pass in seconds, and when they break for the last commercials, she experiences a moment of pure panic. She has made a mistake! She doesn't want it to end!

She hears a whisper—her name—and she looks out into

the darkened studio to see Darcy, her former assistant, standing next to Camera 1. Darcy waves like crazy, and Margaret fights to keep her composure. Darcy works for CNN now. Did she fly all the way up from Atlanta just to be here for Margaret's last broadcast? She must have. It's an incredible gesture.

There is one last human-interest story—at the National Zoo a baby gorilla who lost his mother has cottoned to one of the zebra mares—and then it's back to Margaret to say her final words. She has nothing written down. It's every nightmare come true: Margaret is in a play but didn't memorize her lines. Roger forgot to dress her and she's naked on camera. The teleprompter falls over and smashes, and Margaret has to talk about the new Republican health care bill off the cuff.

She focuses on Darcy, who looks impossibly chic and professional in her pencil skirt and sling-back heels.

"Tonight marks the end of my broadcasting career," Margaret says. "When I first started out as a copy girl in the newsroom of WCBS, I never dreamed I would someday be sitting in this chair."

But that's a lie, Margaret thinks. She *did* dream about it, constantly. She had grown up idolizing the great newsmen of her youth—for back then, they had all been men: Dan Rather, Mike Wallace, Peter Jennings, Tom Brokaw, Ed Bradley, Harry Reasoner, and the greatest of all time, Walter Cronkite. And then, as Margaret was coming into her own, she looked up to Diane Sawyer, Lesley Stahl, Connie Chung, Jane Pauley, and Christiane Amanpour.

Like any dream, hers has required sacrifices. Why that seems true for women more than men, Margaret isn't sure. All she knows is that when Kelley came to her saying he wanted to move the children up to Nantucket, Margaret let him go. She could have insisted he stay in New York. Or she could have left New York and taken an anchor job at the CBS affiliate in Boston. But she didn't do either. She let Kelley go with her blessing; she praised him for quitting his high-powered job trading petroleum futures. She was happy he was taking over the parenting duties.

And yet the most horrible, awful day of Margaret's life was the day she kissed the kids good-bye. Ava was only ten years old. A ten-year-old girl needs her mother. Everyone knew that. Margaret had convinced herself that she would still be Ava's mother; she would just take care of things from afar. She had decided that the best way to parent—especially with Ava—was to lead by example. She would strive for excellence. The kids would see her and then *they* would be inspired to strive for excellence.

Did it work out? Maybe—but there were innumerable lonely nights and countless days where the only word Margaret could find to describe herself was *selfish*. She wanted to be in front of the camera. She wanted to fly to Port-au-Prince, to Fallujah, to Islamabad. She let Mitzi and Kelley do the drudgery, the heavy lifting. Mitzi packed Ava's lunch and delivered Ava to piano lessons. Mitzi bought Ava her first bikini, filled her Easter basket, chaperoned her first girl-boy birthday party at the Dreamland Theater.

Margaret tried to compensate with Ava and the boys by being the Disneyland parent. She spared no expense in taking the kids on lavish trips during her limited vacations, and in buying them whatever they wanted.

She lived with guilt, night and day.

One night during the holidays, when the kids were teenagers, Margaret called the inn from the back of the car; it was after a broadcast and Raoul was delivering Margaret to her apartment. The kids were decorating the Christmas tree, hanging ornaments, eating popcorn, and drinking hot cider in front of the fire. That they sounded so happy only made Margaret feel more lonely and miserable. It was Kevin, her sensitive child, who noticed something melancholy in Margaret's tone, because he dropped his voice to a whisper and said, "The cider Mitzi made is really terrible, Mom. I'm only drinking it to be polite."

Margaret stares into the camera. She wants to somehow convey that her career has not been all glory. It has entailed an equal amount of heartbreak. Margaret is a broadcasting icon now, but she is also a person—one who made choices, one who made mistakes. She wants Darcy and every other Millennial woman out there watching—many of whom idolize Margaret and think of her as a pioneer who broke through very thick, very real glass ceilings—to know that success always comes with a price and that greatness often doesn't allow for balance.

In the end Margaret defaults to her trademark qualities: she is calm, she is reserved, and most of all, she is professional. To nail the landing here doesn't require a display of emotional fireworks. It requires only gratitude and grace.

"It has been my privilege to bring you the news each evening. Thank you for allowing me into your homes and into your lives. Over the past sixteen years, I have visited faraway places. I have dined with presidents and princes. I have seen unspeakable horrors—those inflicted by nature, and those inflicted by man. But I have been buoyed and inspired by the people of this diverse and magnificent country, and by the indomitable strength of the human spirit. God bless each and every one of you. For the *CBS Evening News,* I'm Margaret Quinn. Good night."

The montage plays, but Margaret can't watch. She tells everyone that if she sees photographs of herself from sixteen, twelve, even five years ago, she'll bemoan how much she has aged, but the truth is that the magnitude of what she is leaving behind will make her cry. After the montage ends, the screen goes black. A second later one sentence appears, written in white type: THANK YOU, MARGARET QUINN.

"And...we're out," Mickey says.

There is silence, during which Margaret stares at her desk.

Then Darcy gives a resounding whoop, and the studio bursts into a round of applause.

It's over.

BART

It takes him three days to come to his senses. He doesn't call Allegra and doesn't text her, although her name starts with *A* and is right there at the top of his contacts.

He knows he's being stubborn, stupid, and rude. When he dropped Allegra off at her house on Lily Street after his birthday party Tuesday night, following some pretty serious kissing in the front seat, he said, "I'll call you tomorrow." By "tomorrow" he meant Wednesday. But Wednesday came and went and Bart didn't call, and then Thursday came and went.

What was his problem? Was he being a typical male, playing games? Was he enjoying the thought of Allegra Pancik wondering what had happened, checking her phone in anticipation, possibly even pining for him?

No! Not at all! It was something else; it was the same old thing, his neuroses, his mind sickness. He didn't call Allegra because he didn't feel he deserved to be happy. If the eighteen fallen Marines couldn't feel the sweet sensation of a woman's lips meeting theirs, then Bart didn't deserve to feel it either.

Centaur. He kept thinking of Centaur.

Bart's very best friend in his platoon—his brother, for all intents and purposes—had been Centaur, baptized Charles Buford Duke. Centaur was born and raised in Cosby, Tennessee, in the foothills of the Great Smoky Mountains. He was a huge Volunteers fan; he bled orange and white, he said, and he told Bart about the boats that would line both sides of the Tennessee River on game days. You could walk a mile at least, going bow to stern on those boats, and be enthusiastically offered a cold Budweiser on each one. Centaur didn't have the temperament or the grades for college himself, but when Centaur and Bart met at basic training, Centaur had a girlfriend named Ruby Taylor, who was a freshman at UT, rushing Chi Omega.

How many hours did Bart listen to Centaur talk about Ruby Taylor—how pretty she was, how sweet, how devoted? Centaur had fallen in love with Ruby in third grade at Cosby Elementary. She had kicked him during recess and left a dark-purple bruise, and that was that. Bart had never known a person as blindly besotted as Centaur. Bart saw Ruby's picture. She was no beauty; she had red hair, as expected, but her skin was pasty, her eyes sunken a bit too far in her face, like raisins pushed into dough, her smile too wide, her hips a little wide as well. But that, somehow, made Bart admire Centaur's devotion even more. When they were running around Munich hooking up with buxom blond fräuleins right before they deployed to Sangin, Centaur remained true to Ruby Taylor. It wasn't a hardship to resist temptation, he said, when you were in love—and he hoped that someday Bart knew what that felt like.

Centaur was intending to marry Ruby Taylor as soon as he got home. Even in the darkest days of their capture, even on Centaur's final day, he was talking about marrying Ruby, buying land, building a house, having kids. He wanted five: four boys and a girl, in that order.

Centaur has now been dead for nearly a year. Back in June, Bart received an e-mail from Ruby Taylor, saying she was getting married after her graduation from Tennessee— to one of her teaching assistants, a South African fellow with an unpronounceable Dutch last name. Not even an American. And certainly not an American hero like Charles Buford Duke.

Bart never responded to Ruby's e-mail because he didn't want to hear the story. He already knew the story. When Bart and Centaur's convoy went missing, when they stayed missing for nearly two full years, everyone gave up hope. (No, Bart thinks, not everyone. Not Mitzi.) But Ruby Taylor gave up hope. She fell crying into the arms of her teaching assistant, who smoothed Ruby's hair and told her the future still held promise and light. This all may have happened *before* Centaur died.

What is Bart to think but that girlfriends, women, love, and marriage are pursuits best left to others.

On Friday, Bart wakes up and feels just the opposite. He thinks that if Centaur could see him, he would scream in his face like Sergeant Corbo, the meanest, ugliest, toughest drillmaster in the USMC, and tell Bart to "GO GET THE GIRL!"

Bart spends $150 on a bouquet from Flowers on Chestnut, and he walks right in the door of Bayberry Properties. Allegra is sitting at a desk in the very front of the office. She is wearing a soft white sweater, a patchwork suede miniskirt, and a pair of suede boots. She looks even more beautiful than she did when she was dressed as a geisha. Her dark hair is now long down her back.

"Special delivery," Bart says, holding out the flowers. "For Miss Allegra Pancik."

Allegra sees him and the flowers and puts two and two together, and whereas she has every right to tell him to buzz off for not calling or texting when he said he would, she gifts him a radiant smile.

"I thought you forgot about me," she says.

"Forgot about *you?*" he says. "Impossible."

Allegra floats around the office, holding the flowers up like a trophy.

"I need to find a vase," she says. "And I want to introduce you to my aunt and uncle." She beams at him. "I thought I'd imagined everything that happened Tuesday night. I thought I'd dreamed it."

"Not a dream," Bart says. He suddenly remembers that when he blew out his birthday candles, his wish was that he and Allegra would live happily ever after. "I just had stuff to do the past few days. My family was all visiting, and I pretty much ignored them at the party, so..."

"I know," Allegra says. "I felt so bad about that." She finds a vase under the office's kitchen sink, and she fills it with water. "These are going right on my desk where everyone can see them." She touches his arm. "Thank you, Bart."

He wants to kiss her, but there are other people in the office. Most of them are at desks, on their phones or engrossed with their computer screens, but Bart can't risk compromising Allegra's professionalism. Even now her phone is ringing. He needs to let her go.

"Have dinner with me tonight," he says. "Fifty-Six Union, seven thirty. I can pick you up, or..."

"I'll have my dad drop me off at the restaurant," Allegra says. "And you'll get me home after?"

He nods. "See you then."

When Bart gets back home, he finds Mitzi on the side porch smoking a cigarette. Bart checks the time on his phone. It's three o'clock in the afternoon—four and a half hours until he will next see Allegra. But Mitzi smoking in the middle of the day is a new development, and not a good one.

"What's up, Madre?" he says.

Mitzi waves the smoke away but does not extinguish the cigarette, despite the fact that it is nearly burned down to the filter. "That envelope Eddie Pancik dropped off earlier?" she says. "It was a listing sheet. I'm selling the inn after your father dies."

"You are?" Bart says. He's not sure how to react. Is this good news or bad news? On the one hand, it sounds like good news. Mitzi has made a decision to stop running the inn. On the other hand, selling the inn seems inconceivable. It's the only home Bart has ever known, and it's the only place Mitzi has ever lived on Nantucket, except for a long-ago summer rental. "What will you do then?"

"I haven't decided yet," Mitzi says. "Your father told me you want to reenlist for active duty?"

"He *did?*" Bart says. Bart wasn't sure Kelley had absorbed this piece of news.

"As much as it terrifies me, I think it's a good idea," Mitzi says. "You aren't happy here, that much is obvious. You need a sense of purpose. You need to create a life. They won't send you back overseas, I wouldn't think."

"Probably not," Bart says. There is appeal in going where the action is, but he has also considered officer training school. His dream is to become a drill sergeant at Camp

Lejeune. He would love nothing more than to be on the other side of basic training. He knows firsthand the mental toughness it takes to be a Marine. He was held prisoner for two years; he watched his fellow troops die. And he survived. He is tougher, meaner, and uglier than even Sergeant Corbo. He regards his mother. "I thought you would be against it. I thought you would throw yourself on the ground in front of my feet and beg me not to go back."

Mitzi drops the butt of her cigarette into an empty Diet Coke can on the railing. The Diet Coke throws Bart for a second loop. Has Mitzi been consuming the stuff? Cigarettes *and* Diet Coke *and* selling the inn? Do Mitzi's further plans include moving to Vegas to participate in the World Series of Poker?

"I have some happy news," Bart says.

Mitzi raises her eyebrows in expectation, but it doesn't erase the deep lines of sadness from her face.

"I have a date tonight," Bart says.

He gets to the restaurant early so that he is standing out front when Eddie Pancik pulls up to drop off Allegra. Bart opens her door and helps her out of the car. She's wearing a black knit dress that clings to her unbelievable figure and a pair of leopard-print high heels. She is, in the words of his fellow Marines, *smoking hot.*

Bart pokes his head into the car to address Eddie. "I'll have her home on the early side, Mr. Pancik," he says. "I know she works tomorrow morning."

"Thank you, Bart," Eddie says. "You kids have fun."

Eddie drives away, and Bart takes Allegra by the hand. He holds the door to the restaurant open and ushers her inside. The restaurant is lit by candles, and Bart and Allegra are seated at a cozy, tucked-away table.

"This is so romantic," Allegra says. "This is a real, grown-up date."

"I figured I'd better bring my A game," Bart says. "I know you're used to smooth operators like Hunter Bloch."

"Oh please," Allegra says. "I'm all finished with smooth operators like Hunter Bloch. I want..."

Bart leans forward. He can hear Centaur's voice in his ear, saying, *PAY ATTENTION TO WHAT SHE WANTS!*

"...I want a real man."

A real man, Bart thinks. What does Allegra mean by that? Probably she means she wants someone strong, intelligent, competent. Someone who has achieved something noteworthy: in Bart's case, joined the Marines, been captured, and been held prisoner. If Hunter Bloch were to walk into this restaurant right now and make a snide comment to Allegra or try, somehow, to win her back, Bart would bring Hunter to his knees, using only one hand. But Bart knows there are other elements that go into being a man, qualities that his father and his brothers have that he has yet to develop.

Patience.

Thoughtfulness.

"Let's order a bottle of sparkling water," Bart says. "I don't want you to get carded or have it be awkward."

"You can order a drink," Allegra says. "I don't mind."

"That's okay," Bart says. "I look forward to spending an evening sober with you."

"You're very sweet," Allegra says. "Thank you." She locks eyes with Bart, which is intoxicating enough. Bart thinks about nine-year-old Ruby Taylor kicking Charles Buford Duke right above the ankle bone with her Mary Jane, or whatever shoe little girls down south wore, and stealing his heart forever. Centaur showed Bart the spot on his right leg that Ruby had kicked.

I get it now, Bart thinks. *I get it!* He takes Allegra's hand across the table. There's music in the restaurant—Eric Clapton singing "Wonderful Tonight"—and Bart feels like pulling Allegra up to dance. He's alive, they're alive; it's their first real date and they're going to need to tell their children about it someday, so why not make it a story? Bart stands up.

"Dance with me," he says.

She doesn't say: *Here? Now?*

She doesn't say: *But no one else is dancing. Everyone else is eating dinner, Bart. This is a restaurant, not a nightclub. Everyone will look at us.*

Instead she says, "Okay." She rises and moves into his arms. She fits right under his chin even in her heels. Bart is suddenly very glad that Mitzi taught him to dance when he was young, despite his mighty protestations. Someone must have also taught Allegra, because she is graceful on her feet, fluid and poised.

The song ends. The other diners clap. Allegra curtsies. Bart feels that, wherever he is, Centaur approves.

Everything is fine. Everything is better than fine—until the chicken.

Bart blames himself initially. He wasn't paying attention when Allegra ordered her dinner; he was too busy deciding between the steak-frites and the Nantucket bay scallop special. They agreed to split the mussels as an appetizer, which were delicious in a coconut curry broth over jasmine rice. Bart insisted on taking the mussels out of the shells for Allegra. He was a real man, meaning he would do the lowliest of chores for his beloved. He would plump the pillow for her every night, he would bring her coffee in bed every morning. He would clean the gutters of their imaginary house; he would stop by the store for eggs or butter or tampons without complaining.

During the mussels they talked about their past relationships. Bart wanted to get it all out in the open now, on their first date, instead of later, a month or six weeks later, when his attachment to Allegra, and therefore his jealousy, would be greater.

"You've had boyfriends other than Hunter Bloch, I assume?" Bart said.

"One boyfriend in high school," Allegra said. "Brick Llewellyn. He was my year. Do you remember him?"

"No," Bart said. He didn't add that high school hadn't really been his thing. He'd skipped a lot and done no activities. After school he and his best friend, Michael Bello, had smoked dope, wrecked cars, stolen beer, and thrown parties. If this Brick Llewellyn wasn't an established derelict, Bart didn't know him.

"He was a good guy. Still is. He's very smart, goes to Dartmouth. He hates me. I cheated on him with this jerk named Ian Coburn."

"I know Ian," Bart said. "And you're right. He's a jerk. He drove that red Camaro."

Allegra had a mussel suspended over the bowl. "I learned my lesson with Brick. I hate myself for what I did to him. I won't ever cheat again."

Bart nodded. He hadn't been a saint either, although in his case, he'd never committed seriously enough to anyone to have his extracurricular activities count as cheating. "I had a sort-of girlfriend named Savannah Steppen. She was more like a friend with benefits. That was really it, Savannah and the nameless, faceless conquests I made as a young Marine."

"I remember Savannah," Allegra said. "She was beautiful."

"You're beautiful," Bart said.

They grinned at each other, holding hands across the table. And then the chicken arrived.

Allegra says, "Oh, this looks good."

Bart stands up. His fault: he wasn't listening. If he had been listening, he would have steered her toward the lamb or the gnocchi.

"I have to step outside," he says.

Allegra looks more surprised than affronted, although certainly she is both. It's unspeakably rude: their food has just arrived, it's hot *now,* appetizing *now,* and if Bart leaves, then Allegra can't politely start.

"Is it...do you...?" Allegra says. She must not know what to think. Maybe Bart has to make a phone call, maybe he smokes and can't hold off his craving for nicotine one more second. Maybe he found the story of Allegra cheating on Brick Llewellyn off-putting.

"I don't feel well," Bart says. "I need air." He strides for the door and steps out into the cool night.

He hears Centaur screaming, *WHAT ARE YOU DOING? IT WAS GOING SO WELL!*

It's chicken, man, Bart tells him.

He's not a real man after all. He has issues. He's a mess. His parents tried to get him to see a therapist. Mitzi had an appointment all lined up, and Bart agreed to go, but at the last minute he detoured to the beach instead, where he waited out the hour in his car, radio blaring.

Chicken.

He's afraid of the chicken. No, *afraid* isn't the right word. He can't be in its presence. He can't look at it or smell it, and he certainly can't eat it. Even the word *chicken* makes him ill.

The door to the restaurant opens and Allegra steps out.

"Bart?" she says. "What is it?"

He turns his eyes to the street. He is blowing this date. He has blown it already. Bart feels Allegra's hand on his shoulder. She's touching his new blue cashmere jacket.

"Tell me what's wrong," she says.

Can he tell her? If he tells her, will she understand? She's outside without her coat. He wants to send her back inside, but he can't banish her and he doesn't want to go back to the table.

"When I was... while I was captured...," he says.

She moves her hand to cup his elbow and sidles her body up to his. When she speaks, her voice is in his ear. "Yes, tell me. It's okay, Bart. You can tell me."

"We ate potatoes," he says. "Every day, every night, potatoes—no butter, no oil, no salt or pepper. Just the potatoes, either boiled or roasted in the ashes of the fire."

"Yes," she says.

"And then, one day, we had chicken. There were chickens scratching around the camp. They produced eggs, which the Bely ate; we were never given any eggs. But then there was spit-roasted chicken and we all got some, and it was, I kid you not, the most delicious thing I'd ever eaten, that piece of chicken."

"Yes," Allegra says.

"And then, the morning after we ate the chicken, one of us was chosen. The first day it was Private Jacob Hiller. And we thought, 'Okay, J-Bear'—that was our nickname for him—'is a big, burly guy, maybe they need him to help with digging a hole or fetching water or chopping wood or whatever.' But J-Bear never came back. They marched him to this place called the Pit and they killed him."

"Oh...," Allegra says.

"And it went on like that. We eat potatoes for days or

weeks, then there's a chicken roasting, and the next morning another soldier is taken away and marched to the Pit."

"No!" Allegra says. She's crying softly.

"We never knew when it would happen," Bart says. "Until they roasted the chicken. Then you knew it was coming, but you didn't know who they were going to pick." Bart takes a deep breath of the night air and squeezes his eyes shut. "I'll tell you what, Allegra. I loved the rest of those guys so much that every single time I wished it would be me."

"No!" Allegra says.

Bart shakes his head and snaps back to himself. "I'm sorry."

Allegra says, "I'm going back inside. I'll have them take the chicken away and I'll get the scallops instead."

Bart bows his head. "Thank you," he says.

Allegra disappears through the door, and Bart takes another moment under the black sky and the stars.

He told her.

He told her and she understood. She still likes him, he thinks.

He hears Centaur's voice: *GET BACK TO YOUR GIRL!*

"Okay, okay," Bart says. "I'm going."

AVA

It's a Tuesday afternoon, a week after Bart's party. Ava emerges from the subway, goes to pick up her laundry, and considers Vietnamese food for dinner. She can either get takeout or go to the place on Second Avenue and sit at the bar. A warm, fragrant bowl of pho is what she needs, along with a roasted pork banh mi.

She climbs the four flights of stairs to her apartment, unlocks the knob and the deadbolt, and steps inside to experience the ecstasy of her own place.

Her phone rings. It will be Margaret, not Potter. Potter teaches until seven. It's quarter of six, though, which is too close to broadcast time for it to be Margaret.

Her mother retires at the end of the week. She will finally be free at the dinner hour!

When Ava checks her phone, she sees an unfamiliar number, a 650 area code—what is that?—and it's not a phone call, it's a FaceTime. Who could this be? It's not Shelby's number or any of her siblings'. It's not Nathaniel Oscar, thank goodness, or Scott Skyler. Could it maybe be Kelley, using the phone of one of the hospice nurses?

There's only one way to find out. Ava accepts the Face-Time request.

"Hello?" she says. She hasn't given one thought to how she must look after a full day of teaching, her evening commute, and climbing all those stairs.

The screen on her phone shows a dark-haired man in a yellow polo shirt. There is someone sitting beside him.

"Ava?" the man says. "Ava Quinn, is that you?"

"Yes?" she says. She smiles at the screen, squinting, trying to figure out just who this is. The voice is accented, British, sort of familiar, someone she has spoken to recently—but who?

"It's Harrison, Harrison Fellowes here, calling from Palo Alto. And I have PJ with me. We just called to say hello and to see how you're doing."

Harrison Fellowes? Palo Alto? PJ? Ava knows she has the ability to put this together...she just needs a minute...and then she thinks, *Oh! Harrison! Trish's boyfriend! And PJ! PJ, the total nightmare child!* But wait...why are they calling *her?* Why are they FaceTiming *her?* Ava peers at the picture on her screen. Yes, it's Harrison, and there's a squirming presence next to him.

"PJ?" Ava says cautiously. "Hi, it's Ava."

She waits.

Suddenly there is PJ's face. Possibly it's the novelty of FaceTime that lures him in. After all, how strange is it to be able to see someone who is three thousand miles away?

"Hi," he says.

"Hi, *Ava*," Harrison prompts.

"Hi, Ava," PJ says.

Ava feels tears welling. She can't…this is so…*unexpected*, so…bizarre, really. This must be why Harrison asked for her cell number. He wanted to facilitate this impromptu meeting. It's ingenious. Ingenious and very, very kind.

"Hi, PJ, how are you?" Ava has to come up with something else to ask. "What's new in the world of Minecraft?"

"Something exciting happened," PJ says.

"Oh yeah?" Ava says. "What?"

"I finished building my roller coaster," PJ says.

"Well, all right!" Ava says. "I *love* roller coasters!" She can't believe this is happening. PJ is talking to her of his own volition. Maybe Harrison has offered up a wonderful bribe, but Ava doesn't care.

At that moment Harrison holds up the camera so that they're both visible. Ava hungrily scans the background: They're at home, or in a homey atmosphere. In a den or a library. There are shelves of books behind Harrison and PJ's heads—and a trophy. Maybe one of Trish's sailing trophies or a trophy given to Shakespeare scholars. Or a Minecraft trophy. "We called to say hello to you, our friend Ava, and also to invite you and Potter to Palo Alto for Thanksgiving. Trish and I are hosting this year. It'll

just be us, PJ, and a few fellow academics, so it's sure to
be a horrifically boring time, but we'd love it if you would
join us. And yes, I do know it's short notice and airfare
will be frightfully expensive, but I know that PJ, in particular, would like to see you and his dad. Isn't that right,
PJ?"

"Yes," PJ says. He sounds sincere.

"Oh," Ava says. She personally can't go to Palo Alto. She
must go to Nantucket to be with her family, her father. Potter
was planning on coming with her, but Ava decides right then
and there that he doesn't have to. Not only does he not have
to, he shouldn't. He should go to Palo Alto and spend
Thanksgiving with his son.

Ava says, "Harrison and PJ, I ask for your understanding
when I tell you that I have family obligations elsewhere. So
although I really appreciate the offer, I can't come. But I can
assure you that Potter will come to Palo Alto. Okay?"

"Yes," Harrison says. "That would be wonderful, although
we'll miss our friend Ava. Won't we, PJ?"

There's only a split second's pause. "Yes," PJ says.

"Well, we'll call Potter and confirm that he's free," Harrison says.

"Yes, do that. He's finished teaching at seven," Ava says.

"Ah, well, I teach at four, so I'll try him tomorrow," Harrison says. "If you see him before I speak to him, feel free to
pass on the invite."

"I'll do just that," Ava says. "Thank you for calling. I
mean . . . thank you."

Harrison smiles. He's such a hero! She can't believe he
orchestrated this!

"The pleasure was ours," Harrison says. "Bye-bye, Ava."

"Bye-bye, Ava," PJ says.

The screen goes blank.

* * *

Ava can't wait for seven, when Potter is finished teaching his class. He is going to flip when he hears that *Ava* was invited to Thanksgiving in Palo Alto.

Or is he? Ava wonders. He may be angry that Harrison, of all people, reached out. Ava never told Potter that she and Harrison had a conversation in the lobby that afternoon, and she certainly didn't tell him that she gave Harrison her cell. Potter's obvious first question is going to be *How did Harrison get your number?*

Ava's elation subsides, then morphs into worry. She needs to think about how to handle this.

When Potter calls after class, he sounds weary. Ava forgot that it's midterms, so he has papers to grade for two classes and an exam to administer to a third. He says, "This is why I want you to move in with me. So you're here when I get home."

Ava smiles. She loves that he wants more of her. "You'll be fine. You need some sleep."

"I won't be able to see you until Friday. I'm coming there for dinner?"

"Yes," Ava says. "No! Wait! I forgot Friday is my mother's last broadcast. We're going to the studio. There's going to be champagne in the greenroom after the news, then Drake is taking us to dinner at Upland. Not just us, but Lee Kramer, who heads the studio, and his wife, Ginny, who is the editor of *Vogue,* and Darcy, my mother's former assistant, who is flying in from Atlanta. And Roger, her wardrobe guy, and a few of the producers, and Raoul, my mother's driver, and his wife. There will be twenty of us, I think."

"Just tell me when and what to wear," Potter says. "*Vogue* sounds intimidating."

"You're not intimidated by anyone," Ava says—except, of course, his own son. Around other adults, however, he shines. She can introduce him to anyone—lowbrow or highbrow—and he always fits in. She brought him to Margaret and Drake's wedding, where he knew no one but Ava and Margaret, and he did so well that now he is basically part of the family.

Family reminds Ava of the FaceTime call from Harrison and PJ. Clearly Harrison hasn't reached out yet; Potter would have mentioned it. Should Ava tell him? She decides to follow her gut and think about it overnight. She'll tell Potter tomorrow if he doesn't mention it first.

The next day Ava gets a call from Bart saying he wants to use his Acela tickets and come to New York for the weekend. With Allegra Pancik!

"Wow!" Ava says. "So are you two a thing, then?"

"Yes, we are a thing," Bart says. "I took her out to dinner last Friday night, and I've seen her every day since then, and I want to surprise her with a weekend in New York. I didn't tell her where we're going, but I asked her to take off of work."

"Okay!" Ava says. She hasn't heard Bart sound this animated since last Christmas, when he was still high on his newfound freedom. She's happy for him, but the protective big sister in her wants to advise him not to move too fast or get too serious too quickly. Girls Allegra's age can be flighty, shallow, and opportunistic. Allegra is very pretty and, if Ava remembers correctly, she has a wild streak; she's the polar opposite of her serious, quiet sister. "Do you two want to stay at Drake's apartment? Because if so, I can set that up."

"I don't want to seem like I'm showing off," Bart says. "I want to get a hotel room. Something nice, too. I have my checks from the government saved up. Do you have any recommendations?"

"Let me research it for you," Ava says. "And you and Allegra should plan on coming to Margaret's last broadcast on Friday night. Dinner after—Drake is paying, so you can save at least part of your government checks. It's a group of people. I'll add you and Allegra to the list."

"That would be beyond amazing," Bart says. "Thanks, sis."

Ava finds Bart a room at the Warwick New York on Fifty-Fourth and Sixth for a very reasonable rate, and she adds Allegra and Bart to Drake's guest list. She is busy with all the details, and so she doesn't have time to talk to Potter about the FaceTime call with Harrison and PJ, and Potter doesn't mention it so Harrison must not have called yet. But Thanksgiving is only two weeks away, and Potter will need to book a flight. She worries that Harrison has reconsidered the invite, or that perhaps she misunderstood and she was supposed to be the one to pass the invite along.

She'll broach the topic over the weekend, she decides. After things have calmed down.

Margaret's final broadcast is a big deal, despite Margaret's wish that it not be made a big deal. A story runs at the bottom of the front page of the *Times* on Friday, and Margaret's photo is splashed across the front of the *New York Post* with the headline ANCHORS AWAY. There's also a piece in *Time* magazine and a spread of Margaret's best outfits in *Women's Wear Daily*.

Margaret's only nod to the occasion is that she has chosen, for the first time ever, to wear black on the air. She looks beautiful and Ava tells her so.

Margaret says, "Will your father be watching, do you think?"

"He wouldn't miss it," Ava says. "You know that." Mitzi might space that it's Margaret's last broadcast—or to her it might fall into the category of inconsequential—but Kevin and Isabelle will be there to remind her.

Ava gets choked up from the instant Margaret signs off. There's a compilation of Margaret's most memorable moments over the years.

Margaret in a biker jacket, T-shirt, and jeans doing a *60 Minutes* segment on Sturgis.

Margaret in New Orleans during Hurricane Katrina, her hair plastered to her head from the rain.

Margaret surrounded by American servicemen in Fallujah.

Margaret in Paris after the shooting at *Charlie Hebdo,* in Rome when Pope Francis was elected, in London after the subway bombing, in Washington during Obama's first inauguration.

Margaret with tears streaming down her face as she embraces one of the mothers of the Sandy Hook Elementary victims.

Margaret with Melania Trump at Mar-a-Lago, years before Melania was the First Lady.

Margaret with Queen Elizabeth, the Dalai Lama, George Clooney, Beyoncé, Hillary Clinton, Muhammad Ali, Ralph Lauren, Jennifer Aniston, Bruce Springsteen, LeBron James, Stephen King.

Margaret at Ground Zero, standing in front of the wreckage of One World Trade Center, holding an American flag, wearing an *I Love NY* T-shirt over her dress.

There is champagne in the greenroom once Margaret is finished, and the mood is joyous. Margaret herself seems ecstatic.

She says, "I may just let myself get drunk tonight."

Ava drinks three glasses of Dom Pérignon on an empty stomach, after which she feels very light-headed. Drake instructs everyone to take taxis down to Upland, which is on Park Avenue South. They have a private room, he says.

The network has surprised Margaret with a white stretch limousine. Raoul, Margaret's driver, is also enjoying his first day of retirement, and so there's another chauffeur and plenty of room in the limo for Margaret and Drake, Ava and Potter, and Bart and Allegra.

When Margaret sees the limo, she balks for an instant. Then she grins. "You know who I never got to interview? Liberace."

There's more champagne in the limo. Ava accepts a glass from Drake—it's *Cristal*—and Allegra says, "I feel like I'm in a rap video."

"You know who else I never interviewed?" Margaret says. "Snoop Dogg. Of course, he belongs to Martha now."

The party atmosphere continues at the restaurant, Upland, one of Drake's new finds. There are jars and jars filled with Meyer lemons suspended in liquid, and Ava becomes mesmerized by all those lemons—fifteen or twenty lemons per jar, and shelves and shelves of jars, two whole walls of shelves. Thousands of lemons sacrificed themselves for the decor of this restaurant, Ava thinks, and she may have said this out loud, because Potter says, "We'd better get you something to eat."

In the private room there are high-top tables, a full bar, and long tables of food: kale Caesar, artisan pizzas, platters of pasta with exotic sauces.

"I'll have more champagne," Ava says.

*   *   *

People make toasts: Lee Kramer from CBS; Darcy, Margaret's former assistant; and Drake. Ava can't remember what anyone says, but she cries quietly through each toast. Her mother is such a phenomenal person. She has achieved so much. She is an idol, an inspiration, a national treasure.

Ava is too drunk to make a toast. She will come across as a weepy, sentimental mess.

But then Ava gets an idea. She speaks to the bartender, who calls in one of the restaurant's managers, and Ava makes her request. Turns out, they can accommodate her halfway. They have a cordless microphone and a small amp, but no piano. As they set up the microphone, Ava double-checks the lyrics on her phone.

Potter sweeps Ava's hair aside and kisses her neck. "What are you doing?"

"Oh, nothing," Ava says. She chimes a spoon against a glass, and the room draws silent. Ava is a little nervous about singing without accompaniment, but then she reminds herself that, just as being the most intelligent, gracious, poised, and articulate woman on the planet is Margaret's gift, music is Ava's gift. She can sing drunk or sober, with a piano or without.

This song has long been one of Margaret's favorites, even when it wasn't popular to admit it.

Ava doesn't bother with an introduction; she simply starts singing, her voice pure and true.

> *"Thanks for the times that you've given me,*
> *The memories are all in my mind."*

It's the Commodores, "Three Times a Lady," and by the time Ava finishes, everyone in the room is either singing along or crying. Some are doing both. Even the bartender.

* * *

When Ava and Potter finally leave the party—it is well past one in the morning—Margaret hugs them each good-bye.

To Ava she says, "Sweetheart, that was a beautiful tribute. I didn't deserve it, but I will never pass up the chance to hear you sing."

To Potter she says, "I hope we see you next weekend, but if not, we'll see you on Nantucket at Thanksgiving."

Ava opens her mouth, but no sound comes out.

When she and Potter climb into the back of the taxi, Ava says, "I have something to tell you about." She is so drunk she has no idea if this sentence makes any sense. She should wait and tell Potter tomorrow. But she's too drunk to keep her mouth shut. She has leaped off the proverbial cliff; there's no way to unleap.

"What is it?" Potter says.

"Thanksgiving," Ava says. "We've been invited to California."

"What?" Potter says. "Invited to California? By whom?"

"By Harrison and Trish," Ava says. "Oh, and by PJ."

"What?" Potter says.

Ava starts laughing. She's not laughing because anything is funny. She's laughing because she has already messed this up. She went at it backward. How is she supposed to explain things in reverse?

"I can't go," Ava says. "I have to be on Nantucket with my father. But you . . ." Here she attempts a playful punch to Potter's arm. "You should go. You *need* to go."

"To California," Potter says.

"We were invited," Ava says. "By Harrison and PJ. And by Trish, too, although that was more . . . *implied,* I guess you'd say." *Is that right?* Ava wonders. She occasionally mixes up *imply* and *infer*.

"I think you've had a little too much to—"

"No!" Ava interrupts him. "I mean, yes. I have had too much to drink, most definitely, but this is real. This is really real. On Tuesday afternoon Harrison and PJ FaceTimed me…"

"What?" Potter says.

She can't be derailed. "…and they invited us to California for Thanksgiving. I told them I can't go because my father is dying, but I told them you'd be there. I promised you'd be there. Harrison was supposed to call you himself. He was going to call on Tuesday night, but you were teaching and then he had to teach at four. I thought he said he was going to call you, but now I think maybe I was supposed to pass the invite along."

"How did Harrison or PJ get *your* number?" Potter asks.

"Did you hear me? I promised them you'd be there. So tomorrow morning we need to book you some flights."

"Ava," Potter says.

"I gave my number to Harrison," Ava says. "He asked me for my number when he and Trish showed up that day and Harrison and I went down to the lobby with PJ."

Potter doesn't respond. He's no longer looking at Ava; instead he's looking out the taxi's window at the blocks of Park Avenue South rushing past. Grand Central looms in front of them.

"Harrison said he had an idea, something that might help things with PJ. I wasn't even sure what he was talking about, but now I know he planned on FaceTiming me with PJ and pretending like Harrison and I were friends so that PJ would feel less threatened."

"I can't believe this," Potter says. "You gave Harrison your number. Because stealing my wife wasn't enough. Now he wants to steal away my girlfriend. Who, I would like to point out, is far more precious to me than said wife ever was."

Revisionist history, Ava thinks. Even so, she feels a surge of joy at the declaration.

"It wasn't like that," Ava says. "Harrison felt sorry for me because PJ was being so difficult." Ava pauses. Potter can't deny that his son was difficult. "And his plan worked. When they called me, PJ talked to me. He said hello and good-bye, and he told me he built a roller coaster on Minecraft. He talked to me, Potter. Harrison got him to talk to me."

"Harrison," Potter says, "was overstepping his bounds. This is none of Harrison's business. What is he doing other than confusing my child? You're Harrison's friend and that's okay. You're my friend and that's not okay? Do you see how warped this is?"

Ava has a hard time coming up with a rebuttal that won't insult Potter. What she wants to say is that PJ trusts Harrison; whether Potter likes it or not, Harrison has influence. Harrison's endorsement matters and Ava needs it.

Instead what she says is, "I grew up with divorced parents. You've only known Kelley and Mitzi and Margaret and Drake since they've been best friends. It wasn't always that way. There were lots of years when Mitzi hated my mother, and do you know who those years were the hardest on? Me and Paddy and Kevin. It's hardest on the kids, who have to split allegiances, who overhear one parent they love and trust talking badly about another parent they love and trust. Kids feel the animosity, they sense the competition, envy, and judgment. I don't think that divorce necessarily ruins a childhood, but a bitter divorce can. We are the adults, Potter. We can choose to be agreeable. Now, I'm not saying we will ever be best friends with Trish and Harrison..."

"We won't," Potter says.

"...but we can aspire to be civil. To be friendly, even. It'll make things better for PJ. Don't you want to make things better for PJ?"

"Yes," Potter says. "Of course I do."

Ava lets her head fall onto Potter's shoulder. "Tomorrow we'll look for your plane ticket."

KELLEY

Lara downloads Danielle Steel's *Dangerous Games* for Kelley because he can no longer see the screen of his phone well enough to download books himself.

"I understand this is her best one yet," Lara says. "A political thriller."

Kelley feels a pulse of excitement, but it's fleeting. He won't be able to follow the twists and turns of a political thriller; the main appeal now is the comforting sound of the narrator's voice.

Kelley says, "Did you see my wife last night on TV?"

"Your wife?" Lara says. "Mitzi?"

"Margaret," Kelley says. "Margaret Quinn, my wife."

Lara offers Kelley a sip of ice water. "Mitzi is your wife," she says. "Margaret Quinn is a TV news anchor. And yes, I did see her. She was wonderful, as always. She has such elegance, such grace."

"She's my wife," Kelley says. "No, wait, that's not right. She's my ex-wife. Margaret was my wife before Mitzi."

"That's very nice," Lara says. She places the earbuds in Kelley's ears and starts the book. It's the same narrator as *The Mistress*—Alexander Cendese—and the effect is immediate. Kelley relaxes. His eyes fall closed.

*   *   *

He has a hard time discerning between what's reality and what's a dream. He has dreams that are actual memories, or nearly. He dreams about the first time he came to Nantucket. It had been Margaret's idea. When Margaret was eight years old, she spent the summer with her wealthy grandmother, Josephine Brach, in one of the summer mansions on Baxter Lane in Sconset. She had wanted to re-create that summer for their children—Patrick was eight, Kevin seven, Ava just a baby and nursing.

Kelley had said, "I hate to tell you this, Maggie, but we can't afford any of the houses on Baxter Lane." Instead they had rented an upside-down house facing Nobadeer Beach, but the waves at Nobadeer scared the kids, so they had to drive each day to Steps Beach, so named because it featured a flight of forty-one steps down to the dunes covered with *Rosa rugosa*. It was picturesque but also quite a haul with two kids, a baby, and the amount of paraphernalia that those kids and baby required. The next summer they realized they could buy a beach sticker for a hundred dollars and drive the kids and all the gear right onto the beach at Fortieth Pole. That year they rented a cottage on Madaket Road that had a smell, and the summer after that they rented a soulless time-share condo until they found a house on Quince Street that Margaret really loved.

Kelley has lived at the inn for twenty-two years. The man who stayed in those other houses feels like someone else entirely.

There used to be a restaurant called the Second Story that he loved, but Margaret found the food too spicy. There was a place called the India House, where Kelley took Margaret? No, Mitzi—he took *Mitzi* to the India House every Saturday night of her final trimester with Bart because she had an insatiable craving for their Indonesian peanut noodles with duck. The Second Story is now Oran Mor, although Kelley hasn't been in there since two owners ago—and the India House is just gone.

Mitzi is at Kelley's bedside. Her hair is piled on top of her head.

She says, "I'm putting the inn on the market, Kelley. I'm going to sell it."

Kelley nods. It's the right thing to do.

"I told Eddie Pancik I wanted to sell it only to someone who would keep it an inn," Mitzi says. "I couldn't stand to think of some millionaire knocking down walls to create master suites. But I've come around on that now. If we're going to sell it, we sell it and wash our hands of it and let the new owner create memories of his own here."

Kelley thinks, *People will walk by the house and think, 'I remember when this was an inn. They had a party every Christmas Eve. It was the best party of the year. Kelley Quinn, the owner, used to saber the top off a bottle of champagne. Santa Claus came to that party driving a 1931 Model A fire engine.*

Mitzi is holding Kelley's hand, and he applies pressure. He wants her to know he thinks she's doing the right thing. Whatever happens next with this house won't affect or diminish what they have had here.

They have had so much.

Bart comes in the middle of the night and sits by Kelley's bed. Maybe it's not the middle of the night. Maybe it's late afternoon or early evening. It's November, and the sun sets at four o'clock. It feels late, though. The rest of the house is quiet. Mitzi often falls asleep on the sofa in the living room in front of the fire, and Kelley can't blame her. Jocelyn is the night hospice nurse. Very little gets past Jocelyn, so she must have given Bart the okay to come in.

"Dad," Bart says. "I think I'm in love."

In love. Kelley has lived nearly all of his adult life in love—first with Margaret and then with Mitzi. He has been very lucky in that respect.

Kelley feels like he already knew this about Bart. "The ghee. The ghee."

"The geisha from the party," Bart says. "Yes. Allegra Pancik. I've been seeing her for a couple of weeks. We went to New York together. She's...well, she's the best thing that's happened to me...I don't know, recently? Or ever, maybe? She's lots of fun and she's a good listener. She's patient. She gets me, I think. You know, when I was growing up, I thought the most important thing about my future wife would be how she looked. But it turns out, that's the least important thing. I mean, Allegra is really pretty, don't get me wrong, but that doesn't matter. I like talking to her, I like the sound of her voice; it calms me. I like surprising her, making her happy, seeing her smile when I walk through the door. I like it that she sings off-key and is a rabid Patriots fan, the kind where she screams at the TV. I like that she has insecurities and sees things in herself that she wants to improve. She knows she's not perfect, just like I know that I'm not perfect."

"You're perfect," Kelley says, though his words are unintelligible.

"You're going to meet her on Thursday," Bart says. "She's coming for Thanksgiving."

Kelley thinks, *Thursday is Thanksgiving?*

He reaches out for Bart's hand and tries to squeeze. This is torture! Kelley is here, he's listening, he's present, he has things to say, blessings to bestow, but he isn't having any luck communicating. Or maybe he is. He can't tell.

Bart seems to understand. "I love you, too, Dad," he says.

As Bart stands to leave the room, Kelley thinks eagerly about Thanksgiving. Thanksgiving means Mitzi's corn pudding and her fiesta cranberry sauce. He will have a bite of each, he thinks, and he drifts off to sleep.

EDDIE

The Christys are caught in a stalemate. Raja wants to make an offer on the Medouie Creek Road house in Wauwinet—and Masha wants the inn. Eddie checks in with Raja once a week to see if there has been any movement one way or the other.

"No," Raja says. "She's not backing down."

"Well, neither are you," Eddie says. "Right?"

"Right," Raja says. "I tell Masha again and again: We know nothing about the hospitality business. And I don't *want* to know anything about it. The point of buying a second home is having a sanctuary. A place to relax. But Masha is dead set on it. She's like Jack with his squeaky giraffe. You can't get that giraffe away from him when he's in a certain frame of mind."

Eddie has long joked that the two most useful backgrounds for a real estate broker are psychology and elementary education. Eddie has basically taken on the role of Raja's therapist. He would like to see Raja get his way—and not only because Eddie's commission will be bigger. Eddie wants Raja to win on behalf of all the henpecked husbands in the world. He realizes that the only reason Masha hasn't steamrolled Raja is because the inn isn't technically on the market yet.

But Mitzi has asked Eddie to put it on right after Thanksgiving. She says it will be ready to show—all but the master suite, where Kelley is living—on Christmas Stroll weekend.

The situation with the Christys is so confounding that Eddie is relieved things on his own home front are, for the most part, cheerful. Allegra is exclusively dating Bart Quinn now, and the relationship has completely transformed her. She is always in a good mood, always sweet and solicitous. She offers to help with the laundry and keep the cottage neat and tidy. She smiles, she hums to herself, she sings off-key in the shower.

Eddie says, "It's like she's had a personality transplant."

Grace says, "She's in love."

Grace has also been in a good mood recently. Eddie told her he saw her biking when he was driving the Christys out to Wauwinet, and she said, "Yes, that was me. I've been either biking or walking every day. Trying to lose these last ten pounds."

Eddie says, "Well, I think you look great." And she does! Her skin has a healthy glow; she's trim and fit, and it seems like she's been sleeping better at night. She also went to RJ Miller and had the gray taken out of her part. Eddie didn't notice this per se, but he did see the charge come in on the credit card—two hundred sixty dollars!—and when he asked Grace what it was for, she pointed to her hair and said, "Isn't it obvious?" And Eddie was so chagrined he hadn't noticed that he decided not to give her any grief about the expense.

Grace stays even-keeled when Allegra announces that she's eating Thanksgiving at the Winter Street Inn with the

Quinns, and she even remains sanguine when Hope calls from Bucknell to say that *she* isn't coming home for Thanksgiving either. Instead she's going to one of her pledge sisters' houses in Bethlehem, Pennsylvania, because it's closer to school and Hope needs to get back to campus Saturday; her jazz ensemble has been invited to play at a local coffeehouse.

"Wait a minute," Eddie says. "Neither of them will be home?"

"They're growing up," Grace says.

"What are *we* going to do?" Eddie asks. "Eat by ourselves?" The idea seems small and sad, especially considering they don't have a proper dining room. When Eddie considers how little space they have, he thinks it's no wonder the girls want to celebrate elsewhere. Eddie needs to sell the Christys a house, take his commission, and buy his family a decent-size place to live.

Grace shrugs. "We can either eat with Glenn and Barbie—"

"They're going to Napa," Eddie says, but even if they were staying on Nantucket, Eddie wouldn't want to eat with them. He has to see them every day at the office. He could use a break.

"Okay, then, we'll go out," Grace says. "I'll make a reservation at American Seasons."

"American Seasons?" Eddie says. It's a romantic restaurant and the food is dynamite, but . . . it's not cheap.

"Yes," Grace says, leaving no further room for discussion.

It's only that night as Eddie is trying to fall asleep instead of obsessing about money ($260 for a haircut and color, Thanksgiving dinner at American Seasons, which will necessarily include champagne and nice wine, and Hope's second-semester bill at Bucknell), the Christys, the Winter Street Inn, the ways his life would be easier if he could manage to sell the Wauwinet house to the Christys and the inn to someone else, that Eddie wonders about Grace's new exercise routine and her newly colored hair and, most puzzlingly, her easy acceptance of the news that neither twin will be home for Thanksgiving, historically the most sacred of Pancik family holidays.

It's almost like she doesn't care, he thinks. Like her mind is somewhere else.

On Thanksgiving morning Grace announces that she's going to walk to Children's Beach to watch the Turkey Plunge. The Turkey Plunge is where hundreds of crazy people race into the water to benefit the public library, known as the Nantucket Atheneum. Grace and Eddie have never attended the Turkey Plunge, because when they lived in Wauwinet, it was simply too far out of the way; it started early and the girls wanted to sleep in. Grace always used to cook an elaborate meal—not just turkey, stuffing, and mashed potatoes, but also a crab cake appetizer, caramelized Brussels sprouts, Parker House rolls from scratch, and, instead of pie, a gingerbread and poached pear trifle, served in her grandmother Harper's etched-crystal trifle dish. Madeline, Trevor, and Brick Llewellyn used to join them, as well as Barbie, back when Barbie was single. Eddie carved the turkey and broke out his best vintages of zinfandel, which is the only wine that pairs acceptably with turkey, in his opinion. Between dinner and dessert, Eddie and Trevor used to smoke Cuban cigars out in Grace's garden.

Eddie's heart aches for his old life.

Now that they live in town, they can stroll over to Children's Beach in a matter of minutes, so why wouldn't they go? It makes perfect sense, Eddie tells himself.

At the plunge he sees people he knows, of course. There

are land mines—Eloise Coffin is present with her doltish husband, Clarence, and Eddie steers clear of them, pulling Grace along by the hand. He isn't sure how Grace managed in the aftermath of his indictment. How did she survive both the news of her affair with Benton Coe *and* a husband convicted of running a prostitution ring? How did she hold her head up?

Eddie sees Addison and Phoebe Wheeler talking to Chief Kapenash. The chief waves, and Eddie thinks about joining them for a chat, even though he doesn't much care for Addison.

Grace says, "We can just stand here and be observers, Eddie. This isn't a networking thing."

"Oh, I know," Eddie says. He lets Grace lead him over to a tree where they have a good view of people lining up, preparing to charge the water. Eddie sees Rachel McMann dressed in a black tank suit and a bathing cap decorated to look like a Pilgrim hat. Of course. He sees Blond Sharon and Jean Burton and Susan Prendergast and Monica Delray and Jody Rouisse, Grace's former garden club cronies. Does Grace still talk to them? he wonders. He should ask her. Whom is she friends with now? Whom does she confide in?

The whistle blows. The swimmers race into the water, shrieking and laughing.

"That looks like fun," Grace says. "Maybe we should do it next year."

Eddie would rather eat glass. "Maybe," he says.

After the plungers have dried off and are enjoying hot cider and doughnuts, Eddie sees a man heading toward them. He's wearing a black Speedo, the kind that competitive swimmers wear, and has a towel hanging off his shoulders like a cape. Because he's dripping wet and more than half naked, it takes Eddie a moment to realize it's Benton Coe.

"Eddie," Benton says. He offers Eddie a hand, which Eddie shakes as firmly as he can. "Grace." He bends over to kiss Grace on the cheek.

"How was it?" Grace asks. "Cold?"

Eddie doesn't bother listening to Benton's response; he doesn't care if it was cold or not. All Eddie cares about is Grace's tone of voice and her facial expression. She sounds calm, normal. At first Eddie feels gratified by this; Benton's presence doesn't seem to fluster Grace one bit. But then Eddie realizes that the only way Grace could nonchalantly converse with the man she had a red-hot affair with, who has returned to the island after an absence of two and a half years, is if...

Grace has seen Benton before, Eddie thinks. She has talked to him before.

"It wasn't as bad as I thought," Benton says. He wraps the towel around his waist, shielding his lower half, thank God, but giving both Grace and Eddie a wonderful view of his broad shoulders and rippling abdominal muscles. "So anyway, how are you guys? Happy Thanksgiving."

JENNIFER

Usually, Jennifer loves Thanksgiving at the Winter Street Inn. For starters, Nantucket is easy to get to. Last year was their year to be with Jennifer's mother in San Francisco, which involved cross-country flights and, by obvious necessity, also involved Jennifer's mother, Beverly, who is trying on her best day. Secondly, the inn is cozy and Nantucket is both festive and charming at the holidays. Mitzi is an uneven cook, but she does a pretty good job with this meal and she isn't afraid to delegate. Jennifer has been assigned two salads.

But Jennifer can't think about the salads, or about Thanksgiving at all, until she gives Danko an answer about *Real-Life Rehab*. She promised him an answer by Friday the seventeenth. When Jennifer asks for an extension, he gives her through the weekend, but he says he needs an answer by end of business on Monday or the network will hire their second choice.

Jennifer has told no one about the offer or about the fact that she has lost the penthouse project. She did pick up one small job designing and decorating side-by-side nurseries for a fantastically wealthy couple in Back Bay named the Printers, who just found out they're pregnant with boy-girl twins after twelve years of in vitro. When Jennifer goes to meet with Paige Printer for the first time, she brings along her file of playroom ideas, and Paige loves them so much that Jennifer scores herself a third room to decorate in the Printer home.

The Printer project will take only sixty or seventy hours, sum total, to order for and install. It's a snack, not a meal, but at least when Jennifer tells Patrick that she's "off to work," she's not lying.

She needs to talk to Patrick! But she wants to think the decision through herself first, and giving real consideration to all the factors involved takes time. She bounces back and forth between *Yes, I'll do the show* and *No, I won't* with the regularity of a championship tennis rally.

Yes, she'll do it: There are thousands of interior decorators in the country, and only a couple dozen viable design shows. Jennifer is phenomenally lucky to have been offered a job *as the host*—not a consultant, and not a pretty accessory to a man. The face, voice, and talent of this show will be Jennifer Quinn. The show has a message; it has a heart. They are rehabbing houses in neighborhoods that desperately need hope. And Jennifer, as a former pill addict, is sending her own message. There is life—a good life—waiting for people out there, postaddiction.

No, she won't do it: She doesn't want to be labeled as a pill addict. It's shameful. It's a dirty little secret. Danko said there would be endorsements and that her personal business would take off like a rocket, but who wants a known addict to walk into her home? Who wants a known addict repping his products? Nobody, Jennifer thinks. It will be a stain on her character; it'll be the only thing people will think of when they see her. If she has a bad day, if she loses her temper, if she's weepy or goofy or impatient or temperamental, people will wonder: *Has she had a relapse? Is she back on the pills?*

But perhaps the darkest reason Jennifer would say no to Danko's offer is that once she has announced herself to the country as a recovering addict, she *can't* go back on pills. That door—which Jennifer thought was opening ever so slightly a few weeks ago—would be slammed shut and locked forever.

Both the yes and the no arguments are so compelling that she can't decide between them.

Patrick—she needs to discuss it with Patrick.

But first, for a practice run, Jennifer decides to tell Leanne.

It's after barre class on Saturday morning, and Leanne has asked Jennifer to go for coffee at Thinking Cup. As soon as they get their coffees, muffins, and yogurt parfaits and sit

down at one of the tiny tables, Jennifer leans forward so far
that she can smell the cinnamon on the top of Leanne's cap-
puccino and says, "I have something to talk to you about, and
it's going to be very difficult for me."

Leanne says, "I'm a safe place for you, Jennifer. You
know that." She holds up her palms. "No judgment here."

Jennifer couldn't have hoped for a better response, and
yet she fears Leanne *will* judge her. How could she not? But
Jennifer has to start somewhere; she has forty-eight hours to
make a decision. Whatever Leanne advises her to do, she
decides, is what she will do.

Jennifer says, "About a year before I met you? While
Paddy was in jail? I became addicted to pills. Ativan and
oxycodone."

Leanne gasps, "Oh, Jennifer!"

Here comes the judgment, Jennifer thinks. Leanne won't
want to go to barre class or get coffee anymore. She won't
want to be friends anymore. When people ask who decorated her house, she'll say, "A former pill junkie named Jennifer Quinn."

Leanne grabs Jennifer's hand. "I feel honored that you've
shared this with me. It must have been a difficult time
for you."

Jennifer lets a few tears fall into her latte. "It was," Jennifer says. She blots her face with a napkin and thinks: *Of
course Leanne knows exactly what to say and how to react.*
"You don't think I'm a horrible person?"

"Oh, sweetie," Leanne says. "How could I ever think
that?"

Jennifer proceeds to tell her the rest of the story: How she
met with Grayson Coker, how he hit on her, how she quit.
How Paddy is struggling to get his hedge fund up and running, how both he and Jennifer were depending on the pent-

house project for money. How Jennifer has been approached to host a show on SinTV.

Here Leanne shrieks like a fangirl. "SinTV!"

"But I'd have to reveal myself as a former addict," Jennifer says.

"Do it," Leanne says. "You have to do it."

"I'm not sure that I can," Jennifer says.

"Why not?" Leanne says. "This is your big chance. So you tell the world you're a recovering addict. People will care for five minutes, then they'll forget. And the people who care longer than five minutes are those who are either recovering addicts themselves or who have addicts in their family—and to those people you'll be an inspiration. A beacon of hope."

"You think?" Jennifer says.

"You need to choose bravery over shame," Leanne says. "Humility over pride. Otherwise, you're hiding in the shadows. You think substance abuse doesn't affect the affluent? The sophisticated? That addicts don't live in Beacon Hill or Back Bay?" Leanne leans in. "It affects everyone." She digs into her yogurt parfait. "I, for one, would be behind you a hundred and ten percent. And I can tell you without equivocation that Derek will be behind you as well. What does Patrick say?"

Jennifer raises her eyebrows.

"You haven't *told* him?" Leanne says.

Jennifer picks a raisin out of her bran muffin. She shakes her head.

"Go home now," Leanne says. She helps Jennifer wrap her muffin and secure the top to her latte. "Go home and tell him, and then call me later so I can hear about how wonderful he was."

Patrick is in his office, of course, running through the close of Friday's markets on the computer. The two younger boys are in the den playing Minecraft, and Barrett is at the Celtics game with his friend Saylor and Saylor's father, Gregory. Gregory is in AA—he's very open about this—and Jennifer doesn't think less of him for it, does she? No. She doesn't worry about Barrett when he's in Gregory's care. Why would she? Getting help is a sign of strength, of wisdom.

Jennifer closes the door to the office. "I need you to shut down the computer," she says to Patrick. "I have something to tell you."

I quit the penthouse project.

> *What? Why? Why on earth did you do that?*

It wasn't working out.

> *Wasn't working out? For Pete's sake, Jen!*

Grayson Coker hit on me. He tried to kiss me. He was inappropriate with his hands.

> *What?*

So I walked out. And I quit.

[Deep breath.]

> *When was this?*

A few weeks ago.

> *Weeks ago? And you didn't tell me?*

I thought you'd be angry.

> *I am angry. How* dare *he . . .*

And I knew you'd be upset about the money. I mean, I know we need it. But the good news is, a new opportunity presented itself.

> *What is it?*

A show. A design show on SinTV called Real-Life Rehab.

> *SinTV, as in the network that produces* Swing Set?

[Pause. Jennifer wonders if Patrick, too, watches *Swing Set*.]

Yes.

Does this design show involve swinging?

No. They rehab buildings in bad neighborhoods. They're setting it in Boston. The first house is in Dorchester. They want me to be the host. I'll get paid thirty-five thousand dollars per episode for the first twelve episodes of the first season.

Thirty-five thousand per episode? That's amazing! I'm so proud of you.

But.

But what?

The show is called Real-Life Rehab *for a reason. I have to tell everyone that I'm a recovering addict. That's part of the deal. Nonnegotiable.*

Oh.

What do you think?

I…uh, okay. Wow. I don't know what to think. What do you think?

I think I'm going to do it. I'm going to choose bravery over shame. Humility over pride. Otherwise, I'm hiding in the shadows. I don't want to hide in the shadows. I want the spotlight.

Good for you.

Really?

Yes, really. Come here and give me a kiss.

On Monday morning Jennifer calls Danko and says, "I'm going to do the show."

"Yasssss!" he says. "The studio execs are going to be thrilled. Good for you, Jennifer. You won't regret it. I'll FedEx the contracts to you today, and we'll likely start shooting the pilot just after the first of the year."

Jennifer hangs up the phone. She feels brave and humble. And excited!

Now...*now* she can allow herself to think about Thanksgiving. She will make a kale Caesar with homemade dressing and pumpernickel croutons, and an autumn salad of mixed greens, butternut squash, dried cranberries, goat cheese, and toasted pecans with an apple cider vinaigrette.

Yum.

Mitzi has decided to keep dinner "just family," but even that involves quite a crowd. Kelley and Mitzi will be there, obviously, as well as one or both of Kelley's hospice nurses, as well as Jennifer, Patrick, and the three boys, and Kevin, Isabelle, Genevieve, and baby KJ. Ava is coming without Potter. (*Again* without Potter? This seems odd to Jennifer and she says so to Patrick. Patrick says, "He's in California seeing his son.") Margaret and Drake are coming, just after Margaret's retirement trip to Barbados. And Bart will be there with his new girlfriend, Allegra, who was the girl dressed up like a geisha at his birthday party.

Despite the presence of hospice nurses, and despite the fact that Kelley's speech has slowed down and he can't eat more than a few bites of food, Mitzi has instructed everyone that the holiday is to be treated as it has always been treated in the Quinn household—as a celebration of family, a day of gratitude.

Think how lucky we are, Mitzi writes in the group text she sends. *Bart is home.*

Then she sends a text that says: *There will be no tears, no maudlin toasts, and above all: no family squabbles. There will be turkey with all the trimmings, there will be pie and there will be football.*

And at midnight Mitzi will proceed with her tradition of decorating the inn for Christmas.

That means nutcrackers! Mitzi says. *And the Byers' Choice carolers!*

Jennifer is so happy about her decision and her new career that she doesn't even roll her eyes.

Patrick, Jennifer, and the boys put the BMW on the ferry Thursday morning. The boys go up to the top deck with money for hot dogs and chowder, and Patrick pulls a bottle of Schramsberg sparkling wine and a half gallon of fresh-squeezed juice from the cooler in the back of the car.

"Surprise," he says.

Jennifer beams. He must have sneaked the champagne and juice in alongside the salad fixings. He's the sweetest, most thoughtful man alive; Jennifer loves mimosas on Thanksgiving morning.

"This'll keep us from engaging in family squabbles," Jennifer says as she and Patrick do a cheers with their plastic cups.

"Either that," Patrick says, "or it will make us engage in family squabbles."

Jennifer laughs. It's anyone's guess.

She senses something off as soon as she walks into the inn — but maybe she's imagining it. She had three mimosas on the ferry; she's a little bit buzzed. That must be it. The house is already filled with people, the parade is on TV, and there's the rich, savory aroma of turkey coming from the kitchen. Mitzi doesn't start decorating until midnight, but there's a fifteen-foot Douglas fir in its usual place in the corner of the room next to the fireplace, so there are added scents of woodsmoke and pine.

Jennifer doles out kisses:

Margaret ("I can't tell you how happy I am not to be at that parade!").

Drake ("When you and Paddy go to Barbados, you have to

stay at Cobblers Cove. It's like something straight out of 1957").

Ava ("I made Potter go to Palo Alto. It's a long story. I'll tell you later").

Mitzi ("Did you bring two salads? I hope you brought two salads").

Bart ("This is my girlfriend, Allegra. We used the gift certificate to Fifty-Six Union, so thank you again").

Allegra ("Yes, thank you so much. You're married to Patrick, right? And you have three boys—Barrett, Pierce, and Jaime. Bart made me memorize the family tree").

Kevin ("Hi, Sis. Can I get you a glass of wine?").

"Yes, please," Jennifer says. She can't figure out what it is, but something doesn't feel right. It's as though she's standing in a pocket of cold air. Maybe it's Kelley. His light is fading. Everyone must feel it. "Where's your father?" Jennifer asks Patrick. The boys have vanished upstairs to their room, which has a TV and a PS4. They'll play Minecraft until the first football game comes on, then it'll be all about their fantasy teams. Jennifer won't hear from them again until dinner.

"He's sleeping," Patrick says. "He normally wakes up between four and five, Mitzi says. Dinner is at five thirty."

Kevin returns, holding Jennifer's wine. "For you," he says. He raises his bottle of beer. "I would make a toast about this being the last Thanksgiving at the inn, the last Quinn family Thanksgiving…"

"But nothing maudlin," Jennifer says. She notices Kevin's eyes shining. She tries to change the subject. "Where's Isabelle?"

"Kitchen," Kevin says.

As soon as Jennifer walks into the kitchen, she understands what's off. Isabelle is standing at the stove, basting the turkey.

It's a light golden brown with a puff of savory stuffing at the cavity. Jennifer likes to put everything but the kitchen sink in her stuffing—sausage, pine nuts, dried cherries—but Isabelle is a stuffing purist. She uses only onion, celery, thyme, and sage. She also puts white wine in her gravy—lots and lots of wine.

"Hey, you," Jennifer says. She lays a hand on Isabelle's back and kisses her cheek. "Everything smells *très bon.*"

She feels the muscles of Isabelle's back tense under her silk blouse, and although Jennifer knows it's crazy, as they're standing directly in front of the oven, a chill comes off Isabelle. It's the icy pocket that Jennifer felt earlier.

Isabelle turns around and seems to address Ava, Mitzi, and Margaret—but not Jennifer—in French. Something about *"le bébé."* She returns the turkey to the oven and dashes up the back stairs.

Jennifer feels stung. She hesitates before turning to face the rest of the women in Patrick's family, but when she does, no one seems to notice anything amiss. Ava is opening a bag of marshmallows; she has been put in charge of the sweet potatoes. Margaret is pouring a glass of wine; she has been assigned appetizers, which Jennifer is sure she brought up from Dean & DeLuca. And Mitzi is perusing her spice rack.

"Where are my cloves?" she says.

Ava throws Jennifer a quick look. "You could try making the cider without cloves this year, Mitzi."

Jennifer nearly asks if Isabelle seems okay. Maybe she has postpartum depression. Maybe she is annoyed that while everyone else in the family has been given cushy assignments—salads, cheese and crackers, a vegetable or two—she has been left with the heavy lifting, the turkey, stuffing, mashed potatoes, and three kinds of pie. As though she's still the help!

But Jennifer knows what's really wrong. It's Norah Vale. Isabelle saw Jennifer talking to and hugging Norah Vale.

Kelley makes an entrance fifteen minutes before dinner is served. When his hospice nurse Lara pushes Kelley into the room in his wheelchair, everyone cheers. Patrick takes over for Lara and encourages her to help herself to the artichoke dip, the smoked oysters, and the tapenade. To Lara's credit, she digs in and asks the score of the Cowboys game.

Hospice nurses are people too! Jennifer thinks.

She is on her third glass of wine.

The last time Jennifer went into the kitchen for a refill, Isabelle was at the stove making gravy, and Mitzi was out on the side porch smoking a cigarette.

"Do you need any help, Isabelle?" Jennifer asked.

"Non," Isabelle said.

Kelley can still talk—slowly—and he can eat a few bites of food. He asks for a smoked oyster. Genevieve is awake from her nap, and when she sees Grandpa eating a smoked oyster, she asks for one as well.

Jennifer turns to Patrick and says, "I have ten bucks that says she spits it out."

There's an angry whisper in Jennifer's ear. *"Ma fille est Française."*

It's Isabelle, who is standing next to Jennifer while Genevieve pops the oyster into her mouth, swallows it happily, and asks for another.

Isabelle picks up people's empty glasses, crumpled napkins, and the cheese platter, which has been all but demolished.

Jennifer says, "You shouldn't have to do that, Isabelle. You're doing too much as it is. Let me help you."

"Non," Isabelle says. Her voice is like a warning shot, but

no one else in the family notices. They are too busy celebrating the two oyster eaters. And that, Jennifer supposes, is as it should be.

Jennifer goes up to lasso the boys, and when they come down, everyone is moving toward the table. The TV has been turned off and replaced with Vivaldi. The table sparkles with fine china, crystal, and candlelight. In the center of the table is a horn of plenty, spilling forth gourds and tiny pumpkins, lady apples, pecans and walnuts in the shell. Jennifer snaps a quick picture with her phone as she wonders who arranged it. She couldn't have done it better herself.

Kelley is seated at the head of the table as always. Jennifer finds herself between Allegra and Drake— or In-Law Alley, as she likes to think of it. Isabelle is all the way across the table in the seat closest to the kitchen.

Isabelle glowers at Jennifer, then disappears into the kitchen. She reappears with the turkey, which she sets in front of Kevin. They have agreed that Kevin will carve and Patrick will say the blessing.

Patrick stands and raises his glass. "Our family has so much to be grateful for that it's difficult to know where to start. This time last year I was in San Francisco with Jennifer and the boys, and my baby brother was still missing in Afghanistan. Bart has now been returned to us safely, and I know we are all grateful for that. Kevin and Isabelle have grown not only their business but also their family. Ava has moved to New York and has started a new job. My mother capped off sixteen years as the voice of this great nation and now, I know, hopes to put her considerable talents to even more noble pursuits. I believe I speak for all of us, Mom, when I say how proud we are of you."

Margaret bows her head and smiles at her plate.

"But mostly, today, I am grateful for the man who brought us all here together. Dad, you brought me and Kevin and Ava to this island when we were at impressionable ages. You married Mitzi, bought the inn, and gave us a little brother. You had moments when you were tough, stubborn, and sometimes a real jerk. But not a day passed while I was growing up that I didn't feel loved. It's only now that I have three sons of my own that I can appreciate what an admirable job you did with us. I would like to thank God for this meal, and for this home, and for all of us at this table. But above all, I would like to express my gratitude, now and forever, that you are my father."

"Amen," Bart says.

"Amen," Jennifer whispers.

Ava wipes tears away with her napkin. "No maudlin toasts," she says. "Weren't you on the group text?"

And everyone laughs.

The meal passes pleasantly, and Jennifer's sense of unrest fades a bit. Isabelle is up and down and in and out of the kitchen until Kevin makes her sit down to eat. Everyone praises Jennifer's salads, and Jennifer, in turn, raves about the sweet potatoes and Mitzi's fiesta cranberry sauce, but mostly she praises Isabelle's turkey, stuffing, mashed potatoes, and gravy.

It's like Isabelle doesn't hear her. She doesn't respond.

But no one at the table notices! Everyone is talking about next weekend, Christmas Stroll, and how Eddie Pancik, Allegra's father, has people lined up to look at the inn. Apparently, there are already a few interested buyers.

Patrick raises the question that Jennifer knows has been plaguing him. "Have you thought about what you're going to do with the sale proceeds, Mitzi? Buy another house here?"

"Actually, I've been thinking about the Caribbean," Mitzi says.

The table grows quiet and then Kelley speaks up. His voice is strong and clear, and for one second it's like he's perfectly healthy. "Mitzi doesn't have to decide right now. Let's just enjoy."

"Hear, hear," Drake says.

Jennifer offers to help clear the table and wrap leftovers. She supposes she should be grateful that Isabelle is the way she is—proud, reserved, French. Certainly there are other sisters-in-law out there who would have seen Jennifer with Norah Vale and then talked about it with everyone else in the family behind Jennifer's back. But Isabelle doesn't seem to have told even Kevin. Kevin is his same old self, a bartender at heart, pouring drinks and cracking jokes.

Drake and Margaret are also helping out in the kitchen, but then Margaret says, "I'd love to take a walk through town before dessert."

Jennifer says, "Please, go right ahead. Isabelle and I have things handled here."

Drake and Margaret disappear out the door, holding hands. Jennifer returns to the dining room—ostensibly to see if there are any other plates or glasses that need clearing, but really to double-check that the rest of the family is safely in the living room.

Jennifer hears Mitzi say, "Only five hours until midnight. I'm going to get the nutcrackers out of storage. Allegra, why don't you come with me?"

Ava passes by the dining room on her way down the hall. She has her phone in her hand. She sees Jennifer and says, "I can't hear myself think with all these people. I'm going to my room."

Jennifer closes the swinging door between the kitchen and the dining room and secures it with a latch that nobody ever uses. Then she approaches Isabelle at the dishwasher.

"I know you're angry with me," she says. "And I want to explain."

"No need to explain," Isabelle says. Her English is surprisingly fluent, confirming Jennifer's suspicions that Isabelle pretends there's a language barrier only when it's convenient for her. "Norah Vale is like poison. She was poison to Kevin and she was poison to you. She sold you the pills. Kevin tells me this."

"Right, I know," Jennifer says. "But see, the thing is, Norah has changed. She's going to business school, she has cleaned up her act, she dresses nicely now—"

"How you dress does not change who you are," Isabelle says.

"No, I realize this, but—"

"When I saw you, you were buying drugs from her, yes?"

"I was *not* buying drugs from her," Jennifer says firmly.

"Buying drugs from whom?" Patrick says.

Jennifer whips around. Paddy is looking at her and Isabelle curiously—but not accusingly, she tells herself. He holds up a butter knife. "I flipped the latch. Sorry about that. I just wanted to see if you needed any help."

"I did not buy drugs from Norah Vale," Jennifer says. She knows she has some explaining to do. "A few weeks ago when we were here for Bart's party, I bumped into Norah... do you remember when I went to the sewing center to get that fabric?"

Patrick nods, but Jennifer knows he doesn't remember.

"Well, I bumped into Norah and her brother Danko on Main Street, and we ended up getting coffee at the Hub."

"You didn't tell me you saw Norah," Patrick says.

"I must have forgotten to tell you that part," Jennifer says. What this means is that she left out Norah's involvement on purpose because Patrick had already digested so much and Jennifer didn't want him to short-circuit. And does it really *matter* who the producer of the show is? "Norah and Danko are the ones who approached me about doing the show."

"What?" Patrick says.

"Danko is the producer," Jennifer says. She can suddenly see that the real problem with the show isn't going to be that she's announcing she's a recovering addict, but rather that Norah Vale is tangentially involved. She appeals to Patrick. "You remember Danko? He pulled us out of the sand up at Great Point that one time..."

"Yes, yes," Patrick says. "The tattoo artist."

"He's a television producer now and has been for years. Norah has *nothing* to do with it. She was simply making the introduction."

"You are now involved with some other...project with Norah?" Isabelle asks. "You are keeping her in our lives, when all I wish is for her to be gone?"

"Norah isn't a threat to you," Jennifer says. "Kevin loves you. You have a family and a business and a future."

"She hurt Kevin very badly," Isabelle says. "I'm sure he will agree it's better if she has nothing more to do with anyone in this family."

"I'm sure he will agree with that," Patrick echoes. He looks at Jennifer. "Sometimes I just don't understand what you're thinking."

Jennifer stares at Patrick, dumbfounded. She would like to point out the following:

1. This show has nothing to do with Norah Vale. Danko is the producer.

2. Sometimes Jennifer doesn't understand what *Patrick* is thinking. Such as when he decided it would be a good idea to take the privileged information that Bucky Larimer gave him at his Colgate reunion and use it to illegally make twenty-five million dollars. He broke the law, he lost his job, and he went to jail. As a direct result of this, Jennifer got hooked on pills, and now they find themselves in a precarious financial situation. Needless to say, they wouldn't be having this conversation if not for the poor choices that Patrick himself made.

Possibly, he gets to point two on his own, because his expression and his voice soften.

To Isabelle he says, "Jennifer is going to be working with Norah's brother on a TV show. It's a very big, very exciting opportunity for her, and I support her. I'm sorry this has any tie to Norah Vale. But Norah isn't directly involved."

"And even if she were, she has changed," Jennifer says. "She's nice. I *like* her. I like her far more now than I ever did when I was related to her. And she is no threat to you or Kevin."

Isabelle shakes her head. "Please leave the kitchen," she says. "I will finish this myself."

"So you're still mad?" Jennifer says. "You're going to stay mad unless I renounce any association with Norah? I think you need to grow up, Isabelle."

"Get *out*," Isabelle says.

"What's going on in here?"

Jennifer turns to see Mitzi walk into the kitchen with Allegra in her wake. Jennifer offers Allegra a smile. *If you marry Bart,* she thinks, *this will be your family too!*

"Nothing," Jennifer says. "I was just helping Isabelle clean up."

Isabelle sniffs as only an indignant French woman can and runs the water in the sink. Jennifer refills her wineglass at the fridge. Mitzi shifts her gaze between Isabelle and Jennifer, but they are the model of obedient daughters-in-law. There will be no family squabbles.

AVA

So much for being her own fulfilled, independent person!

She misses Potter more than she ever dreamed possible. He's in Palo Alto, staying at the Westin; the hotel is less than a mile from the bungalow where Trish, Harrison, and PJ live. He arrived on Wednesday afternoon. The plan was that Potter would take PJ out for pizza because Trish had a meeting. But when Potter arrived at the house, PJ refused to go with Potter unless Harrison came as well.

"So it was like an alternate version of *Heather Has Two Mommies* called *PJ Has Two Daddies*. I'm sure everyone at Patxi's thought we were gay."

"What do you care?" Ava asks.

"I don't," Potter says. "But I do care that I seem to have been replaced by a thirty-year-old Brit. Did you know that Harrison is only thirty?"

"That's not *so* young," Ava says. "I'm thirty-two."

"Harrison is very fond of you, by the way," Potter says. "He made a point at dinner to ask about 'our friend Ava.'"

"What did you tell him?"

"I told him Ava was *my* friend and he'd better stay away from her," Potter says.

"How was PJ?" Ava asks. "Did he behave?"

"He was terrific," Potter says morosely. "He told us about school, he ate his pizza, he put his napkin in his lap, he was polite with the server."

"Wonderful!" Ava says.

"But I think it was because Harrison was there," Potter says. "I really messed up, letting Trish take him so far away."

Ava steels herself for the announcement that Potter is moving to California. "It is far away," she says. "I miss you."

"Not half as much as I miss you," Potter says.

On Thursday, Ava tries to throw herself into the Thanksgiving spirit. Potter is with his family and Ava is with hers, and who knows how much longer her family will remain intact? Mitzi has let it be known that this will be the final Thanksgiving at the inn, and they all realize but do not outwardly acknowledge that it will be their last Thanksgiving with Kelley.

If Ava lets herself think about it, she'll dissolve. She planned to spend hours of quality time with Kelley, but his condition has deteriorated so rapidly—even since Halloween—that all he does is sleep and listen to Danielle Steel novels on his phone. Ava offered to buy the same novel down at Mitchell's Book Corner and read it aloud, but Kelley said he enjoys the narrator's voice. He finds it soothing.

He seems very attached to his hospice nurses, Lara and Jocelyn; they are the only ones other than Mitzi who feed him, give him his medicine, and get him in and out of his wheelchair.

There are a few moments on Thanksgiving that make Ave especially upset.

1. In the morning she goes over to visit her best friend, Shelby, and Shelby's husband, Zack, and their baby, Xavier, who is now a toddler. Shelby announces that she is pregnant again, with a girl, and Zack, who has

a penchant for arcane knowledge, informs Ava that a family of a boy followed by a girl is known as the king's choice. There is the son to carry on the family name, and the daughter to marry off and create a dynasty. Ava congratulates Shelby and Zack on getting the king's choice, but secretly she feels left behind. She and Shelby are the same age, but Shelby is married, with a child and a baby on the way. When will Ava's life start moving in that direction? She's happy in New York, but she has nothing permanent.

2. She loves Margaret and Drake, but she sees them all the time in New York. She loves Paddy and Jennifer and Kevin and Isabelle and Bart, but she saw everybody three weeks earlier. She wonders why she didn't go to California with Potter.

3. Bart has started dating Allegra Pancik—in a big way. Allegra comes over to the inn at three o'clock, and she and Bart are joined at the hip. Or, rather, the lips. All they do is kiss! This could have been true when they were in New York at Margaret's retirement party, but Ava didn't notice because she was with Potter. Now that she is missing Potter so badly, she can't even look at Bart and Allegra. She wants to tell them to keep their hands off each other while they're in public—but she will, no doubt, sound like a lonely, bitter old maid.

4. Mitzi assigns Ava the sweet potatoes. Ava despises sweet potatoes. She wants to replace them with a roasted butternut squash dish, but Mitzi shoots that idea down.

After dinner Ava gets a FaceTime call from Potter. She takes the call in her old room, which is buffered from the noise of the living room.

"Hi," she says.

"You're so beautiful," Potter says.

"Are you with PJ?" she asks.

"No," Potter says. "Why?"

"Since you're FaceTiming, I thought maybe you'd have PJ there too."

"That's Harrison's thing," Potter says. "Not mine."

Ava nods. She doesn't say that she thinks the FaceTiming is an effective strategy. "What time are you headed over there?"

"In a few minutes," Potter says. "That's why I called now."

"Is Trish a good cook?" Ava asks.

"Terrible," Potter says. "Harrison does all the cooking, apparently. He invites the friends, he sets the table, he parents the child...he does all the domestic duties while Trish reads and writes and critiques and lectures."

"I'm sure you'll have a good time," Ava says.

"I'm sure I'll have a terrible time," Potter says. "I never want to celebrate another holiday without you."

This makes Ava feel good. "Me either."

"Which brings me to the real reason for my call," Potter says. "I want you to agree to go to Austria with me at Christmastime. We'll spend time in both Vienna and Salzburg. An old friend of Gibby's has a son who works for the ambassador, and he has gotten us two tickets to the Hofburg Silvesterball on New Year's Eve, and I've already booked a room at the Grand Hotel Wien."

Ava gasps. She has seen photographs of the balls in Vienna; they're like something out of a fairy tale—men in white tie and tails, women in gowns and tiaras, a full orchestra, endless waltzes.

"I need a dress!" she says.

"So I take it that's a yes?" Potter says. "You'll go?"

Ava refrains from biting her lip because Potter can see

her and he'll interpret that as a sign of hesitation. What about her father? Ava decides that she will fly back to the United States on New Year's Day and come right to Nantucket. She doesn't start teaching again until January 8, so there will be time for a nice visit.

"I'll go," she says. She gives Potter her brightest smile. The Grand Hotel Wien! A ball at the palace! "Of course I'll go!"

EDDIE

As predicted, Grace wants to start their Thanksgiving dinner with a glass of champagne (Perrier-Jouët, twenty-six dollars per glass), and she orders one for Eddie as well. Then, since she can't decide between the foie gras appetizer and the Nantucket bay scallops, she orders both and adds the caviar option to the scallops for an additional thirty-five dollars.

Eddie is sweating. Grace wanted him to look "nice," so he is wearing a shirt, a V-neck sweater, and a blazer. He removes his blazer and wipes his brow with his napkin. He has two hundred fifty dollars in cash on him, but they are going to exceed that, so Thanksgiving dinner is one more thing that will go on Eddie's sagging credit card.

He tries not to panic. He tries to be grateful. He's grateful he *has* a credit card. He's grateful he has a wife and two healthy daughters.

He needs to sell the Christys a house. He needs to find a different buyer for the Winter Street Inn.

He should never have gone into real estate in the first place, he thinks. It's too risky, too uneven; it's boom or bust. Why did he go into real estate? He has been a broker for over

twenty years, but only now, Thanksgiving Day 2017, is he
questioning his life's most basic decision. He should have
gone to the Benjamin Franklin Institute of Technology and
learned HVAC. HVAC guys never have to worry about their
next paycheck; HVAC guys are buying land on Vieques in
Puerto Rico and building vacation homes.

Grace raises her glass of Perrier-Jouët. "This is really
nice," she says. "Just the two of us."

It *is* really nice, although Eddie is surprised to hear Grace
say so. She doesn't tend to celebrate being alone with him—
and can Eddie blame her? All he does is think about work
and obsess about money.

"How did it feel, seeing Benton today?" Eddie asks. "Was
it…weird?" *Weird* isn't quite the word he's looking for, but
he doesn't have a developed emotional vocabulary, as Grace
will be the first to point out. What Eddie wants to know is:
Does any part of Grace wish that she and Benton were still
together? Does she miss him? Did she see his strong, muscular torso today at the Turkey Plunge and feel desire? Did she
look into Benton's soulful brown eyes and feel love?

"Eddie," Grace says. "There's something I have to tell you."

Here it comes, Eddie thinks. The answer to all of those
questions is yes. And didn't Eddie sense that this morning?
There was *no way* that was the first time Grace had seen Benton Coe. She has been secretly meeting him ever since Benton
got back. When Eddie saw Grace on the Polpis bike path, she
was riding home from a secret rendezvous. She probably wanted
to go to the Turkey Plunge just so she could see Benton do the
stupid, pointless, masochistic swim.

At that moment Grace's appetizers arrive, and because
the table is small, one is placed in front of Eddie—the scallops topped with black, glistening clumps of caviar. Why not
add some gold leaf while they're at it? And yet Eddie would

buy every appetizer on the menu if that would make Grace love Eddie instead of Benton.

Once their server leaves them to enjoy the appetizers, Eddie says, "What is it?"

"I've been talking with Benton," Grace says. "He called with a proposition when he got back from Detroit, and I've met with him three times to discuss it."

Proposition. Met with him three times.

"Three times?" Eddie says. Grace is telling him the exact number of times she has been with Benton. Three! Three is a lot! Actually, it's less than Eddie feared, but he won't tell her that.

"Try the foie gras," Grace says. "I'm happy to share."

How can she be thinking about eating at a time like this? Eddie wonders. Granted, it's Thanksgiving, but Grace is about to detonate the bomb that will destroy their marriage, their family, their lives.

I am not *happy to share!* Eddie thinks.

"Eddie?" Grace says. She's looking at him across the candlelit table. The tables at American Seasons are all hand-painted with different scenes and schemes, and Eddie and Grace are seated at the chessboard table. This seems appropriate. He's the king and Grace is the queen, but he has been forced into checkmate by their former gardener.

"What?" Eddie says.

"Benton has offered me a job. He wants me to come work for him, working in garden design and implementation. His partner left and Benton has more work than he can handle on his own. We always had the same aesthetic, the same sensibility—that was the attraction, I think, more than any-thing else. And he's going to pay me, Eddie…"

Eddie lifts his eyes from the table.

"…twenty-five hundred a week to start. Plus bonuses,

when projects reach completion. I told him I'd talk to you before I gave him an answer. But I want to say yes. The girls are growing up and I'm bored. Also, we could use the money."

Twenty-five hundred a week, so ten thousand a month. With bonuses. A steady income.

But Eddie can't risk having Grace work for her former beloved. Can he?

"What about...your feelings?" Eddie says. "Your feelings for Benton? If I say yes, you can work for him, and the next thing I know, you're sleeping with him? How can I trust you, Grace?"

"I know that part will be difficult," Grace says. "But let me start by saying that my romantic feelings for Benton are dead and gone. I'm fond of him as a friend. And he's back together with McGuvvy. She's still in Detroit now, but she's moving to Nantucket after the holidays and they're going to live together, and their house is also the office." She smiles. "You don't have anything to worry about, although I know my word doesn't stand for much."

Eddie takes a deep breath, then a deep drink of his twenty-six-dollar champagne. He feels like it's Christmas instead of Thanksgiving. Grace is taking a job that will bring in real money! She'll be doing something she enjoys! Benton is back together with McGuvvy!

"Your word is all I need," Eddie says. After all, Grace has placed trust in Eddie as well; she believes he is no longer lying to her or breaking the law—and he's not. He never will again.

Eddie floods with relief, with joy. He picks up his fork and tastes one of the caviared scallops.

"Delicious," he says, and he flags their server to order another one for himself.

PART THREE

DECEMBER

BART

The first weekend of December on Nantucket is Christmas Stroll. It has been this way Bart's entire life, but he never cared, barely noticed, and didn't think to celebrate.

Until this year.

Because this year he's in love.

He's in love!

On the Friday of Stroll, Mitzi wants Bart out of the house because there are interested buyers coming to look at the inn. Bart heads down to Main Street, which is as busy and bustling as it is on any summer day—only now the shop windows are all decked out with snowflakes and glass ornaments, wreaths, ribbons, gingerbread houses, candy canes, and reindeer. Main Street is lined with Christmas trees, each one decorated by a class at Nantucket Elementary School. That was probably the last time Bart was excited about Stroll—when his fifth-grade class came downtown during the school day to hang their ornaments on their tree and Ms. Paul took them to Nantucket Pharmacy for hot chocolate.

When Bart steps into Bayberry Properties and sees Allegra's face, Christmas has a whole new meaning.

She says, "I can take my lunch break now. Want to stroll?"

They hold hands and walk up the street, poking into the bookstore first, then into Murray's Toggery, and then Bart leads Allegra over to the pharmacy for a nostalgic cup of hot chocolate. She takes a sip and gets a speck of whipped cream on her nose.

"I'm in love with you," Bart says.

"What?" Allegra says. "You are?"

"I am," Bart says. He doesn't care if it's too soon, he doesn't care if they're too young, he doesn't care that they both still live with their parents at home. He doesn't even care if Allegra is in love with him in return (okay, maybe he does care, but judging from the glow of her face and the light in her eyes every time she looks at him, he isn't worried; she's in love with him, too), because he gets it now. He gets it completely. The world makes sense. It has meaning, and that meaning is love, and love, for him, is Allegra Pancik.

On Saturday, Allegra has agreed to help her mother decorate for Christmas up at Academy Hill. There's a tree in the lobby that needs trimming, and there is garland to be hung, as well as wreaths for the front door and all of the front windows. The residents of Academy Hill usually come down from their apartments to watch, and Mr. Lazear, who is "seriously ninety years old," according to Allegra, and who used to be the music teacher back in the 1950s, when Academy Hill was a school, leads everyone in carols.

"It's actually kind of fun," Allegra says. "I went with my mom last year. We could really use your help if you know anything about stringing lights or draping garland."

Does Bart know anything about stringing lights or draping garland? He's only Mitzi Quinn's son, and Mitzi Quinn is only the biggest Christmas fanatic south of the North Pole.

"I'm your man," Bart says.

"I can't tell you how grateful I am," Allegra's mother, Grace, says. "Eddie is showing houses all weekend, and he isn't handy anyway."

"No problem," Bart says. He unpacks the artificial tree, and he and Allegra snap its branches into place, then get it covered in white lights. Allegra hangs the ornaments, while Grace sets out a punch bowl, which she fills with juice, ginger ale, and a container of rainbow sherbet, and arranges a platter of homemade sand tarts and peanut butter cookies with chocolate kiss centers.

As Bart hangs the wreaths, the lobby fills with residents, many of whom Allegra walks over to introduce to Bart.

"My boyfriend, Bart Quinn," Allegra says.

"Is this the war hero?" one gentleman asks.

"Bart Quinn, sir, United States Marine Corps."

Once the news circulates that Allegra has a new boyfriend, everyone wants to meet Bart, shake his hand, thank him for his service, and tell him what an honor it is to have him right here at Academy Hill. One of the residents served in Korea with the Army; one of the women was a battlefield nurse in Vietnam. Mrs. Hester, who must be nearly deaf, comments very loudly about how handsome Bart is, and Mr. Reinemo says just as loudly that Bart is a lucky young man to be courting someone as fetching as Allegra.

Then Mr. Lazear enters the lobby singing "Deck the Halls." The next request is for "Jingle Bells," and Bart thinks of Ava—she really and truly despises this song—but everyone in the lobby belts it out with the enthusiasm of schoolchildren. During the endless, empty hours that Bart was being held prisoner, he used to conjure the faces he was fighting for back home, but he never once thought of the elderly. Mostly he thought about babies, kids, people his age who were the future of the country. But now he feels proud that he was also fighting for people who are living out their final years with purpose and dignity, people who have known enemies other than ISIS and the Bely, people who understand the cost of freedom.

Mrs. Hester rummages through a box until she finds the plastic mistletoe, and as everyone sings, she implores Bart to hang the mistletoe in the doorway. He does so, and then Mrs. Hester directs Allegra and Bart to stand beneath it.

"I think they want us to kiss now," Allegra says.

"Well, we can't disappoint them," Bart says. He leans down to kiss Allegra, and the room erupts in cheers.

JENNIFER

**PLEASE JOIN US IN CELEBRATING THE SEASON...
AND THE FORTHCOMING FIRST SEASON OF *REAL-LIFE REHAB*
STARRING BOSTON INTERIOR DECORATOR JENNIFER QUINN
MANDARIN ORIENTAL HOTEL
DECEMBER 9, 2017
6:30–8:30 P.M.
SINTV**

Patrick picks the invitation up off the counter and whistles. "You are the star," he says. "Your name is on the invite and everything."

"Mandarin Oriental," Jennifer says. "Not too shabby." She kisses Patrick on the lips. "I bought you a new holiday tie to wear. It's on the bed."

"Wow," Patrick says. "It's starting to feel like the good old days."

Jennifer knows what he means. She signed the contract for the first season and received a nice fat check, which went right into the bank. Now they have a splashy holiday party to attend, the way they used to when Paddy worked for Everlast Investments. Jennifer bought a red velvet slip dress, as well as a pair of red stilettos from Jimmy Choo at Copley Place. This party will be buzzworthy—the *Globe* and *Boston Common* are coming to cover it. All of the show's sponsors are invited as well as the glittery stars of Boston's social scene. Jennifer was able to invite Derek and Leanne, which is good because Jennifer will need to see friendly faces. Danko will attend, obviously, as well as *Real-Life Rehab*'s director, a thirty-something woman named Layla, who is also a former addict, she confided. In her case, it was cocaine and Valium.

"One to pump me up," Layla said. "One to bring me down."

Jennifer said, "I understand only too well." Still, Jennifer marveled because Layla was even younger than Jennifer. She had unlined black skin, cornrows, the cheekbones of a supermodel, and a degree from Harvard Business School.

On the night of the party, the network sends a car service to pick up Jennifer and Patrick. Alyssa, who is babysitting, and the three boys crowd by the bay window to ogle at the car out on the street.

"Be careful of the tree," Jennifer says. She has been so busy with preparations for the show—she meets Danko and the architect, Matthew, and the contractor, TF, at the house in Dorchester every day—that her own Christmas decorations, which are usually quite lavish, have suffered somewhat. She opted for a slightly smaller tree and used only three thousand of her five thousand ornaments. Christmas Lite, she's calling it this year.

"It seems silly, sending a car," Jennifer says. "The Mandarin isn't that far. We could have walked."

"Let's enjoy it," Patrick says. He buttons his overcoat and slips Jennifer's wrap over her shoulders.

"Bye, kids!" Jennifer calls out. "Bed by ten!" She takes Paddy's arm and descends the steps of their townhouse to the waiting car.

"Good evening, Ms. Quinn," the driver says.

When the car pulls up in front of the Mandarin Oriental and Jennifer steps out, photographers snap her picture.

"I can't believe this," Jennifer says to Paddy. She fears that Patrick might take issue with his role as her arm candy. After all, in their former life he was the breadwinner, the big deal; Jennifer was resolutely "the wife," who did some interior decorating in her spare time. But Patrick is beaming; unless he's putting up a very good front, he couldn't seem happier.

He offers one of the photographers his hand. "I'm Mr. Jennifer Quinn," he says. "But you can call me Patrick."

They are escorted to a ballroom that is completely decked out for the holidays. There's a huge tree, swags of garland, white lights, electric candles, and a three-part jazz combo with a scantily clad woman crooning "Merry Christmas, Baby." Servers circulate with trays of cocktails in champagne flutes. The cocktail is called a Santa Baby and is made with champagne, St-Germain, and blood orange juice. Patrick takes two flutes, one for Jennifer and one for himself.

"Cheers to you," he says.

"They spared no expense," Jennifer says. There's a raw bar set up in a wooden dory, and next to the raw bar are tiered trays of crudités and cheeses, and next to that is an elaborate spread of sushi.

"There she is!" Danko swoops in, wearing jeans, a white

shirt, and a Robert Graham velvet blazer. "You look gor-geous," he says, kissing Jennifer's cheek and simultaneously fist-bumping Patrick. "You both do. Ready to circulate?"

"Circulate?" Jennifer looks at Patrick.

"You go," Patrick says. "I'll find you in a little while and we'll get some food."

She is the luckiest woman in the world, with the most supportive partner. "I'm ready to circulate," she tells Danko.

Everywhere she goes, people fawn. The men kiss her hand, and the women squeal, especially the Millennials, all of whom, Jennifer supposes, watch SinTV and are anticipat-ing a big hit. Jennifer feels like a real celebrity—but all she has done so far is film half a day's promotional material in which she wore AG cigarette-leg jeans, a black scoop-neck bodysuit, and black suede Gucci loafers, which will be her "uniform" on the show. It's professional, classy, simple—or, as Danko says, "the essence of Jennifer Quinn." She also wore bright-red lipstick in all the photos. The shade is Gabri-elle from Chanel's Rouge Coco collection, and Chanel has already promised Jennifer a lifetime supply of the shade.

She meets up with Layla, who is stunning in a silvery-lavender sequin sheath and black cage stilettos, and there are more photographs.

"If only our dealers could see us now," Layla says.

As if on cue, Jennifer spies Norah Vale across the room. Jennifer wants to go over and say hello and thank her again—because look what a big deal this is! Jennifer has money, a new career, a fresh start. She is going to be on TV every week, she is going to be famous—and all thanks to Norah.

Jennifer has given a lot of thought to her interaction with Isabelle over Thanksgiving. She is sorry that Isabelle feels hurt by Jennifer's continuing relationship with Norah, but she isn't sure what to do about it. Should Jennifer have turned the show down because Isabelle feels insecure?

Jennifer meets people from Gucci and Chanel and Adriano Goldschmied and Hermès. The painfully elegant French woman from Hermès mentions that they'd like her to wear their watch as well and maybe the occasional scarf.

Yes! Jennifer thinks. *Yes! Yes! Yes!*

Next Jennifer meets the head of SinTV, Victor Huggins, known to all as Huggy. Jennifer sees Derek and Leanne talking to Natalie Jacobson, formerly of Channel 5 news, but she's afraid to excuse herself from Huggy. He's the boss! Huggy introduces Jennifer to Heidi Watney and Jason Varitek. Where is Patrick? He's going to die! Jennifer then meets a man named Ellis, who gives Jennifer his card. He owns a speakers bureau. He can get her five-figure speaking fees if she's willing to talk about overcoming her addiction. Has she done much public speaking?

"Not really?" Jennifer says. The only place she ever talked openly about the pills was in her support group. And just as Jennifer is thinking this, she sees Sable approaching. Sable led Jennifer's group; she's the reason for Jennifer's recovery.

If Jennifer tells Sable this, however, Sable will say that Jennifer is the reason for Jennifer's recovery.

"Sable!" Jennifer says.

"I'm so proud of you, sweetie," Sable says, pressing Jennifer's hands between her own. "You are going to help so many people."

Am I? Jennifer wonders. If she helps one person, if she provides even one person with hope where before there was only despair, then this whole thing will be worth it. The champagne and the car service are nice. Never having to buy lipstick again is nice; five-figure speaking fees are nice. But helping other people who are as lost now as Jennifer was is the Reason.

Before Jennifer can feel too self-congratulatory, she comes face-to-face with the one person she hoped never to see again: Grayson Coker.

Danko says, "Jennifer Quinn, may I introduce you to Grayson Coker, CEO of Boston Bank. Boston Bank just signed on as the show's presenting sponsor."

Jennifer raises her champagne flute to her lips, but the Santa Baby is gone.

Danko takes the flute. "Let me get you a refill," he says. "I'll be right back."

Grayson says, "Hello, Jennifer."

Jennifer puts a hand up to shield her cleavage. Why did she wear such a revealing dress? She feels positively naked, naked and blindsided. Boston Bank came on this week as the presenting sponsor? This week?

"Grayson," she says. She refuses to call him Coke. "Thank you for your support."

"I only pledged the bank's commitment once I saw you had been named as host of the show," he says.

What? Jennifer thinks. She knows she shouldn't be surprised. Lots of companies wait until a show's host has been named before they commit, but this feels very awkward.

"I owe you an apology," Grayson says. "I'm sorry about what happened in the penthouse. That's not why I'm supporting the show, however. I'm supporting the show because I think it's going to be a winner. And I grew up in Dorchester. Went to South Boston High School. The show sends a strong message."

Jennifer nods. "Apology accepted," she says. She scans the ballroom over Grayson Coker's shoulder, looking for Patrick. She needs Patrick here right this instant. Instead she sees a very tall, milky-skinned redhead coming toward them. The redhead snakes an arm around Grayson Coker's shoulders and leans in.

"I think we've met before?" she says. "I'm Mandy Pell, Grayson's decorator." She winks. "And his plus one."

"Jennifer Quinn," Jennifer says. She tries to keep any gloating out of her smile. Mandy Pell got Grayson Coker's penthouse job and Grayson Coker's affection—for the time being—but Jennifer got the show! "If you two will excuse me, I have to go find my husband."

Jennifer finds Patrick standing with Leanne and Derek and Norah Vale in front of a buffet table that Jennifer hasn't seen yet. It's a taco bar. There is grilled fish, roasted pork, sliced sirloin, pulled chicken, and two kinds of shells. For toppings, there are tomatoes, lettuce, onions, cilantro, shredded cheeses, chunky guacamole, mango salsa, blistered peppers, and sour cream. Jennifer is suddenly *ravenous,* but she greets Leanne, Derek, and Norah, saying, "You've all met, then?"

"Yes," Leanne says. "Norah was just telling us that she used to be your..."

Dealer, Jennifer thinks.

"...sister-in-law," Leanne says. "I think it's simply wonderful that you all are still friendly."

"I've known Paddy since high school," Norah says. "I was the lowly, troubled sophomore, and he was the big, studly senior."

"That was me, all right," Patrick says, and he raises his glass in a mock toast to himself, and everyone laughs.

It is *wonderful,* Jennifer thinks. She remembers when she met Norah Vale. It was summer, and Patrick had invited Jennifer home to Nantucket for the first time. Jennifer wore a Lilly Pulitzer sundress printed with yellow lions because she so badly wanted to fit in and impress. Norah, she remembers, showed up late for dinner at the inn wearing cutoff shorts and an Aerosmith T-shirt. When Jennifer noticed the python crawling up out of the shirt onto Norah's neck, she nearly screamed.

Norah smirked. "Looks real, doesn't it, princess?" she said.

For years they played those roles—Jennifer the good girl and Norah the bad—until...well, until Kevin and Norah divorced and Norah left...until Norah came back...until Jennifer was bad and Norah was enabling her to be bad. Their trajectory has been so *bizarre*. Someone could write a novel about it, but it wouldn't be believable.

And yet here they are.

Patrick says, "As part of her business degree, Norah is doing an internship with SinTV in Fishers, Indiana."

"Fishers, Indiana?" Jennifer says. Isabelle will be happy to hear that! Isabelle will be thrilled—Norah is leaving Nantucket and moving to the Midwest! Then Jennifer gasps. "Wait! Are you going to be working on—"

"*Swing Set!*" Leanne chimes in. She grabs Jennifer's arm. "Can you stand it? I'm so jealous!"

EDDIE

The Christys return to Nantucket over Christmas Stroll weekend, which is both good news and bad news. The good news is Nantucket engraves itself onto the Christys' hearts. Eddie sees it happen as soon as they step off the ferry. They're smitten. No, they're beyond smitten. They're in love. They want this island to be their home.

All Eddie has to do is sell them a house.

"I love the wreath hanging on the lighthouse," Masha says. "Who thought of that?"

"The Coast Guard hangs it," Eddie says. It has become one of the iconic images of Christmastime on Nantucket—that and the little lit-up tree that sits in the red dory in the Easy Street boat basin. Nantucket doesn't disappoint on Christmas. It combines the charm of a New England town with the ruggedness of a seaside village with the tasteful decorating that comes with money and tradition. The town glitters with white lights, evergreens, and velvet ribbon. There are Victorian carolers singing on Main Street. Eddie doesn't know a single woman who can resist Victorian carolers, and certainly not one as impressionable as Masha Christy. She stands in a daze while the carolers perform "Once in Royal David's City" in three-part harmony, then she claps like crazy.

She turns to Eddie. "I didn't even recognize that song and I loved it," she says. "My favorite carol is 'The Little Drummer Boy.'"

"I like that one too," Eddie admits.

"Can we go see the inn?" Masha says. "Please?"

The bad news about the Christys coming over during Christmas Stroll is that the Winter Street Inn will show much better than the house on Medouie Creek Road. Start with the name: the Winter Street Inn. Then take into account that the inn is in town, a stone's throw from the Christmas magic, while Medouie Creek Road is way, way out in the boonies. Eddie will have to mention that in the chaotic summer months the Medouie Creek Road house remains serene, quiet, and breezy. There is no traffic, there are no crowds, no tourists in the street, no heat emanating off the cobblestones.

But to be fair to Masha, Eddie has arranged for them to see the inn at eleven o'clock. It's just past ten thirty now. "Let's go," Eddie says. "We can walk."

They start strolling up Main Street, past all the twinkling shopwindows. There are children and dogs and men in quilted hunting jackets, women in fur vests and woolen hats with faux-mink pom-poms, like the one Grace wears. Eddie stops at the corner of Main and Centre and takes a deep breath. The air smells like evergreen and peppermint.

Across the street Eddie sees a familiar figure in jeans, an Irish fisherman's sweater, and a Santa hat. It's Benton Coe. He's by himself, holding a red Solo cup.

Good grief, Eddie thinks. This is the last thing he needs. He turns to check that the Christys are still behind him—Masha looked ready to be swallowed whole by every shop and gallery they passed on the way up the street—and his eyes dart left and right as he wonders which direction will be more effective in dodging what's right in front of them.

"Hey, Eddie!"

Reluctantly, Eddie seeks out the source of his name. Benton is headed right for him, Solo cup hoisted. From the flush of his cheeks and the way his Santa hat is drooping over one eye, Eddie guesses Benton has been to a party somewhere on upper Main and has enjoyed more than one cup of cheer. Eddie thinks of Grace—but she and Allegra are at Academy Hill, decorating.

"Hello, Benton," Eddie says. He has no choice but to shake Benton's hand and introduce him to the Christys.

"Benton Coe, I'd like you to meet my clients, Masha and Raja Christy. Masha, Raja, this is Benton Coe. He's my wife's..." Well, here Eddie is tempted to say *former lover,* but he holds his tongue. "New employer."

"Yes!" Benton says, grinning. "We're happy to have Grace on board. She's going to be a huge asset to our company."

Masha bats her eyes at Benton. "What kind of company do you have?" she asks.

Eddie grits his teeth. Does Benton Coe have a mesmerizing effect on every woman he meets?

"I'm a landscape architect," Benton says. "I design outdoor living spaces—gardens, of course, but also pools, walks, decks, patios, water features."

Masha nods in awe, like he's just told her he designed the space station, but then Eddie gets an idea.

"As a matter of fact, Masha, Benton designed the outdoor space at the house on Medouie Creek Road."

"You did?" Masha says.

"Yes, I did," Benton says, growing even more animated than he already was. "Are you thinking of buying that house? I *love* that house. I think that outdoor space is one of my favorites on the entire island. Maybe even my favorite."

Thank you, Benton Coe, Eddie thinks.

"Except for Eddie and Grace's old house. That was... well, that's my number one favorite, but my second-favorite is Medouie Creek Road."

"Really?" Masha says.

"The Medouie Creek Road house doesn't have a garden shed, though," Benton says. "Tell you what, if you end up buying that house, call me and I'll build you a garden shed just like the one Eddie and Grace used to have."

"You would *do* that?" Masha says. She's acting like a twelve-year-old meeting Justin Bieber. Eddie would actually be ecstatic about this—score one for Raja and the Medouie Creek Road house!—if he didn't have the horrifying memory of catching Grace and Benton locked inside the very garden shed of which he's speaking!

If the Christys do buy the house, Eddie will tell Raja: *Absolutely no shed! In fact, hire a different landscaper altogether.*

"Well, good to see you, Benton," Eddie says. "We have to be on our way."

"Great to meet you," Benton says, hoisting his cup. "Good luck in the hunt!"

They part ways, and Eddie leads the Christys across Centre and up Liberty.

"Wow," Masha says. "He was handsome."

"Masha," Raja says.

Masha swats Eddie's arm. "He thinks I'm bad," she says. "You should have heard him carrying on about that lady Rachel from the last time we were here."

"She made cookies," Raja says.

Oh dear, thinks Eddie.

As they cross the threshold from the street to the front walk of the inn, Eddie's phone pings. Quickly he checks it. There's a text from Glenn that says: *Full-price offer just came in on the WSI.*

From who? Eddie asks. Then he thinks, *Whom?*

Some guy just called the office offering full market, Glenn says. *I guess he used to stay there.*

"Is something wrong?" Masha asks.

"Not...not, no," Eddie says. "Not exactly. I just received word that the inn already has a full-price offer. It just came in."

Raja smiles.

"But we can still look at it, right?" Masha says. "And if we like it, we can go higher than full price."

Eddie ushers Masha forward. It sounds sketchy, doesn't it? Some "guy" calling in and offering the full price because he used to stay there? Could be a crank, although Glenn is the best in the business at sniffing people out.

He has asked Mitzi not to be present in the house while he's showing it—and yet before Eddie can reach for the knob, she is swinging the front door open, exclaiming, "Welcome!"

"Mitzi Quinn!" Eddie says. "I didn't expect to find you at home." His voice holds a touch of reprimand, but obviously not enough because Mitzi seems unfazed.

"Come in, come in," Mitzi says. "I'm the owner, Mitzi Quinn." She reaches out to hug—HUG!—Masha Christy, a woman she has never met. Masha, being Masha, thinks she has found her soul mate. Their embrace is one of long-lost friends reunited after a war.

"I'm Masha," she says. "And this is my husband, Raja. Thank you for inviting us into your beautiful home."

They all step into the great room, which, Eddie has to admit, presents well. Mitzi has decorated it with what must be a hundred strings of white lights. There are lights on the gigantic tree, there are lights amid the greens on the mantel, and there is an enormous lit evergreen wreath above the fireplace. The room twinkles.

"This looks even more festive than usual," Eddie says.

"I went whole hog with the lights for Kelley," Mitzi says. She smiles sadly at Masha. "My husband has terminal brain cancer and he's blind in one eye."

"Oh, I'm so sorry," Masha says.

"He used to really love my caroling village," Mitzi says. She leads the Christys over to a table all set up with a Byers' Choice Christmas market scene. "The kids used to tease me about my carolers, and Kelley, too, but one night I caught him out here, rearranging them." She laughs, then quickly grows somber. "That's why we're selling."

Eddie tries not to frown. This is why he wanted Mitzi gone! No potential buyer wants to hear about *terminal brain cancer!* They want to imagine a house filled with happy times. They want a place that will make them feel they will live forever.

"Shall we look at the kitchen?" Eddie says.

*   *   *

"Well, I loved it," Masha says once they have toured the entire house save for the master suite. "No surprise there. But..."

But, Eddie thinks. To keep it running as an inn, she'll have to hire a staff: a marketing expert, a reservationist, a general manager, a housekeeping manager, and at least one chambermaid, a breakfast cook, and a maintenance man. The mere idea is not only expensive, it's exhausting.

"But...I think I'd like to look at the other house again," Masha says. "The one on Whatever Creek Road. I'm intrigued by the outdoor space. And I definitely want a garden shed, like that guy said. What was his name?"

"Benton," Eddie says. "Benton Coe."

Eddie forgot that the week following Christmas Stroll is the busiest week in real estate. Everyone who has come to enjoy the holiday charm and whimsy of the island now wants to own a piece of it.

It's Thursday when Raja calls. Eddie hopes that the reason it has taken him so long is because he has been in heated debates with Masha and has emerged victorious.

"Raja," Eddie says. "What's the good word?"

"I've given it a lot of thought," Raja says. "And I keep coming back to the piece of advice my father gave me when I got married."

"Oh, really?" Eddie says. "What was that?"

"He said, 'Happy wife, happy life.' It sounds elementary, I know, but I happen to believe those words are true."

Happy wife, happy life. Eddie has never cottoned to that phrase; he's always cast it aside into a basket of platitudes that includes *Money can't buy happiness.* Of course money *can* buy happiness; denying that makes you sound like an idealistic simpleton. And yet who has subscribed to the adage of *Happy wife, happy life* more than Eddie? He has given Grace his enthusiastic blessing to work for her former lover, just so she will be fulfilled.

"I agree with you, Raja," Eddie says. "A hundred percent."

"So I'd like to surprise Masha and buy her the inn for Christmas," Raja says. "It's what she really wants."

Eddie sighs. He hoped things wouldn't go this way, but he can't begrudge Raja for wanting to make his wife happy at Christmastime.

"I laud you for your selfless decision," Eddie says. "And I'm going to make this happen—if I can. We do already have a full-price offer on the inn, I think. I'll need to check with my colleague to see if that offer is real or just a paper tiger. Even if it is real, we may be able to go above asking. Now, this may result in a bidding war. How high are you willing to go?"

"Twenty million," Raja says. His voice contains the bravado of a man who has just pushed all of his poker chips into the center of the table.

"The inn is listed at six-five," Eddie says. "I would recommend we go in with an offer of seven million and cap it off at seven-five. The inn just isn't worth more than that under any circumstances."

"I'll pay what it takes," Raja says.

"Let me look into it and I'll get back to you in a little while," Eddie says. "Talk soon."

He approaches Glenn's desk and admires a new picture of Glenn and Barbie in the heart-shaped frame there. They're arm in arm at the Schramsberg Vineyard in Napa. Behind them is a fountain featuring a dancing frog. Eddie holds all sorts of opinions about Glenn Daley, but he has to give the guy this: he loves Barbie and treats her like a queen.

"Where are we with the supposed buyer you have for the inn?" Eddie asks. "Is he for real?"

"He's for real," Glenn says. "Wait until you hear *this* story..."

Before Glenn can tell Eddie the story, Eddie sees Allegra waving at him from her desk up front.

"Eddie," Allegra says. "Mrs. Christy is on the phone for you. Line two."

"*Mrs.* Christy?" Eddie says. "Or *Mr.* Christy?" Is it too much to hope that Raja has had an immediate change of heart?

"Missus," Allegra says.

Missus, Eddie thinks. Probably, Raja couldn't keep the secret for more than two minutes and he told Masha what he'd done, and now Masha is calling Eddie to make sure Eddie wrangles the inn away from the other buyers.

"Hold that thought, Glenn," Eddie says. "I need to sort out this mess. Why didn't I go into marriage counseling like Dr. Phil?"

"I ask myself that every day," Glenn says.

Eddie goes back to his desk and picks up line two. "Good morning, Masha," he says. "How are you?"

"Are you ready for me to make your day?" Masha asks.

Eddie closes his eyes. The only thing Masha is going to make is trouble. He can feel it. "Sure," he says.

"I've given it a lot of thought, and I've decided that I want to surprise Raja for Christmas and put an offer on that What-ever Creek Road house."

Eddie's eyes fly open and he lurches forward in his seat. "Wait a minute. What?"

"The one out in Wauwinet. The house with the pool and the home theater. I want to buy it for Raja. Full-price offer, unless you think we can get it for less."

"I think you *can* get it for less," Eddie says. Masha can probably offer twelve-five and close at twelve-eight or -nine. "Let me look at the numbers and I'll call you back in a little while, okay?"

"Okay," Masha says. "But don't tell Raja. I want him to be surprised."

"You have my word," Eddie says.

He hangs up and goes back over to Glenn's desk. "You're not going to believe this."

"Try me," Glenn says.

Barbie stands up from her desk and joins them. "I'm bored. Tell me, too."

Barbie is "bored," and yet Eddie knows that she put a five-million-dollar lot in Shimmo under agreement this morning. That's his sister for you.

"So, since the first week of November, my Powerball couple, the Christys, have been in a deadlock about what to buy. Mr. Christy wanted the house on Medouie Creek Road, and Mrs. Christy wanted the Winter Street Inn. But then, just ten minutes ago, Mr. Christy calls saying he wants to put in an offer on the Winter Street Inn to surprise his wife for Christmas."

"Aw!" Barbie says.

"But I have a buyer...," Glenn says.

Eddie holds up a finger. "Then, just now, I get a call from Mrs. Christy. She wants to put an offer on the Medouie Creek Road house as a Christmas surprise for her husband." Eddie grins. "You know what this is, right?"

"A relief," Glenn says. "Because I have a buyer for the Winter Street Inn."

"It's...it's..." Allegra has clearly been eavesdropping, and now she's snapping her fingers, looking at her father, trying to pull something out of the pocket of her brain where her schooling resides. "It's that story, that Christmas story about the couple that have no money. She cuts her hair to make money to buy him a watch chain, and he sells his watch to buy her combs."

"Exactly," Eddie says. Maybe a year at UMass Dartmouth wasn't such a waste after all. " 'The Gift of the Magi,' by O. Henry."

"It's not really like that story at all," Barbie says.

"It is a little bit," Eddie says. "Because my story, the Christys' story, is *ironic*. And, like the characters in the O. Henry story, the Christys were motivated by their love for each other and their desire to put the other person's happiness first."

"Sell the Christys the Wauwinet house," Glenn says. "I'm putting the inn under agreement with my guy." Glenn leans back in his chair. "This may not be as good a story as Eddie's, it may not be O. Henry, but it's still a story."

"We're all ears," Eddie says.

"My buyer for the Winter Street Inn is this guy who used to stay there. He stayed there for twelve years at Christmastime. So obviously this guy—George Umbrau, his name is—knows Mitzi and Kelley, and he wants to surprise them by paying full price for the inn. In cash. I guess this guy used to make hats—there's a fancy name for it, which I forget—and one of his hats showed up in *Vogue* magazine, and right away someone swooped in to buy up his hat business for eight figures. So he has the six and a half million. He says he's in no hurry; he wants Mitzi and Kelley to stay at the inn as long as they're able, and when they're ready or Mitzi is ready to move on, then he'll take over. And he says he's committed to keeping the inn exactly as it was when the Quinns ran it." Glenn puts his hands behind his head. "Now, is that guy Santa Claus, or what?"

"Santa Claus?" Eddie says, and a lightbulb goes on over his head.

AVA

Like everyone else in America in general and New York in particular, Ava spends the weeks before Christmas shopping. Only instead of shopping for presents, Ava is shopping for clothes to take to Austria!

"I feel so selfish," she tells Margaret.

"Don't," Margaret says. "This is going to be a very special trip for you, I can feel it."

How special? Ava wants to ask. Does Margaret know something Ava doesn't?

Ava and Margaret are on the third floor of Bergdorf Goodman, in couture. Margaret is buying Ava a gown to wear to the New Year's Eve ball at the palace. Initially, Ava told her mother that buying something new was unnecessary; Margaret has closets filled with gowns. Ava could simply go shopping in Margaret's closets. But Margaret insisted that this ball was worthy of a new gown, one suited and tailored to Ava's figure, coloring, and taste.

Ava tries on fourteen gowns before she finds the winner: a strapless ivory silk gown with a gold cord belt. It's a goddess dress with a blouson bodice and a forgiving amount of room in the skirt. The ivory is flattering to Ava's red hair and her complexion, and Margaret has a pair of long gold Mona Assemi earrings that Ava can borrow. They buy gold sandals with a modest heel—optimal for ballroom dancing—and a tiny gold clutch purse.

"Hair and makeup on me," Margaret says. "You're staying at the Grand Hotel Wien, right? I'll call the concierge tomorrow to set it up."

"But you're already doing so much," Ava says. "The dress, the shoes, the purse..."

"I'm lending you my fur shrug," Margaret says. "Don't let me forget to drop it off."

"And my flight," Ava says. Potter is leaving for Vienna on Tuesday, the nineteenth, because he has business to tend to before Ava arrives, he says.

"What kind of business?" Ava asked.

"I'm starting research on my Danube novel," he said.

And before Ava could express her delight—at Columbia, like everywhere else, it's publish or perish, and Potter had been talking about his Danube novel for months—he added, "And I'm arranging for some surprises for you."

Ava will fly to Vienna by herself on Thursday, the twenty-first, and Margaret has insisted on upgrading Ava's ticket to first class.

"You haven't lived until you've flown first class on an international flight," Margaret said. "Besides, I want you to arrive refreshed."

Ava feels like something might be up, something big. Her mother's insistence that this trip is special, something she will want to be fresh and ready for. Potter's tease of surprises for Ava. But Ava won't get her hopes up; she has been disappointed too many times in her life. Nathaniel "surprised" her three years earlier with a Christmas gift of Hunter boots with matching socks. And Scott "surprised" her by getting Ms. Oliveria pregnant.

Ava *wants* to believe in Potter. He did manage to fix the PJ issue—with help from Harrison. When Potter came home from California, he brought a drawing that PJ had done. The drawing showed five stick figures. PJ was in the middle, Trish and Harrison were to PJ's right, and Potter and Ava were to PJ's left. All of the figures were holding hands and the sun was shining above them.

The drawing was more than Ava could ever have hoped for. She made Potter tape it to his fridge.

"Just let me do things for you," Margaret says as she gives the woman her Bergdorf card. She takes a deep breath. "You know how odd it is that it's nearly six o'clock and I don't have to be anywhere?"

"I bet it's odd," Ava says.

"Odd in the best possible way," Margaret says. "Let's go to the café and get a cocktail."

Over the weekend Ava packs everything she'll need for the trip. She has three days left of teaching, and then Thursday she flies. She can't begin to explain how excited she is. Vienna and Salzburg at Christmas! The Mozart! The marzipan! Ava hopes that one of Potter's surprises is a *Sound of Music* tour while they're in Salzburg.

The hills are alive...!

Potter's first surprise is that he swings by Copper Hill to kiss Ava good-bye before he heads off to JFK on Tuesday. It's three o'clock and the school day is officially over, but Ava is in the conservatory with Justice DeMarco, who is working on an independent study project. Justice is composing his own ragtime piece on the piano, which is a noble pursuit, but Justice gets frustrated easily, and he feels that any direction in which he takes the chord progression sounds derivative.

"All ragtime sounds alike," Ava tells him in an attempt to be reassuring.

"But I want to create a new ragtime," Justice insists. "Ragtime a hundred years later."

It's at this point that Potter walks in. He watches Ava at work with Justice, and Ava can't help but notice the awe-struck look on his face. It's the expression of a man in love watching his girlfriend work.

"Excuse me one second, Justice," Ava says.

Justice goes back to banging out the chords while jangling out a melody with his right hand, and Ava pulls Potter behind the door to her office and gives him a juicy kiss.

"I'm really going to miss you," he says.

"It's only two days," she says. She gives Potter another kiss, longer and very inappropriate for the workplace, then she shoos him out. "Have a safe flight," she says. "Text me when you land."

"I love you," Potter says.

"And I love you," Ava says. She walks Potter out to the main hallway and waves to him until he disappears around the corner.

It's ten o'clock that night, and Ava is lying in bed listening to Schubert's Impromptu no. 3 in G-flat Major on her headphones, her eyes searching out the window for what she imagines to be the contrails of Potter's plane.

Ava's phone rings.

Potter? she wonders. It's too late for it to be anyone else. His flight was supposed to take off at 9:45. He texted to say he was boarding, then again to say he was powering down. Maybe they're delayed, sitting in an endless line of jets waiting to head to Europe, and Potter is bored and he wants to hear Ava's voice one last time.

But when she checks her phone, she sees it's Margaret calling.

"Mom?" Ava says.

"Oh, honey," Margaret says.

BART

When he and Allegra have been dating for six weeks and three days, Bart receives an e-mail from the Marine Corps, and suddenly, Bart realizes, he and Allegra have to have a conversation about the future.

He takes Allegra to dinner at the Greydon House, and they are seated at one of the tucked-away tables in the bar. The Greydon House is the new hot spot on Nantucket; Bart remembers when it was his dentist's office. It has been re-imagined as a hotel and fine restaurant. The bar is dark paneled, the lighting is low, the furniture is ornate, and the overall effect is one of an exclusive club. Allegra mentioned that she has always wanted to come here, and since Bart is now in the business of Allegra wish fulfillment, he has brought her here for dinner.

He orders a cocktail called the Grey Lady, which is served in a cod-shaped mug. Normally, he doesn't drink around Allegra, but tonight he needs to share his news and he's not sure how he's going to handle it.

"I got an e-mail today," Bart says. "I've been approved for officer training. I report to Camp Lejeune on January thirtieth."

Allegra nods slowly. "Where is Camp Lejeune?"

"It's in North Carolina," Bart says.

Allegra stares at her salad. It's baby greens with all kinds of treasures hiding—radishes, roasted beets, pumpkin seeds. Meanwhile, Bart got the lobster bisque, which the server poured out of a pewter pitcher tableside. The food here is artwork.

"So you're leaving?" Allegra says. "You're leaving Nantucket?"

Bart reaches for Allegra's hand under the table. They have been so caught up in each other, so busy enjoying the present and learning about each other's past, that the future hasn't mattered. But Bart *did* tell Allegra he wanted to go to officer training school. He told her at the very beginning, that first night at his party. Right? It seems so long ago now; Bart can't remember. Bart's positive he told her. She probably heard him but didn't think twice about it because she didn't realize they would fall so deeply, desperately in love.

They've been together six weeks. Six weeks from now Bart is leaving for North Carolina.

"I want you to come with me," he says.

"You do?" she says.

"I do. You can live with me on the base. You can get a job. You can take real estate classes. We can be together."

Allegra hunts through her salad like she's looking for the answer there. Bart is waiting for her to say she won't go or can't go or she doesn't want to. She's happy on Nantucket, she has a job, she's comfortable. Bart will try to explain that being *uncomfortable* is what helps you to grow. Allegra needs to leave Nantucket and get out of her parents' house— maybe even more than Bart does.

Bart is so sure that Allegra is the woman for him that he won't be told otherwise. Over Thanksgiving, Patrick pulled him aside and told him to "be careful." Patrick said that things between Bart and Allegra seemed to be moving "a little fast."

Patrick said, "Dad can't exactly give you advice, so I'm going to."

Bart was even-keeled with Patrick instead of punching his lights out, which was what Bart wanted to do. Patrick had always been Bart's favorite brother, and all the times when Patrick had acted as a surrogate father, Bart had been grateful. Paddy was younger than Kelley, and way cooler. But Bart is a

grown man now. He has endured things Patrick can't fathom.
Bart isn't going to have Paddy tell him how to live his life.

Patrick does have a good marriage. Bart will give him that.

Long ago Kelley told Bart way more than Bart wanted to
know about Kelley's own marriages. Kelley and Margaret had
loved each other, but they had lived in a pressure cooker. "It
was Manhattan in the nineties," Kelley said by way of explanation, but Bart had no idea what that meant. Ultimately, the
relationship had proven unsustainable. "That sometimes happens when you get married too young," Kelley said.

Bart is sensible enough to realize that his relationship
with Allegra might not pan out. Allegra might be miserable,
unfulfilled; she might prefer one of Bart's superiors—or
subordinates—to Bart. He knows there are risks. But he also
knows that some relationships between young people *do*
weather the storm. It takes hard work, dedication—and good
luck. Bart feels like he's due some good luck; he has had
enough bad luck to last a lifetime.

If Allegra refuses, will Bart leave anyway? Will he say
good-bye to this girl, this new love, this person who is rapidly becoming Bart's best friend on top of everything else?

No. He'll stay. He won't want to, but he will stay on Nantucket for Allegra.

Allegra smiles at him. "I feel like my parents will say it's
too soon. They'll say we barely know each other..."

"It is soon, I realize that," Bart says.

"But I don't care!" Allegra says. "I'll go with you wherever you want. North Carolina, Alaska, Germany, Mars."

"You will?" Bart says.

"Yes," Allegra says. "I will."

Bart drops Allegra off that night, then sits outside her house
on Lily Street until he sees the light go off in her bedroom.

He is so happy he's dizzy. Allegra will come with him. He doesn't have to be alone ever again.

Bart floats up the side steps of the inn until he smells smoke and sees the glowing tip of his mother's cigarette in the dark.

He can't wait to tell Mitzi the news. It will make her so happy. "Mom?" he says.

As he gets closer, he hears Mitzi crying. "We're losing him," she says.

MARGARET

This year Margaret is all about Christmastime.

She buys a tree from the Korean deli on the corner. It's small, but it's the first tree Margaret has owned since she and Kelley and the kids left the brownstone on East Eighty-Eighth Street.

Of course, one can't buy only a tree, Margaret realizes, once her doorman helps her get it upstairs. She has to buy a stand. And lights. And ornaments. She goes to Duane Reade but keeps her sunglasses on in the store so as not to be recognized. It's far worse being recognized now than it ever was when she was working. First of all, when she was working, she rarely ventured out on the street to do everyday errands like this. Second of all, the general population of New York seemed cognizant of the fact that Margaret Quinn was busy and therefore not to be interrupted for photos, political opinion sharing, or reminiscing. Now that Margaret is retired, she has become fair game. When people recognize her, they want to stop and tell her how much they loved her broadcasts, how much she meant to them, how the "new girl" has an annoying lisp. Then they start to talk about Trump, and this is when Margaret always excuses herself.

She gets a tree stand at Duane Reade as well as a box of four hundred white lights. She inspects the boxes of ornaments, but the offerings look sad and cheap. New York is the center of gross consumerism. Surely there must be a store—or many stores—dedicated solely to Christmas ornaments.

It's Always Christmas in New York, on Mulberry Street down in Little Italy, Google tells her. And the Christmas Cottage, on Seventh Avenue.

The next day at the Christmas Cottage, Margaret fills her basket with ornaments. She and Kelley used to collect ornaments when they traveled, and they added those to the ornaments Kelley inherited from his mother, Frances, in Perrysburg and Margaret's from her family. They topped the tree with the angel they had bought from the shop at the Metropolitan Museum of Art, commemorating the day they met. That's how one is supposed to acquire ornaments, Margaret thinks: bit by bit, with each ornament telling a story.

But oh well! Whatever ornaments Margaret used to have went with Kelley to Nantucket. And she and Drake need ornaments, so Margaret continues to pick and choose the prettiest, most tasteful ornaments she can find. The story behind all of these ornaments will be the same: *These are the ornaments I bought at Christmas Cottage on Seventh Avenue once I retired from CBS and rediscovered Christmas.*

That very same afternoon Margaret decides that she is going to string popcorn and cranberries into a garland. She figures out how to do this using Martha Stewart's website. Martha Stewart is a goddess, Margaret realizes. The breadth and depth of her empire takes one's breath away.

The garland requires another trip to Duane Reade—for

fishing line and a sewing kit—as well as a trip to Gristedes for the popcorn, cranberries, and vegetable oil. Nope, forget the popcorn and oil; Margaret buys two packages of Jiffy Pop instead. She has fond memories of watching the foil dome rise over Melanie Jerrod's hot plate in the dorm at the University of Michigan.

By the time Drake gets home from the hospital that night, Margaret has made two pans of Jiffy Pop, which when combined with two bags of cranberries, yielded thirty feet of garland. She poked herself with the needle innumerable times, but the garland looks just as it is supposed to. Margaret has Johnny Mathis carols playing, and for supper she has made a pot of cheese fondue! Not only did she carefully melt the Gruyère, Emmenthaler, wine, and kirsch, she also cubed and toasted a baguette and sliced up summer sausage for dipping. The recipe for fondue was also on Martha's website. It suggested drinking a crisp Riesling, as the dryness of the wine offsets the richness of the fondue.

"Look!" Margaret says as she hands Drake a chilled glass of Riesling. "I made garland. And I bought ornaments! We can decorate the tree, then eat."

"I can't believe this," Drake says. "You were so productive today."

"Wasn't I?" Margaret says. It's astonishing how much one can accomplish when one doesn't have to work. And Margaret didn't check the news all day, not even once.

Margaret dedicates the next few days to shopping for her kids and grandkids, for Mitzi, for Kelley, and for Drake. In years past Margaret had her assistant, Darcy, pick out everyone's gifts, but it's so much more fun to do it herself. She is in the spirit!

On Friday afternoon Margaret goes gown shopping with Ava at Bergdorf's. Margaret doesn't say this out loud, but she hopes it's only a matter of time before they're shopping for a wedding dress.

Over the weekend Margaret turns her vision outward. Saturday afternoon she sits in a warehouse on the Lower East Side of Manhattan for four hours and wraps presents for Toys for Tots. Margaret herself donated nearly a thousand dollars' worth of toys, but when she sees the list of children who wouldn't get anything for Christmas were it not for this worthy program, she nearly cries. There are pages and pages of names.

Ezekiel, age six.

Marco, age nine.

Patrick, age ten. *There's a Patrick,* Margaret thinks. And there's probably also a Kevin and an Ava, children like her own, children who will now find something beautifully wrapped under the tree.

Margaret has never learned how to properly wrap a present, and so she serves as tape maiden to a wrapper named Nell for the first hour. Then Nell takes mercy on Margaret and gives her a quick wrapping tutorial.

Margaret spends Sunday morning telling Drake how wonderful it felt to actually do some good.

"I wasn't sitting at a ten-thousand-dollar table eating rubber chicken at a charity benefit," she says. "It was real. I was wrapping presents for Ezekiel and Marco and Patrick. I think I'm going to find a soup kitchen next."

"Why don't you come to the hospital and read to the kids?" Drake says. "I'll let them know tomorrow, and you can plan to come on Tuesday. I don't know if anyone has ever told you this, but you have a lovely speaking voice."

"Yes!" Margaret says. She can't believe she never thought of this before! She'll go to Books of Wonder, buy some Christmas storybooks, and read them to the children on the pediatric oncology ward at Sloan Kettering.

*   *   *

Tuesday is one of the most memorable days of Margaret's life. She brings four picture books to the children's cancer ward. Two are Toot & Puddle Christmas books by Holly Hobbie. Toot and Puddle are pigs who live in a place called Woodcock Pocket. Toot is an adventurous pig, and Puddle is a homebody. They are best friends, kind of like Ernie and Bert. Margaret has been a fan of these books since Barrett, her oldest grandson, was small. She loves the art, the quaintness of life at Woodcock Pocket, and the inherent kindness and good judgment displayed by Toot and Puddle.

Margaret has also brought *Olivia Helps with Christmas*—another pig! This one is female and headstrong. The Olivia books were written and illustrated by Ian Falconer, who is also one of Margaret's favorite cartoonists for the *New Yorker.* And the last book is *'Twas the Fright Before Christmas,* which is a brilliant amalgam of Halloween and Christmas, told in clever rhyme.

Only five children are well enough to come to story time: Hayden, Christopher, Madison, Jayquan, and Gladys.

Gladys? Margaret thinks. Gladys is five years old. Everything old is new again.

The children seem to like the stories—*Fright* is the big favorite, no surprise there—and Margaret marvels at how kids act like kids no matter how sick they are. Hayden, Madison, and Jayquan have lost their hair, and Gladys is hooked up to an IV. But they laugh and stand up to get a closer look at the pictures. Christo falls asleep, then wakes up with renewed energy.

After the stories Margaret meets the parents. They all want autographs and photos with Margaret. Jayquan's mother, Aileen, says that she first saw Margaret reporting on September 11. Aileen was fourteen years old, a freshman at

Benjamin Cardozo High School. On that day, Aileen says, Margaret became her hero.

Aileen is now Margaret's hero. To have a child this sick is one of the greatest burdens a parent can bear. How do these parents do it? How do they endure? How do they keep upbeat, optimistic, smiling? How do they keep from breaking?

They do what they have to do, Margaret supposes. Her children were all healthy, but if one of them had been sick, Margaret would have made the necessary sacrifices. She would have done whatever it took to get her child well again. Margaret hugs Aileen extra tight and gives Aileen her personal e-mail address.

Drake meets Margaret just outside the ward. "Let me take you to dinner," he says.

"No," Margaret says. "I want to eat here."

"Here?" Drake says. "At the hospital?"

Margaret isn't sure how to explain it. She wants to stay at the hospital until she's sure that her five new friends are asleep. If she could, she would like to tuck them all in. "Please?" she says.

"Okay," Drake says. He leads Margaret down to the cafeteria. There is one artificial tree decorated with paper snowflakes, and one rather sad-looking menorah. They walk through the food line listening to piped-in Christmas music—Straight No Chaser singing "The Christmas Can-Can," which Margaret thinks is catchy. Margaret gets a tuna fish sandwich and a bowl of vegetable soup, and Drake gets the chicken pot pie. They sit down at a table, and Margaret studies the other people eating, many of them with slumped shoulders and hollow eyes.

"How do you do it?" she asks Drake. "How do you keep from getting emotionally involved? How do you keep from falling in love with every single child?"

"It's difficult," Drake says. "But then I remind myself that they don't need me to love them. They need me to be their doctor, to operate, to make them better."

As Margaret processes this, her phone rings. She checks the display.

"It's Mitzi," Margaret tells Drake.

"Answer it," he says.

But Margaret doesn't want to answer it. There's only one reason why Mitzi would be calling now, so late at night. It's after nine.

Maybe Mitzi just wants gift ideas for the kids, Margaret thinks. That's feasible.

"Answer it," Drake says again.

"Hello?" Margaret says.

"Margaret," Mitzi says. "We're losing him."

"No," Margaret says. She closes her eyes. Lou Rawls sings "Have Yourself a Merry Little Christmas." "No, Mitzi."

"Dr. Cherith was just here. And Lara, the hospice nurse. They think he only has a couple of days left. He's not going to make it to Christmas."

"No," Margaret says. Her eyes flood with tears. Drake reaches for her hand.

"Can you call the kids and tell them?" Mitzi asks. "Patrick and Ava? Kevin was here just a little while ago, so he knows. But would you call the other two for me, please?"

"I think it should come from you," Margaret says. "You're his wife."

"You're their mother," Mitzi says. Margaret hears a familiar hardness in her tone. It's back to their old territorial war—who is what to whom. "I need you to do this for me, please. Just call and tell them they have two days, three at the most, if they want to see him."

"Yes, okay," Margaret says. "I'll call them. And Drake

and I will leave tomorrow night after Drake's last surgery. We'll drive through the night if we have to."

"Thank you, Margaret," Mitzi says, and she hangs up.

Margaret will call Ava first, she decides. Ava can drive up to Nantucket with Margaret and Drake tomorrow night if she wants.

Then Margaret gasps. *Austria!*

Oh, sweet child, she thinks.

She dials Ava's number.

KELLEY

Sight gone now in both his eyes. Hearing gone in one ear. He can make noises but no longer speak. He sees his mother, Frances. His brother, Avery. A kid with Popeye biceps and a Southern twang sticks out a hand and says, *Nice to meet you, Mr. Quinn. I'm Centaur.*

Centaur? Kelley says. *That's your name?*

The kid vanishes.

Kelley is very tired.

Is it Christmas yet? Kelley wanted to make it to Christmas. But Kelley would also like to be granted permission to let go.

Mitzi's voice. "George bought the inn, sweetheart. He paid the full listing price. He says we can stay as long as we want. He says he won't change a thing. He and Mary Rose are going to keep it just like it's always been. Isn't that good news?"

George? Kelley thinks. *Who is this George person who bought the inn?*

Then he thinks: *Oh. George.* Kelley has some vague protest, but he can't possibly articulate it.

He punched George once, right in the kisser. George had deserved it.

George will do a great job of running the inn, Kelley decides.

Mitzi's voice. "Potter is on the phone. He has something he wants to ask you."

Mitzi sounds coy. Who is Potter? Harry Potter? Kelley made it through the first book only.

"I'll give him your blessing," Mitzi says. "Our blessing."

Is it Christmas yet?

He feels someone rubbing his feet. Lara, not Laura.

Kevin's voice. "I love you, Dad."

A tiny, soft hand on his cheek. Genevieve!

Isabelle says something in French. Kelley remembers the puzzled look on Isabelle's face seconds after Kelley found Mitzi and George kissing in room 10.

George is buying the inn.

Mitzi's voice. "It's December twenty-first. The winter solstice," she says. "It's the shortest day of the year. It'll be dark by quarter past four. So dark, so early."

Mitzi touches his face. "It's okay, Kelley," she says. "We are all going to be okay."

It's permission, he realizes. He can let go.

It's the winter solstice.

Do you know what the best thing about the winter solstice is? he wants to tell Mitzi.

After today the days will get longer.

AVA

Both her mother and Mitzi give her a pass. By the time she gets to Nantucket, Kelley may well be unconscious. He'll never know if Ava is there or not. She should go to Austria like she planned.

"Your father would want you to be happy," Mitzi says.

Kelley may never know, but Ava will know. He's her father. Her spirit sinks at the thought of missing Austria, a place she has always wanted to go at the most magical time of year with the man she loves. Potter is still on the plane. She will call him in the morning and tell him she won't be joining him.

In the morning she has a text from Potter that says: *Landed safely. Checking into hotel and crashing.* Ava tries calling him, but she gets his voice mail. She calls the hotel, and they put her through to the room but there's no answer. He must be sound asleep.

She sends a text that says: *My father has a day or two left. I have to go to Nantucket tonight. I love you.*

And then she sends a second text that says: *I'm so sorry.*

Ava goes to school to teach. Her mother and Drake are leaving the city at seven o'clock, but Ava doesn't want to wait that long. She books a five o'clock flight to Boston and squeezes herself onto the last flight from Boston to Nantucket on Cape Air.

Austria will always be there, she thinks. She feels bad about abandoning Potter at Christmastime, but he is a good person; he will think she's making the right decision. Potter's parents were killed in a car accident; he never got to say good-bye.

*   *   *

She tries not to think about Potter or Austria or Kelley or a world without Kelley; she doesn't respond to any of the texts between Patrick, Kevin, and Bart discussing travel plans. She focuses only on logistics: Uber to JFK, the hour-long flight from JFK to Boston, the walk through Terminal C to gate 27, home of Cape Air. Ava has an hour before her flight to Nantucket. She can finally relax.

Wine, she thinks.

She sees an empty chair at the bar right next to gate 27.

"Is anyone sitting here?" she asks the guy on the neighboring stool.

He turns. They lock eyes.

Not happening, she thinks.

"Ava," he says, and he gives her that familiar wicked grin. It's Nathaniel.

"What?" she says. "Are you ... ?"

"I'm going back to Nantucket for Christmas," he says. "My parents are taking everyone skiing in Tahoe, but I fell off a ladder this fall and tweaked my back, so I can't ski. Plus, I can only take four or five days away, so I thought I'd just go back home. Hang at the brewery the whole time, probably. See some friends. In fact, you know who I'm supposed to see tomorrow night is your old friend Scott Skyler."

"Scott?" Ava says.

"I said I'd help him serve the holiday dinner at Our Island Home, then we're going out drinking." Nathaniel arches his eyebrows. "You could come!"

No, thanks, Ava thinks.

"We could surprise Scott. I show up, bring you along. He'll flip. You know that other chick, the English teacher? She really put him through the wringer. She's sixteen kinds of crazy."

"Roxanne," Ava says.

"I'm meeting him at five tomorrow," Nathaniel says. "Early bird special and all that. I can pick you up."

Ava signals the bartender and orders a glass of wine. "I'd love to," she says. This isn't remotely true. The last thing she wants to do is climb aboard the same old merry-go-round with Nathaniel and Scott. Ava can't believe they're friends now, friends who make plans together! "But I can't. My father is very, very sick." Her wine arrives in the nick of time, because Ava feels tears building and the last thing she wants to do is cry in front of Nathaniel, thereby giving him reason to comfort her. She clears her throat. "I'm going home to say good-bye."

"Good-bye?" Nathaniel says. "Is he that sick?"

Ava nods. "Brain cancer. He's got... a day or two left, I guess."

"Oh no, Ava. I'm sorry. I didn't know."

"Please," she says. "Let's change the subject."

"Okay," Nathaniel says. "Let's see... you live in New York now. How do you like it? Are you still dating the ridiculously handsome guy I met last Christmas?"

"Potter," Ava says. "Yes." She holds up a finger and rummages through her bag for her phone. There is one missed call from Potter but no voice mail and no text.

At that instant the seven-fifteen flight to Nantucket is called.

"There's our chariot," Nathaniel says. He plunks some money down on the bar. "I've got your wine."

"No," she says.

"Ava," he says. He touches her cheek. "It's me."

Ava spends forty-five minutes in the dark cabin of the Cessna staring at the back of Nathaniel's head. She thinks about the years they were together, how crazy in love she was. Nathaniel was always just out of her reach in those days. Three years ago at Christmas he went back to Connecticut and got entangled with his high school girlfriend. He broke Ava's heart. Then, when Ava started dating Scott, Nathaniel came back with a vengeance. He proposed, even.

But it had never been right with Nathaniel. It had never been real.

And Scott...Ava's relationship with Scott was more viable. She thought they might end up together—but then he flaked out. Scott Skyler was the biggest disappointment of Ava's life, a far bigger disappointment than Nathaniel because Nathaniel had been so unreliable to begin with.

Ava can't believe the two of them are now friends. She hopes they'll be very happy together.

She loves Potter. She misses Potter.

When they land at Nantucket Airport, Nathaniel says, "Do you want to share a taxi?"

"Kevin is picking me up," Ava says.

Nathaniel says, "I'm sorry about your dad, Ava. Call me if you need me."

Ava smiles. If there's one thing she knows for sure, it's that she won't need Nathaniel Oscar. "I will," she says.

The inn is quiet when Ava gets home, and all of the lights are out except for the lights on the tree, the mantel, and the wreath. It's pretty in the living room and it smells good. There's the usual glass canister filled with ribbon candy, that old deceiver—looks so alluring, tastes so terrible.

Ava longs to sit down at the piano and play some carols, something soothing—"O Little Town of Bethlehem" or "Away in a Manger"—but she doesn't want to wake Kelley or disturb the peace of the house. She'll see everyone in the morning.

She tries calling Potter one more time before she goes to bed, but she gets no answer.

Paddy arrives at eleven the next day with Jennifer and the boys, and Margaret and Drake come at noon. Kevin goes to Sophie T's for pizzas, and Jennifer sets up Monopoly in the kitchen. Bart, Allegra, and the three boys play, and Drake agrees to serve as banker. Ava knows the game is meant as a distraction. They're having a vigil. They're waiting for Kelley to die.

Patrick and Kevin are talking about how George is buying the inn. The terms are incredibly favorable—Mitzi can stay for as long as she wants. And George plans to keep everything the same, so for as long as George and Mary Rose have tenure, the Winter Street Inn will live on.

"It sounds like a gesture on his part," Kevin says. "An atonement, maybe, for getting involved with Mitzi."

Ava can't get wrapped up with the fate of the inn. She's still waiting to hear from Potter. She eats a piece of sausage and mushroom pizza; she watches her nephew Pierce put up hotels on St. James Place and Tennessee Avenue. Ava's favorite property was always Marvin Gardens; she wonders why that was.

Finally her phone pings. Ava checks the screen. The text is from Scott Skyler. It says: *Nathaniel just told me about your dad. I'm on my way over right now.*

"No," Ava says.

Everyone at the table looks up at her. She fakes a smile. "I'm going to my room to take a nap. I don't want to be disturbed for any reason. Except if Dad wakes up. That's the *only* reason. Is everyone clear on that?"

"Clear," Drake says. "Allegra, it's your turn."

Allegra rolls the dice.

*   *   *

Ava must fall asleep, because the next thing she knows, someone is tapping on her door. She sits up. It's getting dark outside, but that doesn't mean it's late; today is the shortest day of the year.

"Come in?" Ava says.

Margaret pokes her head in. "Ava, sweetie?"

Ava starts to cry. Kelley must be awake, and they've agreed they will go see him in reverse order of birth. Bart first, then Ava, then Kevin, then Patrick. *See him,* however, is merely a euphemism for *say good-bye,* and Ava can't say good-bye to her father.

She just can't.

"Mommy?" Ava says. Margaret is a competent, strong woman; she is a fixer. She needs to fix this. *Let's go back,* Ava thinks. Back to Ava's first memory of Kelley, of her parents together. She was three or four years old. Kelley came home from work and Margaret embraced him. They were kissing, and Ava made a tunnel of their legs and crawled through.

"There's someone here for you," Margaret says. "Can you come out, please?"

Someone here for her? Scott! Ugh! Margaret wasn't in the kitchen when Ava said she didn't want to be disturbed, and for whatever reason, Margaret has always been a fan of Scott.

"I don't want to," Ava grumbles.

"Oh, I think you do," Margaret says.

Dutifully, Ava gets to her feet and follows Margaret down the hall.

The living room is empty. Everyone is in the kitchen; from the sound of things, Ava's nephew Barrett is going bankrupt.

And then Ava sees Potter, standing over by the Christmas

tree. He gets down on one knee and holds out a velvet box, in which is nestled a diamond ring.

"Ava Quinn," he says. "Will you marry me?"

When the time comes, an hour later, for Ava to go in and see her father, she does so alone, with the ring on her left hand.

She sits in the chair next to Kelley's bed. Kelley's eyes are open, but Ava knows he can't see anymore. Mitzi is on the other side of the bed, holding Kelley's hand.

"It's Ava, honey," Mitzi says. "Ava is here. She has something to tell you."

"I'm getting married, Daddy," Ava says. "Potter asked me to marry him, and I said yes." Ava holds Kelley's other hand and tries not to think about walking down the aisle without this man at her side. She gets to have this moment with him; she gets to tell him the news. She is grateful for this, so grateful.

Kelley makes a sound. Maybe it's a breath or a sigh, Ava thinks, but maybe he's trying to speak.

I'm so happy for you, Ava. My little girl.

"I love you, Daddy," Ava says.

She squeezes his hand, and a trace of a smile crosses Kelley's lips.

MARGARET

Time remains a mystery to Margaret. A game of Monopoly can consume an afternoon, and an hour on the treadmill seems like forever. But a lifetime passes in an instant.

On Thursday evening Lara, the hospice nurse, comes into the kitchen.

"It won't be long now," she says.

Margaret stands in the hallway outside of Kelley's room as first Bart, then Ava, then Kevin, and finally Patrick go in to say good-bye to their father. Margaret has witnessed all kinds of difficult things in her life, but nothing quite as difficult as seeing her grown children crying when they emerge from the room.

When Patrick comes out, he says, "It's your turn, Mom."

Margaret didn't think she would take a turn. It seems selfish and maybe even improper. Mitzi is in the room, at Kelley's bedside, where she should be. She's his wife. Margaret is... who is Margaret to Kelley anymore? His former wife? The mother of his three older children?

His best friend, she thinks. She has known him longer than anyone.

Drake appears beside her. The Monopoly game must have finally ended. As if reading the indecision on Margaret's face, Drake says, "Go in and say good-bye. You'll regret it if you don't."

Margaret nods. He's right, of course. She cracks open the door and sees Mitzi standing by the bed, holding Kelley's hand, staring lovingly at his face.

"Is he awake?" Margaret asks. "Or... ?"

Mitzi nods and beckons Margaret forward.

"He asked for you," Mitzi says.

He did? Margaret thinks. Kelley can no longer speak, so it's not likely he "asked" for Margaret, but Margaret is grateful for the lie, or the exaggeration, or the intuition. Maybe Mitzi feels that if Kelley could talk, he would ask to see Margaret. In some strange way, this whole story—the inn, the kids, even his marriage to Mitzi—started back in New York City on the day that Kelley and Margaret met.

Margaret leans down so that her voice is in Kelley's ear.

"Hey there, old friend," she says. "It's Maggie. I just want to say..." Here, Margaret chokes up. She takes a moment to compose herself and squeezes Kelley's hand. "I want to say thank you, Kelley Quinn. For all the years we had. For our three remarkable, miraculous children. And for your love. Because despite everything, there was always love."

Kelley's eyelids flutter.

Margaret kisses Kelley's cheek, then she releases his hand. She backs up a step at a time, and she watches as Mitzi climbs into the hospital bed with Kelley and rests her head on his chest.

She's going to hold him until he passes, Margaret thinks. It's beautiful and right—but it's also really, really sad. Tears flow silently down Margaret's face.

Drake is standing in the open doorway, waiting for her. He puts an arm around her shoulder, but he knows not to rush her out. She looks into Drake's eyes.

"I never thought it would end," she says.

"I know," Drake says.

But *does* he know? Margaret turns to take one last look at Kelley, but the person she sees in the bed is herself, in the moments after she gave birth to Patrick. The baby had just been laid on Margaret's chest, and Kelley was next to her, both beaming and weeping.

"We have a son, Maggie," he said. "A healthy baby boy."

Margaret remembers how it felt to hold a newborn, the love expanding inside her until she was sure she would burst. Life seemed like a golden ribbon, unspooling into eternity. They were parents. It was all just beginning.

"Come to bed," Drake says.

"Yes," Margaret says. "Okay." She knows it's the right thing to do. She follows Drake out into the hallway and closes the door behind her, leaving Kelley and Mitzi in peace.

ACKNOWLEDGMENTS

Here is the true and crazy story of the Winter Street series.

In the summer of 2013, the folks at Little, Brown called to say they had had a book fall off their holiday list and they wondered if I could write a Christmas book in four weeks. At that time, I was in the middle of writing *The Matchmaker,* which, as some of you know, is an emotionally wrenching novel, and not wanting to get distracted, I said no. I was intrigued, however, by the idea of a Christmas novel, and so I assured them that I would write one the following year. I came up with an idea for a Christmas trilogy, set at an inn, featuring a blended family with a lot of issues. (A *lot* of issues.) I wanted to title the first book in this trilogy *Christmas with the Quinns.*

Not only did no one at Little, Brown love my title, they weren't keen on the idea of a trilogy. I couldn't blame them: I was an unproven quantity in the holiday market, and they wanted to test the waters to see how a Christmas novel written by the "queen of the summer read" would sell. I handed in a manuscript for *Winter Street* (which is an actual street on Nantucket, although there is no inn and I'm fairly certain the real residents of the real Winter Street now have people peering in their windows. Sorry!), but I had intentionally given it a cliffhanger ending. And voilà! A contract for two more books appeared.

The ultimate irony took place in the summer of 2016 when my editor, Reagan Arthur, called to ask if I would be willing to write a *fourth* Winter Street book. A fourth book in the trilogy? I felt I had tied everything up at the end of *Winter Storms,* but after I gave it some careful consideration, I realized I could write a "double sequel" and include some of the characters from *The Rumor* and weave their stories together.

And so, we have my editor, Reagan Arthur, to thank for this book, which was, in the end, a pure joy to write. I have dedicated this novel to her not only because she is responsible for its existence but also because she is the secret of my success. This is the fifteenth novel I have done with Reagan as my editor. Her sensibility is the one I hold in the highest regard; her opinion is the one I consider above all others. She is always right, and the past fifteen novels of mine have been made better—so much better!—because of the platinum standard of her editing.

I will confide here that my favorite character has always been Margaret Quinn and that my inspiration for her is/was the guilt that I myself feel because my career requires me to spend so much time away from my children. I, like Margaret, have two boys and a girl. It is the plight of working mothers everywhere, I suppose, to try and do two jobs at once. I decided that one way to make myself feel better was to make Margaret a hero; in the first novel, *Winter Street,* she saves the day. Hopefully, I have also conveyed her humanity so that every working mother can see a bit of herself in Margaret.

As always, I want to thank my family and my friends-who-are-like-family: you know who you are (after so many books, everyone else knows who you are, too!). Of special note is my darling pal Elizabeth Almodobar, who shared the Nantucket real estate stories that got my imagination fired up.

I wrote two thirds of this novel on the island of St. John USVI, a second island which has become not only home to me but also a sanctuary. For those of you who are lamenting the end of the Winter Street series, I have (possibly) happy news. I will write a new trilogy set on the island of St. John coming to you in the fall/winter of 2018. I only hope I can do justice to that breathtaking island and all of the fascinating people who live there.

Thank you to all of my fans and devoted readers who have followed along with the Quinns the past few years. Some of you have said you love these novels best of all my work, and in some sense, I do as well. The Quinns will always be dear to me, and they will live on in my mind and in my heart.

In closing, I would like to thank my children: Maxwell, Dawson, and Shelby. The older you get, the more you amaze me with your talents, your gifts, and your innate kindness. How did I get so lucky? Being your mother is an honor. You make every day feel like Christmas. (Okay, *nearly* every day.) I love you.

ABOUT THE AUTHOR

Elin Hilderbrand, the mother of three 3-sport athletes, is an aspiring fashionista, a dedicated jogger, a world explorer, an enthusiastic foodie, and a grateful three-year breast cancer survivor. She has called Nantucket Island her home since 1994. *Winter Solstice* is her twentieth novel.

...AND *WINTER IN PARADISE*

Irene Steele's idyllic life—house, husband, family—is shattered when she is woken up by a late-night phone call. Her beloved husband has been found dead, but before Irene can process this tragic news, she must confront the perplexing details of her husband's death.

Following is an excerpt from the novel's opening pages.

IRENE: IOWA CITY

It's the first night of the new year.

Irene Steele has spent the day in a state of focused productivity. From nine to one, she filed away every piece of paperwork relating to the complete moth-to-butterfly renovation of her 1892 Queen Anne–style home on Church Street. From one to two, she ate a thick sandwich, chicken salad on pumpernickel (she has always been naturally slender, luckily, so no New Year's diets for her), and then she took a short nap on the velvet fainting couch in front of the fire in the parlor. From two fifteen to three-thirty, she composed an email response to her boss, Joseph Feeney, the publisher of *Heartland Home & Style* magazine, who two days earlier had informed her that she was being "promoted" from editor in chief of the magazine to executive editor, a newly created position that reduces both Irene's hours and responsibilities by half and comes with a 30 percent pay cut.

At a quarter of four, she tried calling her husband, Russ, who was away on business. The phone rang six times and went to voicemail. Irene didn't leave a message. Russ never listened to them, anyway.

She tried Russ again at four thirty and was shuttled *straight* to voicemail. She paused, then hung up. Russ was on his phone night and day. Irene wondered if he was intentionally avoiding her call. He might have been upset about their conversation the day before, but first thing this morning, a lavish bouquet of snow-white calla lilies had been delivered to the door with a note: *Because you love callas and I love you. Xo R.* Irene had been delighted; there was nothing like fresh flowers to brighten a house in winter. She was amazed that Russ had been able to find someone who would deliver on the holiday, but his ingenuity knew no bounds.

At five o'clock, Irene poured herself a generous glass of Kendall-Jackson chardonnay, took a shower, and put on the silk and cashmere color-block sweater and black crepe slim pants from Eileen Fisher that Russ had given her for Christmas. She bundled up in her shearling coat, earmuffs, and calfskin leather gloves to walk the four blocks through Iowa City to meet her best friend, esteemed American history professor Lydia Christensen, at the Pullman Bar & Diner.

The New Year's Day dinner is a tradition going into its seventh year. It started when Lydia got divorced from her philandering husband, Philip, and Russ's travel schedule went from "nearly all the time" to "all the time." The dinner is supposed to be a positive, life-affirming ritual: Irene and Lydia count their many, many blessings—this friendship near the top of the list—and state their aspirations for the twelve months ahead. But Irene and Lydia are only human, and so their conversation sometimes lapses into predictable lamentation. The greatest unfairness in this world, according to Lydia, is that men get sexier and better-looking as they get older and women...don't. They just don't.

"The CIA should hire women in their fifties," Lydia says. "We're invisible."

"Would you ladies like more wine?" Ryan, the server, asks.

"Yes, please!" Irene says with her brightest smile. Is *she* invisible? A week ago, she wouldn't have thought so, but news of her "promotion" makes her think maybe Lydia is right. Joseph Feeney is sliding Irene down the masthead (and hoping she won't notice that's what he's doing) and replacing her with Mavis Key, a thirty-one-year-old dynamo who left a high-powered interior design firm in Manhattan to follow her husband to Cedar Rapids. She came waltzing into the magazine's offices only eight months ago with her shiny, sexy résumé, and all of a sudden, Joseph wants the magazine to be more city-slick and sophisticated. He wants to shift attention and resources from the physical magazine to their online version, and, using Mavis Key's expertise, he wants to create a "social media presence." Irene stands in firm opposition. Teenagers and millennials use social media, but the demographic of *Heartland Home & Style* is women 39–65, which also happens to be Irene's demographic. Those readers want magazines they can *hold,* glossies they can page through and coo over at the dentist's office; they want features that reflect the cozy, bread-and-butter values of the Midwest.

Irene's sudden, unexpected, and unwanted "promotion" makes Irene feel like a fuddy-duddy in Mom jeans. It makes her feel completely irrelevant. She will be invited to meetings, the less important ones, but her opinion will be disregarded. She will review layout and content, but no changes will be made. She will visit people in their offices, take advertisers out to lunch, and chat. She has been reduced to a figurehead, a mascot, a pet.

Irene gazes up at Ryan as he fills their glasses with buttery Chardonnay—the Cakebread, a splurge—and wonders what he sees when he looks at them. Does he see two vague, female-shaped outlines, the kind that detectives spray-paint around dead bodies? Or does he see two vibrant, interesting, desirable women of a certain age?

Okay, scratch desirable. Ryan, Irene knows (because she eats at the Pullman Bar & Diner at least once a week while Russ is away), is twenty-five years old, working on his graduate degree in applied mathematics, though he doesn't look like any mathematician Irene has ever imagined. He looks like one of the famous Ryans—Ryan Seacrest, Ryan Gosling. Ryan O'Neal.

Ryan *O'Neal?* Now she really *is* aging herself!

Irene has been known to indulge Lydia when she boards the Woe-Is-Me train, but she decides not to do it this evening. "I don't feel invisible," she says. She leans across the table. "In fact, I've been thinking of running for office."

Lydia shrieks like Irene zapped her on the flank with a cattle prod. "What? What do you mean 'run for office'? You mean *Congress*? Or just, like, the Iowa City School Board?"

Irene had been thinking Congress, though when the word comes out of Lydia's mouth, it sounds absurd. Irene knows *nothing* about politics. Not one thing. But as the (former) editor in chief of *Heartland Home & Style* magazine, she knows a lot about getting things done. On a deadline. And she knows about listening to other people's point of view and dealing with difficult personalities. Oh, does she.

"Maybe not run for office," Irene says. "But I need something else." She doesn't want to go into her demotion-disguised-as-promotion right now; the pain is still too fresh.

"*I* need something else," Lydia says. "I need a single man, straight, between the ages of fifty-five and seventy, over six feet tall, with a six-figure income and a sizable IRA. Oh, and a sense of humor. Oh, and hobbies that include grocery shopping, doing the dishes, and folding laundry."

Irene shakes her head. "A man isn't going to solve your

problems, Lydia. Didn't we learn that in our consciousness-raising group decades ago?"

"A man *will* solve my problems, because my problem is that I've got no man," Lydia says. She throws back what's left of her wine. "You wouldn't understand because you have Russ, who dotes on you night and day."

"When he's around," Irene says. She knows her complaints fall on deaf ears. Russ joined the Husband Hall of Fame seven years earlier when he hired a barnstormer plane to circle Iowa City dragging a banner that said: *Happy 50th Irene Steele. I love you!* Irene's friends had been awestruck, but Irene found the showiness of the birthday wishes a bit off-putting. She would have been happy with just a card.

"Let's get the check," Lydia says. "Maybe that barista with the beard will be working at the bookstore."

Irene and Lydia split the bill as they do every year with the New Year's dinner, then they stroll down South Dubuque from the Pullman to Prairie Lights bookstore. The temperature tonight is a robust thirteen degrees, but Irene barely notices the cold. She was born and raised right here in eastern Iowa, where the winds come straight down from Manitoba. Russ hates the cold. Russ's father was a navy pilot and so Russ grew up in Jacksonville, San Diego, and Corpus Christi; he saw snow for the first time when he went to college at Northwestern. Privately, Irene considers Russ's aversion to the cold a constitutional inferiority. As wonderful as he is, Irene would never describe him as hearty.

Lydia holds open the door to Prairie Lights and winks at Irene. "I see him," she whispers.

"Don't be shy. Order something complicated and strike up a conversation," Irene says. "It's a new year."

Lydia whips off her hat and shakes out her strawberry-blond hair. She's a pretty woman, Irene thinks, and, with the confidence she's displaying now, not at all invisible. Surely Brandon, the fifty-something barista with the thick spectacles and the leather apron—better suited to welding than to making espresso drinks—would be intrigued by Professor Lydia Christensen? She coauthored the definitive biography of our nation's thirty-first president. Herbert Hoover has gotten a bad rap from history, but most Iowans are kindly disposed toward him because he was born and raised in West Branch.

As Lydia marches to the café, Irene floats over to the new fiction. She loves nothing better than a stack of fresh books on her nightstand. What an enriching way to start the new year. Irene spent her New Year's Eve taking down all of her holiday decorations and packing them neatly away. She left the boxes at the bottom of the attic stairs. Russ is due back late tomorrow night or early Thursday morning, he said, and once he returns, he will be fully at her disposal. He left for a "surprise" business trip two days after Christmas. The man has more surprise business trips than anyone Irene has ever heard of and in this case, he was leaving Irene alone for New Year's. They had quarreled about it the previous afternoon on the phone. Russ had said, "I'm fully devoted to you, Irene, and I strive to see your point of view in every disagreement. But let's recall who encouraged whom to take this job. Let's recall who said she didn't want to be married to a corn syrup salesman for the rest of her life."

Their conversation, repeated for years nearly verbatim, ended there, as it always did. Irene *had* pushed Russ to take the job with Ascension, and with that decision came sacrifice. Russ is away more than he's home, but he does call all the time, and he sends flowers and often leaves her a surprise gift on her pillow when he goes away—jewelry or a pair of snazzy reading glasses, gift cards to the Pullman, a monogrammed makeup case. He is so thoughtful and loving that he makes Irene feel chilly and indifferent by comparison.

Also, and not inconsequentially, his new job affords them a very nice lifestyle, luxurious by Iowa standards. They own the Victorian, with its extravagant gardens and in-ground swimming pool on a full-acre lot on Church Street. Irene had been able to renovate the house exactly the way she dreamed of, sparing no expense. It took her nearly six years, proceeding one room at a time.

Now the house is a showpiece. Irene lobbied to have it featured in the magazine, but she encountered resistance from Mavis Key, who thought it would seem like shameless self-promotion to splash pictures of their own editor's home across their pages. *Talk about navel-gazing,* Mavis had said, a comment that hurt Irene. She suspects the real problem is Mavis's aversion to Victorian homes. Like Irene, they are out of fashion.

Mavis Key can buzz right off! Irene thinks. Irene's house is a reflection not only of years of painstaking work but also of her soul. The first floor has twelve-foot ceilings and features arched lancet windows with layered window treatments in velvet and damask. The palette throughout the house is one of rich, dark jewel tones—the formal living room is garnet, the parlor amethyst, and the kitchen has accents of topaz and emerald. There are tapestries and ornate rugs throughout, even in the bathrooms. Irene's favorite part of the house isn't a room per se but rather the grand staircase, which ascends two floors. It's paneled in dark walnut and at the top of the second flight of stairs is an exquisite stained-glass window that faces east. In the morning when the sun comes up, the third-floor landing is spangled with bursts of color. Irene has been known to take her mug of tea to the landing and just meditate on the convergence of man-made and natural beauty.

Irene supervised all of the interior carpentry, the refinishing of the floors, the repairs to the crown molding, the intricate painting—including, in the dining room, a wrap-around mural of the landscape of Door County, Wisconsin, where Irene spent summers growing up. Irene also hand-picked the antiques, traveling as far away as Minneapolis and Portland, Oregon, to attend estate sales.

Now that the house is finished, there is nothing left to do but enjoy it—and this is where Irene has hit a stumbling block. When she tells Lydia that she needs "something else," she isn't kidding. Russ is away for work at *least* two weeks a month, and their boys are grown up. Baker lives in Houston, where he day-trades stocks and serves as a stay-at-home father to his four-year-old son, Floyd. Baker's wife, Dr. Anna Schaffer, is a cardiothoracic surgeon at Memorial Hermann, which is a very stressful and time-consuming job; she, like Russ, is almost never around. Irene's younger son, Cash, lives in Denver, where he owns and operates two outdoor supply stores. Neither of the boys comes home much anymore, which saddens Irene, although she knows she should be grateful they're out living their own lives.

There was a moment yesterday around dusk when everyone else in America was getting ready for New Year's Eve festivities—showering, pouring dressing drinks, preparing hors d'oeuvres, pulling little black dresses out of closets—that Irene was hit by a profound loneliness. She had spoken to Russ, they had quarreled, and right after they hung up, Irene considered calling him back, but she refrained. There was nothing less attractive than a needy woman—and besides, Russ was busy.

Irene plucks the new story collection by Curtis Sittenfeld off the shelf; Curtis is a graduate of the Iowa Writers' Workshop, which Irene happens to believe is the best in the country.

She hears Lydia laughing and peers around the stacks to

see her friend and Brandon engaged in conversation. Brandon is leaning on his forearms on the counter while the espresso machine shrieks behind him. He hardly seems to notice; he's enraptured.

So much for being invisible! Irene thinks. Lydia is glowing like the northern lights.

Irene feels a twinge of an unfamiliar emotion. It's *longing,* she realizes. She misses Russ. Her husband spent years and years gazing at her with love—and, more often than not, she swatted him away, finding his attention overwrought and embarrassing.

Irene is distracted by a buzzing—her phone in her purse. That, she thinks with relief, will be Russ. But when she pulls out her phone, she sees the number is from area code 305. Irene doesn't recognize it and she guesses it's a telemarketer. She lets the call go, disappointed and more than a little annoyed at Russ. Where *is* he? She hasn't heard from him since midafternoon the day before; it's not like him to go so long without calling. And where is he this week? Did he even tell her? Did she even ask? Russ's "work emergencies" take him to various bland, warm locations—Sarasota, Vero, Naples. He nearly always comes home with a tan, inspiring envy from their friends who care about such things.

Irene notices the time—nine o'clock already—and realizes she has forgotten to call Milly, Russ's mother. Milly is ninety-seven years old; she lives at the Brown Deer retirement community in Coralville, a few miles away. Milly is in the medical unit now, although she's still cogent most of the time, still spry and witty, still a favorite with residents and staff alike. Irene visits Milly once a week and she calls her every night between seven and eight, but she forgot tonight because of her dinner with Lydia. By now, Milly will be fast asleep.

Not a worry, Irene thinks. She'll stop by to see Milly on her way home from work tomorrow. It'll be a good way to fill up her afternoons now that her hours have been cut. Maybe she'll take Milly to the Wig and Pen. Milly likes the chicken wings, though of course they aren't approved by her nutritionist. But what are they going to do, kill her?

The idea of Millicent Steele being finally done in by an order of zippy, peppery wing dings makes Irene smile as she chooses the Curtis Sittenfeld stories as well as *Where'd You Go, Bernadette,* by Maria Semple, which Irene had pretended to read for her book club half a dozen years earlier. With the house finished, she now has time to go back and catch up. Irene heads over to the register to pay. Meanwhile, Lydia is still at the café, still chatting with Brandon; her macchiato lets off the faintest whisper of steam between them.

Lydia turns when she feels Irene's hand on her back.

"Are you leaving?" Lydia asks. Her cheeks are flushed. "I'll probably stay for a while, enjoy my coffee."

"Oh," Irene says. "Okay, then. Thanks for dinner, it was fun, Happy New Year, call me tomorrow, be safe getting home, all of that." Irene smiles at Brandon, but his eyes are fastened on Lydia like she's the only woman in the world.

Good for her! Irene thinks as she walks home. It's a new year and Lydia is going after what she wants. A man. Brandon the barista.

The wind has picked up. It's bitterly cold and Irene has to head right into the teeth of it to get home. She ducks her head as she hurries down Linn Street, past a group of undergrads coming out of Paglia's Pizza, laughing and horsing around. One of the boys bumps into Irene.

"Sorry, ma'am," he says. "Didn't see you."

Invisible, she thinks.

This thought fades when she turns the corner and sees her house, her stunning castle, all lit up from within.

She'll light a fire in the library, she thinks. Make a cup of herbal tea, hunker down on the sofa with her favorite chenille blanket, crack open one of her new books.

Maybe the "something else" she's seeking isn't running for office, Irene thinks. Maybe it's turning her home into a bed-and-breakfast. It has six bedrooms, all with attached baths. If she kept one as a guest room for family, that still left four rooms she could rent out. Four rooms is manageable, right? Irene has a second cousin named Mitzi Quinn who ran an inn on Nantucket until her husband passed away. Mitzi had loved running the inn, although she did say it wasn't for the faint of heart.

Well, Irene's heart is as indestructible as they come.

What would Russ say if she proposed running an inn? She guesses he'll tell her to do whatever makes her happy.

It would solve the problem of her loneliness—people in the house all the time.

Would anyone want to come to Iowa City? Parents' weekend at the university, she supposes. Graduation. Certain football weekends.

It has definite appeal. She'll think on it.

When Irene opens the front door, she hears the house phone ringing. *That* will definitely be Russ, she thinks. No one calls the house phone anymore.

But when Irene reaches for the phone in the study just off the main hall, she sees it's the same 305 number that showed up on her cell phone. She hesitates for a second, then picks up the receiver.

"Hello?" she says. "Steele residence."

"Hello, may I please speak to Irene Steele?" The voice is female, unfamiliar.

"This is she," Irene says.

"Mrs. Steele, this is Todd Croft's secretary, Marilyn Monroe."

Marilyn Monroe, Todd Croft's oddly named secretary. Yes, Irene has heard about this woman, though she's never met her. Irene has only met Todd Croft, Russ's boss, once before. Todd Croft and Russ had been acquainted at Northwestern, and thirteen years ago, Russ and Irene had bumped into Todd in the lobby of the Drake Hotel in Chicago. That chance meeting led to a job offer, the one Irene had been so eager for Russ to accept. Now Todd Croft is just a name, invoked by Russ again and again. The man has become synonymous with the unseen force that rules their lives. *Todd needs me in Tampa on Tuesday. Todd has new clients he's courting in Lubbock.* "Todd the God," Irene calls him privately. And yet everything she has—this house, the swimming pool and gazebo, the brand-new Lexus in the garage—is thanks to Todd Croft.

"Happy New Year, Marilyn?" Irene says. There's a hesitation in her voice because Irene can't imagine why Marilyn Monroe—Irene has no choice but to picture this woman as a platinum blonde, buxom, with a beauty mark—would be calling. "Is everything . . . ?"

"Mrs. Steele," Marilyn says. "Something has happened."

"Happened?" Irene says.

"There was an accident," Marilyn says. "I'm afraid your husband is dead."